THE NEEDLE ON FULL

Caroline Forbes

ONLYWOMEN PRESS

Published by Onlywomen Press, radical feminist and lesbian publishers, 38 Mount Pleasant, London WC1X 0AP.

Cover design Angela Spark.

Typesetting: D'Silva Typesetters WC1.

Snake was first published in 'Spinster', volume 1, number 2, 1980.
The Needle on Full and *Transplant* were first published in 'Crystal Crone', 1980.
Marianna and the Graduation was first published in THE REACH and other stories; lesbian feminist fiction, ed. by Lilian Mohin and Sheila Shulman, Onlywomen Press, London, 1984.

Printed and bound in Great Britain by Redwood Burn Ltd., Trowbridge, Wiltshire.

British Library Cataloguing in Publication Data
Forbes, Caroline
  Needle on Full.
  I. Title
  823'.914 [F]   PR6056.063/
  ISBN 0-906500-19-2

CONTENTS

For my mother

I would like to thank Caroline Gilfillan and Lilian Mohin without whom, as they say, this book would not have been written. Also thanks to my friends who have listened to my ramblings over the years it has taken to get this far.

THE NEEDLE ON FULL

The thin electronic whine of the alarm woke her up. She groped round for the switch to turn it off, trying to move quietly so that she would not disturb the mound that lay beside her in the bed. After all it was one of the few mornings in the year when he did not have to get up. Outside it was still dark and she shivered as she looked out of the window, she hated these days, but in winter it was even worse. Far below she could see the parking lot lit by the harsh orange lights, surrounded by a high wire fence to keep out poachers. She could see her husband's car sitting amongst the rest waiting for her. She could always pick it out from the others even though they were all the same make. They looked like huge fat beetles, their underbellies low on the ground, bloated, but his easily the oldest, a grandmother to the rest, slowly ticking her life away while the others still shone with newness.

She turned away from the view abruptly and started getting dressed. She had no time to be day-dreaming this morning. Already she could hear the murmur of others like her getting up, having whispered conversations, making tea. The walls in these blocks were little more than paper. She didn't eat much for breakfast, preferring to get out on the road and take extra sandwiches for later so she would get a good place in the queue. She had dawdled too long in the bedroom to have time for a hot drink and she cursed herself for being so late as she grabbed the bag she had packed last night, her coat and scarf and the car keys, and slipped silently out of the flat.

Thankfully the lift was working, the stairs could put an extra twenty minutes on the journey and she liked to stand in the lift for those few minutes to regain herself before the long drive ahead. By the time she got to the parking lot she could see others like herself armed with bags and blankets heading for the row of cars. There were a few nodded hellos but mostly they were all too busy, too fraught to stop and talk. Not that they did much socialising in this block, not like before when she and Jim had lived over on Southside, where the blocks were smaller and even cosy sometimes. She hadn't wanted to move, but he had waited years to get over to where the pickings were better, the rides longer and the tips higher. That was what you got for marrying a driver she supposed as she fiddled the key into the car door and slid behind the steering wheel, dumping her things on the passenger seat. It took her a while to remember where everything was. These were the only times she ever drove the car, and the last time it hadn't been so dark and she had forgotten where the light switch was and how to move the seat forward. But soon she was backing out, feeling the engine respond to her direction and she relaxed as the car joined the trail the others had left before her and headed west, leaving behind the faint light of a December dawn.

After picking her way carefully through the side streets, (years of practice had taught her the best routes for this operation) she joined the motorway that stood on high concrete legs, straddling the poorer area of Northside before it swept down through the parks of the West and out into the sprawling suburbs of London. She checked the fuel gauge carefully, Jim had cut it fine this time, and she prayed there would be enough to get her there. But he was a good man and had always tried his best, even if it meant cutting down on his lifts a few times. She shook her head; they had been so short of money since they had come North and she knew he had been working long hours to pay for the extra luxuries they enjoyed. Still, there was nothing she could do about it now except get to the depot as fast as possible and hope they hadn't cut down on the rations again.

Now she was out on the main road there was nothing to do except listen to the traffic reports on the radio and watch the road. The car drove easily, fitting into a steadily growing stream of black cars just like it, all headed the same way like birds on a migration. And it was a bit like that, she thought. Every two months they all headed back to the depot to fill their great metallic bellies with the petrol that was their life-blood. As the dawn began she could see the tall blocks lining the road, a few lights glimmering behind drawn curtains as the early shift workers prepared for another day. She had always hated the idea of being a factory worker, it had been one of the main reasons she had married Jim, to escape that fate. As a driver he had been able to offer her more, even the possibility of qualifying for a travel permit so that they could eventually get out of the city, even for a few days. But that had been over fifteen years ago and the glamour she had seen then had gone. Every time she thought they might get on top of things there was always a new rise in prices, or the petrol ration was reduced, so they stayed where they were. And now that Jim had got the pitch on Northside she could see little hope of her ever getting out of it all.

She checked the dials once again, petrol, oil

and water. The car was in need of an oil change after
the last two months of continuous driving and she
could hear the familiar grating that came as the oil
light got brighter, until, if she left it, the engine would
seize up. She looked at the clock and tried to relax, at
the rate she was going it wouldn't take that long to
get there and she had enough fuel. The plastic seat
covering creaked beneath her and she could feel it
sticking to her legs. She hated this job, hated having
all the worry of whether the car would make it,
whether the traffic would be bad and how long she
would have to wait in the queue. In all the years she
had been married she had never missed a turn.
Because she and Jim had no children, and she was
rarely ill, there had never been a reason why she
should. After all, it was accepted that that was what
you did if you married a driver, and it hadn't seemed
much in exchange for the advantages of more money
and some freedom of movement in the city. But after
doing this trip every two months for so many years. . .

The sky was nearly light now and she could see
the blocks thinning out, slowly being replaced by the
detached houses that marked the beginning of the
Controllers' zone. Near the motorway the houses
were quite small, but Jim had told her of the lifts he
took sometimes, out beyond those streets to where
you could not see one house from another and they
all had big gardens and trees around them. Of course
they had their own cars but occasionally they still
needed the services of a driver and the tips were
always good for those lucky enough to get them.

The road was getting crowded now, the cars
moving bumper to bumper at a steady fifty miles an
hour. She would have to pay more attention to the
driving, she could not afford to have an accident.
And of course they did occur; cars that had mis-
judged their petrol would come to a slow and silent

halt and, if the driver behind was not concentrating, it could be the start of a huge pile-up. Up and down the central divide patrolled break-down vans waiting to tow those unfortunates off the road and leave them to the long walk home, if they could not get a lift or find someone willing to give them a little petrol. And these days when the Controllers kept such a tight rein on the fuel supplies, there was little or none to get on the Black Market. Once upon a time it had been quite easy to get an extra gallon here and there, but not anymore. Now, unless you had the right documents and passes, money was no good.

As she drove she saw a couple of cars stranded, their drivers leaning cold and tired against the bonnet, waiting for the cars going back in the hope of some petrol or at least a lift home. One of the women looked white and frightened with scared eyes that seemed to follow Sally as she drove by and she promised herself she would give her a lift on the way back. She knew what the woman was frightened of, she had heard tales of severe beatings and even murder, if a driver's wife returned empty-handed from one of these expeditions. In fact she could see no reason why these women could not simply get a lift to the depot, borrow a can and be able to return to their cars and drive to the depot as well. But it was the Controllers' way of ensuring that no one used more than their quota of petrol, and because it was so harsh it normally worked. Most of the women she saw were young, inexperienced, the older ones like her would never allow such a thing to happen. It only took two months with no income and the long struggle out of debt that would follow to happen once, to make both the drivers and their wives learn to treat their allowance with some respect.

Ahead of her was a car from Eastside, its yellow

numberplate glinting in the winter sunlight. Behind her was another Northsider, another green numberplate but on a much newer car. Both cars were driven by women. It was rare to see one that was not. Most men only qualified as drivers after they were married, they all knew what they would have to do otherwise. The stories of two or three days delay in the delivery were numerous and true and they were much happier to sit at home and wait. Only North and East were out today, South and West would do the same trek next month. She thought back to the Southside days when she and Jim were just starting out. There were so many ways round the rules then, it was possible to sneak petrol across the river and help each other out. Now with the police blocks on the tunnels and bridges and the river patrols it wasn't worth the risk. The penalties were severe too. Back then, a stiff fine or a short jail sentence was the price you paid, now it was anything up to ten years for the mildest form of petrol fiddling. She shook her head impatiently, sometimes she hated the clear, smelly liquid that seemed to be the most important thing in her life. When she looked at those huge tanks surrounded by barbed wire and guards she wanted to see them burn to the ground, then what would the Controllers control?

A beep from the car behind pulled her attention back to the road. She had wandered off onto the hard shoulder for a minute. Sally waved her thanks out of the window and set herself to drive the last miles as carefully as possible. It was just as well she had started paying attention for, as her eyes flickered across the dials, she was appalled to see the temperature gauge just entering the red. The faint hiss of steam came in through the open window and, cursing herself for not checking the water before she left that morning, and Jim for not doing it himself as he had promised, she slowed down, indicated, and pulled onto the hard shoulder. She came to a halt by one of the concrete pillars that supported the road on its journey through the suburbs.

Outside the car it was cold and she pulled her jacket close round her body. Gingerly she lifted up the bonnet and, with her hand wrapped in her scarf, unscrewed the top of the water tank, jumping back as the boiling liquid sprang up in a frantic attempt to escape the pressure it was under. She stood looking at it for a few minutes, listening as the bubbling subsided. There wasn't much she could do except wait till it cooled down and then go on and hope it wouldn't happen again. She looked at her watch, there was a good six hours before they closed the depot, that should be plenty of time, even if she had to stop again. But she was worried, if she was at the end of the queue she might have to take low-grade petrol, or, even worse, not the full amount. She was not afraid of Jim, not even if she came back with nothing, but all the bills, the rent for the pitch, the new flat. She leant against the driver's door and looked at the road, watching the endless stream of black cars going past her. One of the breakdown trucks waved over to her from the central reserve but she nodded and waved back that she was alright, well what could they do after all?

'Do you need any help?'

Sally turned round abruptly at the sound of a voice to see a young woman climbing over the crash barrier at the side of the road.

'Who are you? What are you doing here?'

'Oh, I was just passing and I saw you, so I thought I'd come and see what was the matter. I've done a bit of mechanics in my time you see and I know how serious a breakdown could be for you. My name's Harriet by the way, Harriet Mitchell.'

She stared at the hand outstretched towards her, then looked up and caught the expression of interest in the younger woman's clear blue eyes. She didn't know what to think. Such a thing was unheard of, the drivers looked after themselves, they did not expect such casual interference in their dramas. She looked nervously up and down the road, wondering what the others would think if they knew what was happening. She wished she knew what to do, she tried to think what Jim would do, but of course he had never done this trip, he didn't know what it was like. And still Harriet Mitchell just stood there, smiling, with her hand out ready to shake. Sally wished she would go away, didn't she know that pedestrians were not allowed on the motorway? In fact no one was allowed on the road without a driver's permit, if the police patrols came by they would both be in trouble.

'Look, why don't you just go? I'll be alright. I wasn't paying attention and the car overheated but it'll be alright in a while. I'll still be able to get to the depot and if you hang round here we might both never get anywhere, the patrols will be along soon.'

'Just let me have a quick look, you might have something wrong that will get worse, and then what? I won't be long and I've got eyes in the back of my head for patrols so don't worry about that.'

Harriet had dropped her hand, though she was still half smiling, and had walked round to the front of the car and started peering into the engine. Sally still wanted her to go away but somehow she couldn't do anything about it. She leant against the barrier and watched as the woman bent down over the engine, muttering to herself and fiddling with various hoses and clips. How old was she? It was difficult to tell. She might be only nineteen or twenty, but her manner seemed older, more assured.

She had not spoken to her like the teenagers in the block, who had that 'you'live in another age' way, she had spoken to her quite normally, one woman to another as though this happened every day. Sally watched her body lift a little and then bend over further into the depths of the engine. She watched the bones of her shoulders move under the skin that showed above her shirt collar. She watched how her blonde hair fell towards her face in a curve on each side, leaving a slightly grey neck exposed. She put her hand up to touch her own hair for a moment, feeling how the perm was growing out and the grey was beginning to grow in.

'You've got a leak in one of the radiator hoses, I've got a piece of rubber patching that should fix it. I'll just go and get it. I won't be long.' Harriet stood upright now, tall and thin. Sally felt she had to stop this, regain control in some way. As Harriet turned to go, she grabbed her arm and pulled her back.

'Wait, why are you doing this? Are you trying to get me into trouble or something? You don't know me, I don't know you or where you come from, or what you're doing hanging round the motorway looking for drivers in distress so you can be some kind of knight in shining armour! Now I suppose you're off to report me for fraternising with a pedestrian off bounds, I hear the rewards are very generous these days!' She stopped, turned round and was silent for a moment. She could feel Harriet's blue eyes making her cheeks blush like a girl. Harriet smiled and pressed a cool hand against her burning cheeks.

'I just want a lift to the depot, and you know no one stops on the way there if they can help it. I don't mean you any harm, honestly I don't. Now I won't be a minute.'

While Harriet was gone Sally could relax a little.

She looked at her watch and was astonished to find that it was only fifteen minutes since she stopped. She watched the traffic stream past. With a bit of luck it would work out alright, although the bulk of the cars had been past her, there were quite a few still on the road and plenty of time. Maybe it was good this woman had come by, at least she might mend the car until she got it back to Jim. But now she had to give her a lift as well. It would not look good, two in the car. The patrol could pick her up for that, the other woman would certainly not have a travel pass or she wouldn't be trying to cadge a lift from her. She wondered why she wanted to get to the depot at all. She had no hope of getting any petrol for herself, drivers who were stranded had enough trouble, no one would help someone like her. Why didn't she want a lift back to the city? After all what was beyond the depot, except more Controllers and then nothing?

'See, I wasn't long, it'll be fixed in a minute. You'd better keep an eye out for the patrol, I think they should be along very soon now.'

'How do you know?'

'Oh, I've timed them; they don't always behave the same, but I think they prefer to. It makes it simpler to fill out their log sheets you know. None too bright these patrols!' She laughed and hung her thick leather jacket over the barrier and rolled up her sleeves. She paused with her hand on the radiator, 'By the way, what's your name? I'd like to call you something.'

'Sally, you can call me Sally if you want.'

Sally watched for the patrol. It was easy to spot now the cars had thinned to a trickle. Harriet slipped into the car and hid under the blanket on the floor and Sally put on that look of despair to fool the patrolmen. They pulled in beside her, the big white van in stark contrast to the black cars it herded and controlled.

'What's the matter with you lady, having some trouble?' They never helped, this was just part of the game.

'No, it's alright, just overheating, everything's okay.'

'Overheating eh! What you or the car?' Laughing to each other at their joke they looked her up and down. The driver got out of the car and came round for a better look. She felt her muscles stiffen and could hardly restrain herself from blurting the whole story out before they found Harriet, after all it was not her fault. He peered in the engine for a minute and nodded to himself.

'Have you been trying to fix this lady?' He had come up right beside her, the peak of his cap throwing a harsh shadow across his face.

'No, well yes, just a bit. But I think it's alright now.'

She knew she should not let them scare her so much. They were only trying to upset her, there were still enough cars on the road to stop anything worse happening. The patrolmen had learnt a long time ago that there was one thing all the women would stop for. After two patrollers were found dead, tied to the crash barriers, the warning had been taken seriously. He was still beside her, slightly behind her shoulder, grinning round into her face.

'Well as long as it's going to be alright, lady.' His body lurched into hers and she felt his hand grab her bum. She pushed him sharply away, ready to run to the road for help.

'Come on Greig, we haven't got time for any trouble, we're due up at the depot.' His mate had wound up the window, slid into the driving seat and started the van. He turned to her once more and laughed.

'It's a lovely day for a walk!'

The van disappeared leaving her feeling angry and frightened. Her knees were shaking and she was thankful to sit quietly in the driving seat and watch Harriet finish the repairs through the window.

She had even begun to doze off when Harriet opened the passenger door and sat down beside her.

'It's done now, it should be fine, although you should get some more hoses soon or it will happen again.'

Sally sat up, startled by the woman's voice.

'Thanks, thanks a lot, you've been a great help.' She still nursed a small hope that the women would simply get out and say goodbye, taking herself off back to her own world. She felt exhausted by the whole episode.

'That's okay, I like to help women if I can.' She smiled a wide open smile that left Sally feeling both suspicious and vulnerable. She still did not know what this woman wanted from her and although she had to admit that she had saved her neck over the car business, and that she had not made any demands on her apart from a request for a lift, Sally still felt she must have some ulterior motive in the way she was carrying on Sally tried to speak with more authority, disguising her own anxieties and fears.

'Listen, before we go on, and before the patrol comes back, would you please tell me again what you want? I am very grateful for the help you've given me but I can't help feeling you want something more from me in return. If it's money, you can forget it because I haven't got any.'

'You know what I want, I want a lift as far as the depot and that's all, I promise. If you think I'm being funny with you or something then maybe it's just because I like you, and I'm interested in you.

For the first time Sally relaxed and laughed, infected by Harriet's approach to the situation.

I don't mean to unsettle you or make you angry. I'm not 'after' anything, apart from the lift.'

'What do you mean! You don't even know me, we've hardly spoken since we met!'

'But sometimes I think you can tell you're going to like people as soon as you set eyes on them, don't you think?

Sally stared at her. She was disconcerting. One minute she seemed so confident, the mechanic living outside the law, the next she was coming out with platitudes Sally hadn't heard since she was at school. She looked more closely at her.

'How old are you?'

'Eighteen.'

'I see.'

Sally said nothing for a few minutes. Harriet was wiping her hands carefully on an oily rag.

'I suppose you think I'm really young and all that. Lots of people say I'm young for my age, as well, but I don't care. I manage okay. I mended your car didn't I, and I know you're going to give me a lift in the end, aren't you?' She laughed and leant over towards Sally, her hand resting lightly on the older woman's arm.

'Well, I suppose you're right, I don't think I was ever going to throw you out of the car, I must say. But I still don't know why you want a lift to the depot at all.'

'Don't you think we'd better start driving there, you don't want to be too late in the queue or you won't get a full tank.'

Sally swore and started the car. For a minute she had forgotten all about the petrol and the depot, she had been enjoying sitting in the warm car with the winter sun coming in the back window, just talking. The motorway was fairly empty now as she pulled off the hard shoulder and picked up speed.

The car seemed to be fine, the temperature gauge hardly registered anything.

'The car's going okay.'

'Yes, I told you, it will be alright for a few hundred miles at least, then it could break down again unless you get new hoses.'

'Oh, Jim will take care of that I'm sure, he's very good at repairing the old car. We've had her for years.'

There was a long pause beside her.

'Is he your husband then, this Jim?'

'Yes.'

'What's he like, do you love him and all that?'

Sally was surprised at the question. 'Whatever do you want to know about that for? I suppose I love him, I don't really think about it that much.'

'Did you love him when you married him?'

'I think so. I wanted to because he was a driver and I thought that was very romantic. My mother wanted me to marry him and as the council approved it seemed the best thing to do. He's good about money for me and he doesn't drink or gamble or treat me badly, so I don't have anything to complain about, even if he isn't the most exciting company.'

'Do you have any children?'

'No, I did think about it for a while, but at the beginning we didn't have enough money and then it just didn't happen, and although we talked about adoption for a while I realised in the end that I didn't really want a child anyway.'

'I see.'

Harriet's answer brought Sally back to earth.

'Why are you always talking about me and my problems when I'm trying to find out about you? What is an eighteen-year-old girl who should be home with her mother or her husband, doing out on the road alone trying to get lifts?'

Sally looked at her, quick flashes from the road ahead to the side of her face, seeing beyond the blonde hair and blue eyes to the thinness of her cheeks, the bluish smudge under each eye, she was very young to be looking so drawn. As Harriet started to talk, Sally slowed down so she could pay more attention, she knew the queue would start soon and this privacy would be over and suddenly she wanted to know everything about her.

'I just want to get out, out of the city. I've never been out, my family didn't live in a park zone so I couldn't even have that when I was little. I've heard things about what it's like out there, that you can live without the city, without petrol and electricity and all that. I've heard it's really pretty, and people can do what they like, and don't have to work in factories and live in big blocks and take pills all the time to keep sane.'

Sally could feel the words pouring out in a great rush, a release of pressure.

'I know it might sound mad to you but I've found out a lot of things. It is possible to do it if you can only get out of the city. In the end I just started walking, but I thought that if I came this way I might get a lift as far as the depot, and surely the countryside musn't be much further than that.'

'But what about your family?' Won't they miss you at home? And I'd have thought you'd be courting by now.'

'Oh no, I'm not interested in getting married. That's why I got an apprenticeship to be a mechanic, then you don't have to get married until you've finished. My father got it for me, but he's been transferred to Security A so I hardly ever see him now, only on public holidays. He wouldn't notice I was gone for months.'

'What about your mother?'

'She's gone with him. They weren't allowed to take me because I was sixteen, too old to qualify as a child so they wouldn't allocate a flat big enough or give me security clearance. I'm glad now, I would never be able to leave if I was in Security A.'

Sally was silent, thinking about that area of the city surrounded by barricades and checkpoints where only government officials and essential services were allowed. This girl could be the daughter of someone important. She shivered at the thought of them being caught, it certainly put a new and frightening light on the situation.

'Have you thought about what will happen if they catch you?'

'Of course I have, but I was just going crazy in a one room unit, I just had to get out. I know it's a risk but I had to take it.'

'And what about me? If I had any sense I'd turn you in myself. I might get a reward you know, and they certainly won't be too pleased with me, if and when the authorities catch up with both of us.'

'But you won't, will you?'

Ahead Sally could see a dark blur on the road, the end of the queue was in sight at last. Harriet could see it too and Sally could sense a flash of fear run through her body like electricity as she stiffened beside her. Her own body responded, her heart beat fast as she slipped the car into a lower gear, slowing to avoid that moment when the car would stop and they would be left in silence without the gentle hum of the engine to cover up their breathing.

'No. I won't turn you in.'

As she spoke Harriet reached over and took her hand, pressing it lightly between her own. Sally could feel her armpits prickling with sweat and she drew her hand nervously away, gripping the gear stick as

the car came to a smooth halt at the end of the
queue. Ahead of them they could see the high storage
tanks against the skyline.

It was dark now. They had sat in the car all day,
only moving a few feet forward. Behind them a few
other late-comers had joined the queue, but there was
a delay in the delivery, and the word was that it
could be at least another ten hours before all the
cars were filled and could return to the city. Sally
stood leaning back against the car smoking one of
her last cigarettes. She had rationed them very
carefully but they would soon run out. She was
hungry too, the sandwiches and the coffee were gone,
and although the food wagon had been by, and would
come again, she could only take enough for one and
then had to share it with Harriet, who now lay curled
up asleep in the back of the car. Sally wondered
about her. She could have gone by now. They were
at the depot, had been there all day, having whispered
conversations about everything under the sun. Sally
hadn't asked her to go either, she knew she didn't
want her to go although it was mad to carry on. She
had been drawn a little into Harriet's world and it had
shaken her so much that she felt cut adrift at the
thought of Jim and the flat and her life over the past
years. She wished the car had never broken down,
wished she had never met Harriet, even wished the
patrol had found her and taken her away. Every time
she tried to think clearly about the situation, she
could see only Harriet's thin face and long body
slouched in the seat, her eyes full of expectancy. She
tried to think back to her own youth. She had
thought about the outside then, thought about what
happened beyond the city. They all did, they were
even taught about it in school. But it had just been
a phase, she had been caught up in marriage and

papers and passes and those dreams had to be shelved. She looked up and down the queue, seeing other women talking and smoking. Did they ever think about anything other than their everyday lives, she wondered. When she had lived on Southside, she had talked a little about it to one of her friends in the block. But they had agreed that it must be pretty awful, just like the reports said. Her picture of the countryside was one of a wasteland, where a few workers had to live to keep up primary services and defence. Now her head was full of Harriet's romantic notions of beautiful hills and woods and fields, like in old picture books. She knew things used to be like that, but could they really be the same now? She could no longer sort out any pattern of truth in it all.

She stubbed her cigarette out on the tarmac, grinding the end under her shoe and went back to the car. It was cold inside without the engine going, but she could not spare the petrol to keep the heater running. She sat behind the driving wheel looking out at the huge illuminated petrol depot. The first time she had seen it at night it had seemed like a fairytale castle, the complicated networks of pipes and massive tanks picking up the lights and reflecting them back out. Now it seemed like a prison, the barbed wire and searchlights, the silhouettes of the guards patrolling day and night. She turned her head, wondering how she could ever do this trip again.

A whisper came from the back seat.

'Why don't you come and sleep back here with me? It'll be much warmer with two of us.'

Sally hesitated, surprised because she wanted to, afraid to have any more contact with such a disturbing influence. She thought how tired Harriet must be, having to hide under the blanket all day to escape detection. She still couldn't understand why she didn't leave. But she wanted some comfort, some-

26

thing to stop all the crazy ideas she was having that crowded her head, so she got out of the car and went round to the rear door and got in beside her.

Harriet was half lying, half sitting across the back seat. She had taken her jacket off to use as a pillow, and her thin bare legs were propped up against the back of the front seat. She pulled her legs back to allow Sally to get in and opened up the blanket that was wrapped round her to include the other woman. Sally felt embarrassed suddenly. Now she wished she had stayed in the front seat where she was protected from those eyes. Even in the darkness she felt she was being watched, being judged. She sat stiffly, her hands in her lap, smoothing the crinkles out of her skirt, noticing the bulge of her stomach and the thickness of her thighs and wishing they were not there.

'Why don't you lie down? There's plenty of room, you don't look very comfortable like that.'

Sally thought she was laughing at her. She must pull herself together and stop acting like a schoolgirl. After all, what was she embarrassed about? When Harriet was her age she would probably have more weight on her than she wanted, though she was beginning to wonder whether either of them would survive to see that day.

'Come on Sally, I'm not going to bite you, you know!'

'I'm just getting settled, I'll take my shoes off first.' She leaned forward, glad of something to do and pulled off her driving shoes, wriggling her toes inside her stockings, hearing the rustling of the nylon. With an effort she pulled off her jacket and lay back along the seat, her head resting awkwardly a few inches above Harriet.

For what seemed hours there was silence, only the slight brushing sound as Harriet brought her arm down off the back window ledge and eased it under

Sally's head so that she was resting more comfortably. Sally could feel the heat from the other woman's body flowing along the line of contact between them. Harriet seemed relaxed, her arm resting lightly round Sally's shoulder. She thought about what Harriet had said about marriage and men during the hours they had been talking, she certainly didn't seem very perturbed about this situation, almost as though she was used to it. Sally felt confusion mounting in her, she struggled to sit up a bit, resisting the desire to move in closer to the warmth that was there. She turned round and caught Harriet's eye. She looked serious, concerned, even a bit nervous herself. The sight of her made Sally shiver, but she didn't know why.

'Why haven't you gone?' The whisper seemed deafening.

'Because I wanted to stay with you a bit longer.'

'Are you one of them?'

'What do you mean, "one of them"?'

'You know,' Sally brushed her upper lip with her finger, feeling the drops of perspiration on the fine brown hairs that grew there, 'one of those kind of women that don't like men.'

'I like women if that's what you mean.'

Sally felt unsatisfied, unclear. She wished she had never started this conversation but she couldn't go back now.

'I mean, do you, well do you, I mean more than like them? Oh God I can't say it properly! Not now, everything seems to have gone mad.' She didn't dare look at her, she could only feel her own heart beating and her body rigid, each muscle locked solid.

'When I was fourteen I had this friend, this schoolfriend. We used to go everywhere together, we were inseparable. When I was sixteen and my parents moved to Security A they gave me a one room unit in the block next to her family. She stayed there one night after we had been to a block party, we'd had quite a bit to drink and we stayed up for hours talking. I suppose we just realised that it couldn't last, that one day we would both be married and then everything would be different. One thing led to another and we just started cuddling each other and crying and laughing. Well it ended up with her collapsing into bed with me, and when we woke up in the morning, and looked at each other, it was just different. After that she used to stay nearly every night. She used to pretend she was on night shift so that her parents wouldn't suspect anything.'

'What happened?'

Harriet shifted her long body on the seat. 'Oh, she was assigned to a different area and then she got married. I don't think she could really handle it, not when it was so difficult.'

'And what about you?'

'I just couldn't get married, not after that.'

'Have you met other women? Other women like you I mean.'

'Oh sometimes, but it's very hard you know, impossible to really work anything out. That's one of the main reasons I want to get out. Maybe out there it will be easier. Do you mind very much?' Her sudden question made Sally stop her mind from wandering dizzily off somewhere.

'No I don't think so. I've never really thought about it, but I don't seem to mind. I think I guessed already, I just wanted to know.'

The silence settled again. Harriet didn't move, though Sally knew she was awake. Outside she could hear the sounds of footsteps as women idled the night away. She sat up and leaned forward to press the knobs down to lock all the car doors. She felt safe, this was her car, a familiar friend that had served her

well for years. She looked over her shoulder at
Harriet and felt that shiver again. She wanted to put
her arms round her, to comfort her for the loss of
her friend, to help soften the blow on those thin
young bones. She lay back beside her, nestling into
the space beneath Harriet's arm, letting her arm lie
across Harriet's body. She could feel the change of
mood fill the whole car. Harriet let her hand slide
down under Sally's arm, pulling her closer, letting
both their bodies slip down the smooth seat until
they were below the level of the window, cuddled
close under the blanket. Sally felt sick with nerves.
Maybe Harriet didn't want to do anything, after all
she was much older, married, just a lift to the depot
and some warmth through the night. She wanted to
say something, to ask, but she didn't know what to
say. While she was thinking desperately, Harriet
lifted her head and drew Sally closer, till their cheeks
touched. When her voice came she couldn't recognise
it.

'Do you want me?'

Harriet didn't reply, simply turned Sally's face
and kissed her, letting her tongue gently slide
between her lips. As she moved, Sally could feel her
body throbbing, her clothes felt hot and uncomfortable. Harriet gently pulled her head away and began
to undo the buttons on Sally's shirt.

'Let me do that,' she whispered, shy at the
thought of her body. Harriet giggled and released her,
pulling her own shirt off and her T-shirt over her
head. Sally fumbled with her clothes, managed to get
her stockings off and her skirt and blouse without
emerging from the darkness of the blanket. She lay
back, exhausted at the effort, feeling the lunacy of
the situation and, for a minute, wishing very sincerely
that it wasn't happening. Harriet had wriggled out of
her jeans and knickers and lay naked and silent,

waiting. Sally could see her white-skinned shoulders poking out of the blanket, catching the light, and she reached over to touch one of them, ran her small hand over the boneyness and then down onto the warm muscle of the arm. With a final effort of will she sat up and reached her hands round and undid her bra strap, turning away so that Harriet would not see her, and pushed her knickers off to join the pile of clothing on the floor of the car.

Finally she was still, aware only of her breathing and of their two bodies, so different, rising and falling with each breath. Harriet moved round so that she lay facing her and let her hands run down over the skin of Sally's chest, over her breasts and down across her stomach. She pulled her stomach muscles in sharply, sensitive of the fat there, but she just heard Harriet laugh in the darkness and press reassuringly. Her own body responded, surprising her with its strength. She kept her eyes tight shut as her own hands traced the lines on Harriet's face, touching the deep shadow she had seen under her eyes. She fell back as Harriet's hand pushed down harder, she was lying on her back now, looking up through the fall of blonde hair on her chest to the dark outside the car. The blanket prickled against her sweating body and she could think of nothing except a great release and relief as her body opened up and Harriet's fingers worked a kind of magic, unlocking doors sealed inside her for years.

She couldn't tell how much time passed. Her own hands were alive with the touch of Harriet's body, her fingers wet. She was fascinated by what she had discovered. Harriet lay with her arm over her face breathing hard, she laughed softly and turned to look at Sally.

'Well, that was good wasn't it!'

Sally nodded, still too wrapped up in it all to

speak. She let her hands move over the woman's body, curling her fingers in the thick pubic hair.

'Do you feel good?' It was like a child asking for approval Sally thought. She nodded again and let herself rest.

The sound of car doors slamming woke Sally up. It was still dark, though she could just make out a glimmer of light on the horizon. She managed to pull her clothes on under the blanket without waking Harriet, and got out of the car to investigate whether the queue had finally begun to move. She wandered up the line of cars, pulling her jacket round her and watching her breath cloud up round her head. Another woman stood by the bonnet of the next car.

'Is it moving yet?'

'Not yet, but it won't be long now, the green flag's up over the tanks so they're ready for us at last.'

She walked back, rubbing her eyes, waking up at last to her situation. What was she going to do? What had she done? She waited a few moments outside the car trying to collect herself. She couldn't help feeling very pleased with herself, sensing an ease in her body that she hadn't known before. But what about Jim? Her whole life back there? She turned to look down the road towards the city. Over the buildings she could see the faint orange glow that shone all night to mark the heart of the metropolis. Jim would be starting his second day without her. She knew he would be sound asleep after a night out with the other drivers, the flat would be a mess, full of dirty dishes and empty bottles his friends brought round. She knew all drivers were the same, they expected their wives to clear up. It wasn't that Jim was so untidy himself, but she did wish that sometimes, when she got back from one of these long trips, she would find the flat clean. Going Back. The thought of it made her stop in her tracks. How could she be worrying about Jim's mess when she felt so strange about the idea of going back at all? She nodded a greeting absently to one of the breakdown teams as they drove past. What would she tell Jim? Maybe she should say nothing about it, forget it had ever happened, send Harriet on her way and settle back to real life again. She knew she could do that, though it made her feel rather lost and afraid to think about it. There would be an hour or so yet till the delivery, at least, so she could put off deciding what to do for a while.

The food truck made its way slowly down the line. Sally picked up a mug of coffee and a cheese roll and went back to the car. She got in the front seat, leaned over and gently shook Harriet's shoulder.

'Wake up Harriet, I've got some coffee here for you.'

Harriet stirred, muttering in her sleep, then she opened her eyes, blinked and yawned noisily. She reached out her hand, took the mug and gulped down a couple of mouthfuls, awkwardly propped on one shoulder.

'You'd better get dressed while it's still dark otherwise you'll be stuck under the blanket. They say the delivery will be in about an hour. The green flag's up so it won't be long.'

'Okay, Boss.' Harriet smiled and passed the cup back, 'Anything you say!' She looked sideways at her, rather nervous all of a sudden, Sally thought. Her voice sounded very young.

'How are you this morning, how are you feeling?'

Harriet's voice made the previous night come flashing back to her, sometimes like a film, sometimes just the sounds and the feelings. It was difficult to think it had actually been her doing it, unless she looked at the pale face watching her.

'I feel fine, really good.' She smiled, she didn't

know what more to say. She didn't know what else she felt anyway, it was all so confused with what she was going to do about it. Maybe once she had sorted that out she would have time to think properly. She reached over to the back seat and took Harriet's hand.

'Honestly, I feel okay. But what about you?'

'Oh I'm okay too.' There was a silence for a time. 'What do you think we should do now?'

Sally laughed. 'Oh I see, I thought you were the one with everything so worked out, and now you want to know what I think we should do!'

'I hadn't planned on anything like this.'

'I'm sorry, I didn't mean to laugh at you. It's just that it seems quite clear to me. You want to go on to the countryside and try and find your paradise or whatever out there, and I have to go back to the city with the car. What else can we do?'

'You could come too.' She had said it in a very quiet voice but it struck Sally like a blow. She had hoped, with half her soul, that Harriet would want to be rid of her, then she would not have to make the agonising decision.

'How could I? I've got the car! What about Jim?'

'We could take the car with us, use it till the petrol runs out, or dump it once we get out there. I've heard some drivers just go crazy and drive off and never come back.'

'They probably get caught, Harriet.'

'Not all of them, surely, and if we did it carefully, not straight up the motorway, but back towards the city and then off onto the side roads. We could make it, I'm sure. There's only one road block at the boundary, and if we got through that we'd be away! I have found out quite a lot about it remember. As for your Jim, that's up to you I suppose.'

She was getting into her clothes as she spoke and Sally couldn't help but watch for the flashes of white skin as either the blanket or her clothes slipped off. Harriet looked up and caught her eye.

'Could you go back, after last night?'

She was so romantic, Sally thought. And yet it was more than two bodies in the night. Could she go back after the talking, the ideas, the feelings that had poured out of her like sweat. She turned away, sitting and staring at the familiar view beyond the windscreen. Ahead she could see a faint blue smoke, exhaust pipes belching, the queue was moving. It would not be long now, it never was once the gates were open. With fifteen positions and operators it was a quick job once started. She turned back to Harriet.

'You'd better get down under the blanket, we'll be moving soon.'

She settled into the driving seat, glad of something to do, unwilling to go on with the conversation. She knew she would have to decide soon. She even knew what she would decide, but not yet, she didn't want to do it yet.

Within half an hour they were moving. Already the other carriageway was packed with cars heading back into the dawn, roaring off with the confidence of a full tank. She could see a few familiar faces going past her, normally she would have spent the night with them, her friends, up at the top of the queue Now she had to wait, edge forward and wait again, till, after another hour, it was her turn to drive through the big wire gates into the yard and up to the pump. She could feel her hands sticky on the steering wheel. In the back Harriet lay still under the blanket and Sally prayed they would not bother to look inside the car. She got out to talk to the attendant to make sure he didn't peer in while he was filling the car as they often did.

The man smiled at her as she came up. 'It must

have been a bit of a wait for you people this time. They had a blockage on one of the top pipes, it took them all night to clear it.'

'It's okay as long as we can get the quota now.'

He started the delivery, inserting the metal nozzle into the petrol tank at the side and switching it on, then leaned back against the car to wait till the filling was completed.

'Haven't you heard, lady? The quota's had to be put down again. There's not enough to go round and you're a bit late I'm afraid.'

'How much?' asked Sally. She felt defeated, after all this to have failed to get the full quota.

'Thirty instead of forty.'

'So much!' She had never known such a big reduction.

'There's nothing I can do about it lady, it's regulations, you know what it's like these days. When I started working here there was no problem, petrol for everyone. I don't know what things are coming to these days. Here's your oil, lady, just one pint this time.'

Sally took the oil and wandered off, no longer listening while the attendant droned on. He must have been repeating his story to every customer today, she thought. But ten less, that was so much. She knew what a difference it would make. What would Jim do? She got back in the car, forgetting why she had got out in the first place. Only thirty. If she went back there would be no let-up.

'Alright lady, that's your lot!' He replaced the pump and waved her on.

She pulled out of the filling bay and onto the motorway. It was morning proper now, cloudy and cold but not too bad, she thought. As they picked up speed, Harriet emerged from under the blanket.

'What's happening? Where are you going?'

Sally could see the sudden panic in her eyes. She paused, though she knew she had already decided. Her eyes rested on the fuel gauge and she smiled. The needle flickered just below the full mark. Twelve hundred miles, if they made it, she thought.

SNAKE

I'll manage it in the end, it wasn't so hard this time. It won't be long now for that fat man in his velvet office. He thinks he's so safe from me. Just a body filed away in his mind and labelled 'used', 'had'. But I'll get there in the end. Every day I'm getting stronger, my mind concentrates harder and for longer. I can already feel the skin around me, warm and dry, shining, feel my backbone stretch and bend. But it's so tiring, exhausting. But I will do it in the end, he won't stay so safe, that great man.

Her family tell her to try and forget. Both mother and father suspect that she has exaggerated the story. After all she is over thirty and they cannot say she is attractive. She has stayed at home, lives her secluded life in a room over the garage. Before, her mother would often go and chat to her over a cup of tea, now she is barred, everyone is barred and they seldom see their only daughter. Her mother shakes her head as she picks roses in the garden, pricking her fingers on the thorns because she is not paying enough attention. What would become of her? She has never had a boyfriend, has never seemed to want one. The fashion magazines she buys her are always returned unread, she never wears make-up, never seems to make any effort to look anything other than dowdy. And since the summer she has stopped talking even to them. Her mother has tried to suggest she see a psychiatrist but she always refuses, her brown eyes suspicious and untrusting behind the thick brown hair that falls over her shoulders. Still, recently she has seemed happier, some of her old light has come back into her eyes and she has begun to smile again. Maybe she has got over it at last.

He thinks he can get away with it. Thinks I'm just another mousey secretary that he can refresh himself with. They don't believe me, my family. Not even my brother who thinks he's so liberated in his commune in the countryside. They wouldn't believe me now unless they saw me, and they never will. But I must stop thinking about them and concentrate. Lie still, feel my legs melt inside my skin, melt and join. Feel my arms and fingers turn into a line of smooth muscles, my head smooth down into my neck, my body narrow, eyes blink, jaw widen. Open, shut. Longer, longer, ever slender. Try to move, flick my toes inside the skin. Watch the mirror, see my new self. Yes, for a few moments I am there as I want to be. Now I must sleep. Tomorrow I will try again for longer. I must build up my stamina.

Her father sits by the fire, half-watching the television. Tired after a day at the office. He knows he will not see his daughter. Only at the weekend he sees her now, out in the garden doing her exercises. He wonders why sometimes. She has always been on the dumpy side and has never bothered before. He loves her but he does not understand her, she is so different from her brother. He was a rebel when he was young, had gone off to live in some commune

39

in the sixties with his long-haired friends. But now he has settled down to family life and his father can talk to him about the price of petrol and the problems of the Common Market. He can spoil his grandchildren even if they are illegitimate. He has got used to the ways of his son. But his daughter is still a mystery to him. She has always been at home, always obedient and helpful in the house, but never forthcoming. He rubs his balding head and switches channels with the automatic control on his lap. Dissatisfaction fills him. Since the summer she has changed so much he doesn't know what to do. What can he do?

He will be at home now. Sitting with his wife and children, the perfect husband and father. If he knew what I was doing, plotting. I can't help but laugh. I can feel my heart beat with excitement as I know the day is drawing near. Tonight I managed it for half an hour and I do not feel too exhausted. I could watch myself clearly, see the coils winding across the floor, see the light of the fire catch on the colours of my skin. The exercises have made me so much stronger. But it still takes too long, I must be able to speed it up. There will be so little time. Now I can sit and rest. Sit back and feel the glow in my body. Not since then have I felt like this. He took that away with his fat white hands and heavy, hurting body. He thinks I'm still that mousey secretary that he can take and use deep in the back stockroom, surrounded by his wealth in neat cardboard boxes. Now I can laugh. He doesn't know how little time he has left. It was so much easier than I thought.

He sits behind his big teak desk, flicking over the pages of the diary in front of him. Board meetings, buyers visits, golf matches stretch before his eyes. He is doing very well, next year he will start on the Japanese market, things are looking good. Sometimes he thinks about her. He wonders why he wanted to do it. Just because she never looked at him, never smiled when she brought his coffee in the office every morning. He had begun to hate her for it. Had had to make her see his importance, his power. And she was so ugly with her fat round body and square white face. Not like his wife with her long brown legs and slim figure. He is a 'legs man' so he tells them at the club. But she doesn't know that, she should have been more attentive, it was really her fault. Today she smiles at him as she leaves the small cup filled with black coffee on his desk. She even turns and smiles as she leaves the office, closing the thick door noiselessly behind her. Well, she is efficient, does her work neatly and accurately. He will not sack her as he has done before. She does not mention it so he will forgive her.

I am not working hard enough. I must learn more about the secrets of my new self, feel my muscles bend and stretch, control my eyes as they slide round, taking in such a new perspective. It is so strange that I can do it at all. It was just an idea, a dream of revenge, but now it has become real and I must think about it, control it. Tonight my mother knocked at the door and disturbed my other self. It was difficult and I must tell her not to bother me again in the evenings. I see she is worried. She think I am crazy. Maybe I am but I will not be changed by her or her doctors. Afterwards I will think everything out, when it is all over.

She dries the dishes and sits at the kitchen table, weary from the day. She is worried. She doesn't know what to do about her daughter. She feels too old to cope any more. Her husband sleeps in the sitting room. They are both too old, she feels, her daughter must look after herself. She went to her room this evening, wanted to talk to her. But her daughter only hissed and told her to go away. She is always busy in the evening. Her room is always locked when she is at work. It makes her angry, this secrecy, but what can she do. She is too tired.

Today I feel jubilant. I have reached my goal. For hours I lay curled up, smooth coil upon coil by the warm fire. I am beautiful, strong. I will not be stopped. I have timed the change and it is fast enough. I will be in time, for tomorrow is the day.

He is busy this morning. It is stocktaking and there is much to do. He loves to walk around, watching the clerks and secretaries hurrying and scurrying, adding up his wealth. He smiles at them. He thinks he is a generous boss. Doesn't worry too much about office pilfering, is understanding about family losses. Only sometimes he feels he must make a point. The girls in the typing pool smile back. They say his bark is worse than his bite. They have never been inside his office. He watches them and approves. She is smiling today as well. She is working deep in the stock room. He walks along the end of the room seeing her bending over between the high walls of boxes and packages. Sees the flash of white leg at the top of her black stockings as she stoops. She turns and walks towards him. Tells him that she will have to work late. He has so much wealth he believes her. Her face is full of concern. He tells her he will stay too, he can phone his wife. She nods and he feels the sweat rise out of his skin.

Now is the time. He is so foolish, so stupid to think I would forget. I can see his hulking body as he pours himself a drink. He offered me one but I refused. I will not make any mistakes this time. It is so simple, I tell him about the high parcel that I can't reach at the end of the room. He plays the gentleman and goes to fetch it. NOW. The light is switched off and I can hear him calling out in the blackness. Concentrate, concentrate. I am so excited it makes it difficult, but I can and will do it and now my brown coils lie snug beneath the desk, waiting.

For a moment he panics. Caught in the blackness he is powerless. But he is a strong man. The lights have fused, a power cut, he can fetch candles. Maybe it will be better this way. He smiles again. He calls to her but she does not answer though he hears something in the dark. She will have gone for a torch, she is very efficient after all. Slowly he feels his way back to the front, gropes for the light switch. He does not understand. The light is on again, she must have turned it off deliberately. But that is foolish, it is nothing, an accident maybe. He goes to the desk and sits behind it in the leather chair, waiting for her.

Her mother is pleased. She sings to herself as she tidies up in the living room. She picks up the newspapers and fold them neatly and stacks them under the stool. She looks up at the picture of her daughter on the mantelpiece. She is so much better. Although it was so terrible, what happened to her boss, she has got over it very well. In fact her mother hasn't seen her so well and happy for a long long time. She puts the newspaper cuttings about it in the drawer in her desk. So strange to die of a snake bite, and they never even found the snake. She shivers and shuts the desk up quickly. She won't think about that any more. Today she is going to have tea with her daughter.

MARIANNA AND THE GRADUATION

It was in those rare, sweet afternoon sleeps she dreamt of Marianna. Just a flash of black hair, black eyes and a turn of the shoulder and Marianna was gone into the curling shrouds. She would remember the dream for a few minutes after waking, and dwell on the recurring image, wondering what it meant, trying to recapture it, hold onto it before it faded but never succeeded. Lying on the narrow bed in the cubicle, she would feel a sense of loss that made her bones ache. The bare walls leant over her, denying her dreamworld with their bland beige surfaces, washing out that rare flash of black. She would study the fine mesh of the ventilator in the ceiling, endlessly counting the squares as her dream disintegrated, each tiny square a reinforcement of the reality that segmented her, cutting through her brain with its sharp metal lines.

Once she wrote it all down in an effort to think why she should dream such a dream. For several rest periods she studied the paper secretly, away from the prying square eyes of the ventilator shaft, but the task got her nowhere and just made her head ache. She didn't even know why the woman was called Marianna, just that she was — Marianna, black hair, black eyes sparkling with life for a moment and then gone so swiftly. So little to have, yet so permanent that each time the dream came back she knew she had dreamt it many times before. She knew there was something else, something she did not know. Something she could not remember but that she should know, something that mattered.

She eased her body off the bed and stretched wearily as the sound of the dinner alarm filled her cubicle with its shrill ring. She switched it off and sat down again heavily on the bed, rubbing her eyes. She felt like crying but she knew that the others would look at her oddly if they heard her, not really the right thing to do. She could go to the Guardians, they would be kind to her at least, but what more could they do; after all they were only there to teach and look after all the physical needs of their charges. What could they do with a lot of meaningless dreams? She scratched her thin brown hair and started getting dressed for dinner. It took her a while to get herself sorted out. It was often like that after the afternoon sleeps; people would be late down for their meal. The Guardians didn't seem too worried about it so she took her time. In front of the narrow window she stood and gazed out at the grey courtyard and the grey walls opposite. She hated that view, smiled when she thought it would only be another few weeks and she would never have to see it again. She tugged her tie straight, pulled her tunic over her shoulders and wriggled it down over her grey skirt, flattening it over her hips and buttocks. Only two more weeks and she would be free. This thought brought some life back into her and she pulled her belt tight over the tunic as if pulling herself back under control. It was a good half hour after the alarm sounded when she finally left the room, sealed the lock and made her way to the dining room to eat. It was two flights down and the echoing thud of her boots on the stairs filled her head, reassuring her of her own world so that by the time she got to the bottom she felt completely herself again, the dreams of the afternoon once more forgotten.

The Guardians were there, waiting for them, and so waiting for her. They smiled at her from the dais as she joined the queue. She could never really tell them apart but as they all cared for her and the others the same, often said the same kinds of things, it didn't seem to matter. Ahead of her in the queue were other girls, majors like herself, nearly ready to leave the Institute, already adults in their bodies, just waiting for that final graduation. Behind her came the minors, a mass of little smiling faces, giggling to each other while they waited. She laughed at the thought that she had been one of those little minors herself not so long ago, and now she was a major and ready to leave. She turned back to the head of the queue and concentrated on standing straight and dignified; she was not a child anymore.

The general clatter of the dining room made her feel relaxed, this was the reality she understood and felt at home in. She collected her tray from the server and went to a table to eat. No-one else sat at the table with her and for a moment that confused her. She frowned as she tried to snatch at something in her mind but it was gone and forgotten and she settled to enjoy the food. She ate with concentration and then sat back with her cup of wine, sipping it slowly, feeling the red warmth of it mix with her blood. A voice broke her contemplation.

'Lyn, may I sit with you?'

She looked up into the face of one of her fellow majors and nodded to an adjacent chair. The newcomer sat down and was silent for a moment, gazing into her own cup of wine.

'Lyn.'

'Uhuhh.'

'Do you ever think about this place, about what

happens here?'

'What do you mean?'

'Well, you know, them, the Guardians, how they treat us, always smiling, going on about things, you know.'

'No, I don't know, Sarah, I don't know what you're talking about.'

'Oh you must see it, you must. They are doing something to us, I'm sure of it. I've watched them you know, they watch me all the time, and you, that's why I thought you must know what I'm talking about.'

'Are you okay, sure you're not getting sick or something!' Lyn laughed and pressed her hand against the other girl's forehead in mock concern. 'Feels like you're getting a fever to me.'

'Listen to me, Lyn. This is the only chance I may get. I thought you would understand. If you won't, well, more fool you. Just remember that they are always watching you, always.'

Lyn frowned and stared at the other woman who was still staring intensely into her cup. Lyn could see a few drops of sweat on her upper lip and her knuckles were white where she was gripping the cup.

'Are you sure you're alright? I could get one of the Guardians to help you.'

Sarah twitched with fear. 'No, there's no need for that, I'm fine, honestly. I just thought you might have known something more than the others, but, well, it doesn't matter really.' She swallowed the remains of her wine, got up, bowed slightly and formally to Lyn and left.

As the doors of the dining room swung behind her back two of the Guardians rose from the dais and followed her out of the room. Lyn watched them go, watched their grey cloaks flow out behind them. She saw when the second Guardian got the hem of her cloak caught round the corner of the door, breaking a spell as she called out with annoyance and then laughed as she stooped to get it free. When she rose her eyes met Lyn's. Clear as a cat's eyes they chalenged her, dared her, invited her. Lyn turned back to her cup of wine.

Class next day was hard, mathematics and microcomputer dynamics. Hours of figures and equations to be absorbed, leaving no time for contemplation of any kind. Only after her lunch when she was finishing her wine did Lyn give Sarah a thought. She had not been in class, her red hair was unmistakeable, and now when Lyn looked round the dining room, she could see no sign of her. She found this idea unsettling; Sarah should be there, she was in the set so she should be there. A feeling of disquiet grew as she remembered their conversation. Maybe Sarah had really cracked up or something. She could ask the Guardians but she didn't want any trouble, not so close to graduation. She didn't really care about Sarah, it was just that the whole incident had made her feel funny and she didn't know why. She gulped down the dregs of the wine and got up suddenly, deciding to go and get some air before afternoon class began.

That night, back in the cubicle, suddenly she was cold and frightened. The walls were leaning in on her and she could feel their cold breath on her face. She huddled under the blankets for some comfort. She couldn't get that face out of her head, that pale frightened face bent over a' mug of red wine. She had come to her for help and had been sent away, Lyn had sent her away and now it was too late. She had asked the other majors in her group, casually mentioned Sarah's absence during the afternoon break. They had looked at her strangely, they couldn't ever remember seeing her, but how could they have forgotten, they must have seen her. But it was not their fault; she had come to her, Lyn, for help and had got none and now she was gone. Above her the grill gaped down, a mouth full of little square teeth, sharp, ready to bite at her as she felt herself disintegrating. Bits of her could drift up there on the cold air, the teeth were waiting, the mouth grinning. She wrapped the blanket more tightly round her body so that nothing would escape; her eyes could just make out the shadows in the room through the thick weave of the blanket. She shut them tight.

'Lyn.'
She rose from her seat at the back of the class.
'Please go to your House Guardian's office, she wishes to see you.'
Lyn bowed, left the room, and walked down the corridor, feet clicking on the stone slabs. Out into the courtyard where she stopped for a minute to look up into the sky and breathe the cool fresh air. She caught sight of a fly buzzing at one of the first floor windows, trying to get in, not understanding the glass. She walked on, into the block, up the stairs, down the corridor to her door.
'Come in Lyn.' The answer came before she had time to knock. Inside the room, all warm and grey and comfortable, the Guardian led her to a chair and sat her down and then settled into another opposite. Behind her head Lyn could see the fly at the window. It was still hurling itself at the glass. Maybe she could say she was hot and make the Guardian open the window. Maybe she couldn't. She sat back in the chair and waited.
'You have not been sleeping very well recently, my dear,' said the Guardian.
'No.' Lyn suddenly felt edgy.

'We understand you see, we want to help you. We know what a hard time this can be.'

'I don't know what you mean. I just don't sleep very well, but it's okay, I can always sleep in the afternoons.'

'Ah yes, the afternoons.' The Guardian moved round to stand behind Lyn and started massaging her scalp and neck. Lyn began to relax as the strong fingers eased the tension out of her muscles, lifted the pressure off her skull, she hadn't felt like this since . . . since Sarah had talked to her.

'What happened to Sarah?'

'You must not worry about Sarah. She was sick, we had to send her away to get well. She wasn't like you, you are special and will get our special attention.'

Lyn's eyes closed. The Guardian's fingers were so comforting, so relaxing. She didn't feel cold anymore. She opened one eye and saw the fly. She opened both and it was still flying against the window, reckless stupid thing; she could hear it crashing its body into the glass, the shudder that went through its thorax every time it failed. She closed her eyes again.

'Why don't I sleep well? I always used to sleep well.'

'Try not to worry about it, you can always come to us in the night if you get scared, we will help you.'

She had to do something about the fly. Even with her eyes closed she knew it would still be there, she could feel it.

'Guardian?'

'Yes my dear.'

'Will you open the window, just for a moment, I feel so hot, please.'

'I'm sorry my dear, these windows don't open, I'll turn down the heating for you, you're probably over-tired because of this not sleeping.'

'She opened her eyes wide. The fly had gone. Had it known about the windows all along? Probably, she thought, She didn't know very much, not enough, she wanted to know more.

'And what about Marianna?'

'Who is Marianna, Lyn?'

She could not answer. She didn't know why she had asked the question, she just knew it had to be asked. Something about it was like Sarah, Sarah had made her ask. No, Sarah was gone, Sarah didn't know Marianna, only she knew Marianna.

'Who is Marianna, Lyn?'

'I don't know, I don't know! Don't you know Guardian?' She turned, twisting her head out of the woman's hands. 'You must know her if I know her, you know everything about me!'

'I think you must go back to your room now, Lyn. I hope you sleep better tonight and we will see about other things tomorrow. Remember graduation is very near now, you must be well for that.'

'Yes Guardian.' It was as though Marianna's name had never been mentioned. She left the room.

The Guardian sat for some time after the girl had gone, wondering what she was doing. Was it all really worth it, the suffering, the doubts? So many failures, so many Sarahs. And then she thought of Marianna and smiled.

That night Lyn dreamt of Marianna. A dream at night, not in the dozy, quiet afternoon but in the thick night. This time the black hair seemed to envelop her so that she fought to find a way through. There was no face in the hair, no flashing eyes to light the darkness, just the thick strands that caught across her teeth in her mouth, filling her with panic, a ball of fear that rose through her body until it came out of her mouth in a cry of terror that woke her up. She lay gasping on the bed, staring up at the grid, not daring to move, to think what was happening to her. She lay for hours just feeling every muscle tight and stiff under the blanket. She felt as if she were suddenly paralysed, that she could never move again, except to twist her eyes around in their sockets to gaze first at the grill, then the wall, the door, the grill again. She could not see to the window behind her head and the thought occurred to her that it was gone, bricked up because she was gone, like Sarah, like Marianna. Somewhere they too might be lying, paralysed like her, bricked in, locked up because they had done wrong, offended the Guardians. They had said they would help her sleep well, they would know what was happening. She squinted up at the grill, they would be watching her now through the square holes, seeing how she responded, monitoring every reaction on a thousand shiny dials. She made herself relax, controlled her heart so that its beating no longer made the walls vibrate. They would not catch her out that way, she would make sure of it.

She forced herself to sit up, push the blankets back and turn round to see the window. It was there of course, no bricks. She stood on the bed and reached up with her fingers towards the grill. She could see no peering eyes, no lenses or microphones, only the black emptiness of the ventilation shaft. The door opened when she turned the handle, allowing her a view of the deserted corridor with its thin light coming from the Guardian's office. The door was ajar, she could go down there, get comfort for the nightmare. She went back to bed, getting warmth from the rough familiar blankets. She had to think; something was happening, maybe she was going crazy, maybe not, maybe this just happened when you got older, another change like the one that had happened in her body. She did not know anymore what she felt like, who she trusted, where she was.

She lay still, she would just wait until morning and then work it out. When sleep came it was heavy and empty of dreams. When the Guardian looked in on Lyn on her nightly rounds, she found her curled in a tight ball, clutching her pillow, and she pulled the blanket up carefully over Lyn's bare shoulder.

* * * * * *

'We have decided it will be tomorrow. You have today to prepare yourself. You have been told what will be expected of you.'

Lyn could not tell which of the Guardians had spoken because she had been watching the dust in the air, lit by a rare shaft of sunlight, coming from the skylight high in the roof of the main hall. Now she turned back to the dais. They really did all look the same, smiling faces in their grey gowns and mortar boards. They reminded her of the minors, maybe they thought of all the Guardians behaving like minors, running around with their gowns on and all. A sharp hiss from behind her brought her back to reality and she adopted a more respectful position. She looked round at the other majors, there seemed such a lot suddenly, or maybe she had never noticed before, never bothered to get to know them. There had not seemed much point in getting to know them, though at that moment Lyn could not think why.

In the far corner she saw a flash of red and her brow tightened. She moved imperceptibly to get a better view and was in clear sight of a red-haired girl. There was something in her face that made Lyn feel that terrible confusion again. She could not name her, could not remember her, and yet there was something about her.

'Remember girls, this is your chance to show how well you have learnt here. We have much need of your skills and this will be the beginning of your chance to repay all that has been given you here.' The Guardian went on with her speech but Lyn had stopped listening. She was obsessed with the redhead, constantly scratching at her brain for a memory that was suffocated by sleep. She wished the speech was over, they had heard it all before and she wanted to get out and have a closer look at the girl. All the Guardians were speaking now, intoning some kind of prayer, a blessing, before they bowed and walked silently out of the hall.

In the dining room Lyn found the red-haired girl sitting at a table with a mug of wine. Lyn looked at the white mug, at the pale face, and finally, as though under torture, her brain spat out the memory.

'Sarah!'

The pale face looked up at her. The eyes were empty, smiling empty eyes.

'Sarah, don't you remember? It's me Lyn, Lyn!'

The face smiled again, 'Lyn. Lyn, why don't you sit with me?'

'You don't remember do you? You must!'

'What is there to remember? Please don't look so troubled, it is graduation tomorrow, surely it's a day to look forward to. Here, have some of my wine it will help you relax.'

Lyn pushed away the proffered cup and sat staring into the pale face, too stunned to speak. This woman had forgotten her entirely, completely, as though they had never met. And yet it had happened, either that or she was really going mad, a mad woman with mad dreams.

Mad dreams: she could feel that black hair floating across the back of her thin, aching neck. Sarah's face blurred as tears spilled over, flooding Lyn's eyes, the ache of her loss hit her in the stomach. All she could see was that vacant, smiling, pale, empty, lost, stupid face; she punched her fist hard into it, saw the blood spurt out of the nose, felt the crunch of her knuckles into teeth and ran.

* * * * * *

Lyn shivered as the night air crept into her bones, seeking every entrance into her body through her clothes. The sweat of fear, of escape, had long since dried, leaving her feeling dirty and clammy. She was crouched in a ditch, hiding under rotting bracken like a hunted animal. Above her thick clouds covered the sky so that the darkness was complete, giving her no clues as she had tried to stumble her way forward. Now she would wait till the morning, she didn't want to risk going the wrong way, maybe even finding her way back there, where she had come from. She huddled up more deeply under the leaves. She had heard no pursuit when she ran, had only caught a glimpse of grey cloaks rustling, only heard a few voices raised in agitation as she flung herself round corners and down empty corridors, deafened by the sound of her boots, the beat of her pulse and the huge rasping of her breath. She had found the way out without difficulty, she had known it would be there, a doorway that finally took her out. Out beyond the walls, the courtyards, the wire grills and empty, empty cubicles, out into the real world where the ground was rough, where long grass whipped her legs as she ran, crying, fists flailing, tripping over fallen branches until the ditch had come up to meet her, to give her a little shelter, a little rest.

That night she slept long and deep. Even in the cold air she slept a sleep empty of terrors, empty of confusion. A sleep that let her fingers uncurl and lie softly among the leaves, a sleep that soothed her body, unwound her muscles so that the early morning sunshine warmed right through to give her strength. And when she woke she remembered. She remembered Sarah, she remembered the dreams of Marianna, and somewhere at the edge of her mind she even caught a glimpse of her, a glimpse of the black hair rippling somewhere far away. She remembered the Guardians, the Institution, she remembered that she had run away and that today should be Graduation.

She lay on her back and waited until wakefulness had filtered through her whole body, and then slowly pulled herself upright and climbed out of the ditch to see where she had got to.

All around her was a wide open moorland covered by rough pasture, bracken, low bushes and stubby trees, nowhere was cultivated, no paths or roads led across the land as far as her eye could see. Behind her in the distance lay the grey shadow of the Institute, the only break in the straight line of the horizon. She must have run and scrambled miles in the dark to have got so far, and yet when she looked out ahead of her there were only more endless miles of the same flat open countryside. Out of the shelter of the ditch the wind blew so strongly that she could scarcely look into it without tears coming to her eyes. The wind blew from the direction of the Institute so she saw it through a haze, through tears, through a veil of fears and lost memories. She walked away, putting her back to the grey walls and her eyes to the far distant horizon.

All day she walked, till hunger and exhaustion forced her to stop and rest as the sun set. The wind was relentless, and though she was walking with it, not against it, still it wearied her, rushing her too fast, making her stumble and fall in the many holes and ditches that covered the moorland. Her clothes were covered with mud and torn by brambles, her feet felt sore in her boots though she didn't dare take them off in case she could not put them on again. And the worst of it was that it seemed she had not progressed at all. Still the grey shadow hung over the west, still the horizon ahead gave her no promise of change or help.

She made a pile of bracken and collapsed on it, depression, loneliness, fear, all fought for her soul. She couldn't even start thinking about why she had run. It all had to do with her dreams and with Sarah but she was too tired to concentrate. All she could think of was a warm dry bed, a mug of wine and the comfort of those firm walls to keep out of the wind. And even them, the Guardians, even to see a face that would smile at her, give her some comfort. After all, that one had said she was special, so why had they not looked after her? She buried her head in her arms, overcome by self-pity, and cried for all that was lost.

* * * * * *

When she woke the first thing she saw was the grill, the square holes gaping down at her, mocking her, grinning at her thin body huddled under the blanket. Her whole body and soul sighed with the failure of it all, the uselessness of everything. She got out of bed and went to the narrow window, the view had not changed. She sat on the bed, empty, vacant, she could not even cry but just sat watching her body sag, her shoulders curl round, her breasts droop till she felt she could just slide into the floor, admit defeat.

Hours seemed to pass without a movement, no sound from within the room except the sound of her own breathing, no sound outside the room. The corridors were empty now, there were no other majors; graduation was over, they had all gone.

Somewhere below the minors would be in their classes, blissfully unaware of what was happening. There was only her now, one major left behind.

From the seemingly far far distance she heard feet walking down the corridor. Not the thud of a major's boot but a smoother, softer, more rhythmic tread. The swing doors squeaked as the feet entered the last stretch of passage to Lyn's door. Lyn lay rigid, listening to the approaching danger with every part of her body. When the knock came she spasmed and pulled herself up and into the corner of the bed with the blankets wrapped round her. When the door opened she turned her face away and closed her eyes, waiting for whatever it was to happen. But all she sensed was that someone came in quietly and was now sitting next to her on the bed. She opened her eyes and saw her. A young woman dressed in brown working clothes that looked grubby and patched, an old green woollen cloak and leather boots encrusted with mud. As their eyes met, hers black and alive, Lyn's narrow, bloodshot, untrusting, she pushed the hood of her cloak back and her black hair fell down, a wild tangle like a thousand spiders' webs.

'Lyn.'

Lyn knew now that she was mad and simply pulled the blanket more tightly round her shoulders and turned to face the wall.

'You know who I am, don't you? You know I am Marianna.' The woman reached her hand out tentatively towards Lyn who shrank back into the corner.

'We were such friends once weren't we, you do remember? I remember, I remember all the days we spent together; we often went outside then, out onto the moorland when we should have been in class.'

A corner of Marianna's cloak fell across Lyn's hand as she leant towards her. Lyn froze at the contact. Dreams had become reality, this was something that she would not believe. She tore her eyes away from the vision and screamed up at the grill.

'No no no! I will not remember, I will not! There is nothing to remember! I will not be mad!'

She scrambled away from Marianna across the bed and waited for her to disappear as dreams must. This did not happen, only the door opened and the grey figure of a Guardian came in and sat by the black-haired woman. They spoke closely between themselves, nodding towards Lyn. She could not work out why the Guardian was talking to her dream and somewhere still there was the image of a red-haired girl who had been driven insane, or who, maybe had driven her insane.

The Guardian moved over to her.

'Listen to me Lyn, listen to me, who am I?'

'My Guardian.'

'That's right my dear. And what am I here to do?'

'I thought you were here to look after me, but, I don't know, I don't know what's happening anymore.'

'Just trust me a little longer and then you will understand.' She took Lyn's hand in hers and Lyn wanted to bite the hand, to kick and run, and yet she could do nothing. The hand that held hers had cared for her all her short life, had fed her, clothed her, played with her and taught her. What else could she do but give in to it?

'I said once that you were special and I meant it. You are special because you have managed what so many others cannot. You have come out of the Shock. No, wait, no questions till I have finished. You think you are mad, you think someone is trying to attack you, you fear us who have loved you all your life. We understand, we too have gone through the awakening, for that is what it is, an awakening that will shake us, that will give us responsibilities and greater fears than all your contemporaries from the set will feel. You have begun to remember, to have the whole view of your life with you. You will remember more and more as time goes by and you will no longer forget. There are only a very few like you, Marianna is one too. She left because she thought you had forgotten her completely. She did not know that you still carried her image, that one day you might remember and go and seek her out on the moorland. It was she who brought you back to us to get help.'

Lyn looked from one face to the other. Her brain twisted and struggled with the words, waves of fear, wanting, the ache of loss, she didn't know what to say. She wanted it all, and she wanted to go back to when it never happened.

'I know it's hard, but there is plenty of time to find out all that must be uncovered. And there is much joy as well as grief, that you must believe. Now I must leave you; there are many things that have to be prepared. After all in a few weeks there will be another group of majors. Marianna will explain everything to you and then you are free to go when you are ready. Come and see me first though, and I will tell you many stories that you can carry with you wherever you go.' She touched Lyn slightly on the shoulder and left.

Marianna had gone over and opened the window onto the courtyard.

'This view was never much good was it!'
'You've been in here before?' whispered Lyn.

'Of course! Lots of times. We were close you know, please try to remember.'

'I do remember something, but I thought it was a dream.'

Marianna came and sat on the bed again, reached her hand out again. This time Lyn felt herself stretch out and take the hand and allow herself to be pulled gently out of her corner until she was sitting next to the dark-haired woman on the edge of the bed. She nearly started to smile and then she remembered.

'Sarah, what happened to Sarah? What did they do to her?'

'They had to help her, Lyn, they weren't hurting her. She nearly had remembered but it had come out all wrong. Apparently it does sometimes, people only remember all those bad feelings, like how you felt, only Sarah never moved on. They thought it would be better just to let her forget again. Otherwise she would have gone crazy, killed herself or something. What else could they do!'

'And the rest of the majors?'

'They just go on as they are. Only a few come through like you have. After a certain age, when it's graduation, there's no more chance that it will happen, we get too fixed, so after that everyone just does whatever they do best.'

'But why, why is this thing happening? What is the Shock?'

'I don't know the whole story myself, you must ask the Guardians, but thousands of years ago they say there was a terrible war where many many people died, nearly everyone, and horrible things happened. When the few survivors started to build up a life again, they could not bear to remember what had happened so they just forgot. They couldn't bear to be close to people in case it happened again so people were easily forgotten; it was a protection against a terrible pain and guilt. The children were the same, no-one really cared about anyone. Then a few, just a few, started to remember and they tried to help others to remember. It's still only a very few now and only the girls, the boys seem too deep into it, almost like they are asleep all their lives, though

I don't really know why that should be. I suppose it must have something to do with what happened then.'

Lyn was in a daze. She no longer felt that she was crazy, she felt more relaxed with Marianna than she had felt for ages. Yet suddenly hearing all this new information, that made life seem so different, filled her with fresh doubts and fear. She let Marianna put her arm around her.

'But why you and me, why not Sarah?'

'I don't know, Lyn, I don't know about Sarah, maybe she just didn't have anything good enough to remember.'

She was in the middle of doing the dishes when they landed in the back garden. Normally she would have missed them but as Frank had been kept late at the office (her lip twitched with disbelief) they had not eaten until later than usual. He would never have seen them land. His visits to the kitchen were rare, only using it as a way out to his precious garden.

She was just getting to grips with the burnt-on mince at the bottom of the casserole dish, rubbing away with an antique scourer that had lost all its scour and was rapidly becoming a soggy mass in the dirty water. She was just cursing Frank because if he hadn't been so late, the dinner would not have been dried up, she would not still be in the kitchen, there would have been time to go to the pub, etc., etc. A combination of red, yellow and blue lights flashed through the window, illuminating the kitchen through the limp, patterned curtains. It was already dark outside so the effect was bewildering. Before she had time to devise any theories for this situation, a strong smell of burning grass hit her nostrils and when she looked from behind a corner of the curtain, her view of the garden was obscured by a swirling cloud of smoke.

Her first thought was that that wretched family next door were having yet another fireworks party. That again they would come round in the morning and apologise for things getting 'a little out of hand' after they'd kept them awake all night and left the cat in a state of shock. But she remembered that Frances had told her they were going away, off for the family holiday somewhere abroad. Margot had not really bothered to listen where, if she did she might want to go and that would never do, not with her Frank being the way he was. Well if it wasn't that, she really couldn't think of much else. Frank involved with terrorists who were now going to bomb them? She laughed. World War Three? Well, she had read their copy of *Protect and Survive* and she knew it couldn't start with illuminations in the back garden. She stared out of the window, the smoke had settled now, the singeing smell slowly evaporating. Only a couple of orange lights still shone, blinking softly in the darkness. She cupped her hands round her face to make it easier to see and was just able to make out an object of some kind on the lawn. It must be those children, she thought. Maybe they didn't go away. She must have got the dates wrong. They were so spoilt, another of those computer toys. She left the dishes in the sink, wiped her hands on the tea towel, ready to go out and tell them to take themselves and their toys out of Frank's garden. One final glance through the window and she decided perhaps she wouldn't go out just yet, she would call Frank. There was more light in the garden coming from a square opening in the round object that she could see nearly filled the lawn. The light was very bright and illuminated several small figures that were moving round the garden. They looked very little like children.

'Frank!' She called out to her husband asleep in the armchair in the front room.

'Frank, come here, quick!'

He grunted a bit and slumped further into the

chair, the paper crumpled on his lap.

'Frank, for heaven's sake hurry. You should see what they've done to the lawn, and the tomatoes. They've started on the tomatoes. Oh my God!'

Margot was now transfixed in front of the sink watching in horror as the creatures pulled up one after another of her husband's prize tomatoes.

The mention of tomatoes helped bring Frank back to consciousness. He pushed the paper onto the floor and struggled to get his bulk out of the chair, grumbling about quiet evenings and armchairs and the rights of a working man to get a bit of peace at the end of the day. Pushing his feet into his slippers, he shuffled into the kitchen.

'What the hell's the matter with you, Margot! What are you going on about?' He came up behind his wife, pushing her out of the way to have a look.

'The tomatoes, Frank. Look at your tomatoes, what they're doing, and the lawn, it'll be ruined!'

He squinted out into the garden. On the lawn he could see the round object about the size of his greenhouse, the open door, the light that shone from it. He could see several figures busy in his garden. Two were pulling up all of the plants along his herbaceous border, another two were bombarding his apple tree with tomatoes and then making strange squealing noises and running away as the apples came dropping down on top of them. There seemed to be more of them running in the shadows, carrying armfuls of plants and vegetables back inside the glowing doorway. The veins in Frank's neck began to swell with rage as he watched his garden being systematically destroyed.

'Frank,' Margot's tone was hushed. 'It's one of those flying saucers isn't it, and them, they're little green men.' Margot had seen *Close Encounters*, had cried her way through *ET* three times. She knew.

'Now come on Margot, pull yourself together. It'll be those kids from next door up to no good. You know what they're like, no respect for other people's property, no discipline these days. Just wait till I get my hands on them!' With that he reached for his coat from behind the back door and pulled it on with a struggle.

'Oh, be careful, I'm sure next door's away, and they don't look like children to me!' Margot stretched out one arm in a feeble attempt to stop her husband, but she could not pull herself away from the window and the sight of the little figures now tearing up just about anything they could see and carrying it back inside their craft. She was fascinated by their thin black silhouettes darting round the garden. When they started on Frank's prize roses she could even feel giggles rising in her throat. All that effort he had put into them, pruning, fertilising, pesticides, plant foods, the only thing in his life she had seen him really care about, all down the drain in the time it took for one good wrench to pull them out of the ground. They must be very strong, she thought, as she watched them showering what was left of the lawn with rose petals.

Frank's face darkened with fury.

'That's it, that's the limit! My best floribundas, ruined, ruined!' He grabbed the broom, pulled open the back door and disappeared into the garden.

Margot hovered nervously just inside the door, watching as he blundered across the lawn towards them, brandishing the broom and yelling all kinds of dire threats as to what he was going to do to them. She couldn't help but think he looked a pretty ridiculous figure. Even if they were just children dressing up, they probably wouldn't take much notice of him.

At first it seemed as though she might be wrong.

They all stopped what they were doing, heads on one side, and watched as he approached. One of them extended some kind of thing like a radio aerial out of its head towards him. They grouped together so they were in a line, seven identical silhouettes waiting for Frank.

Frank had got to the edge of the herbaceous border and was face to face with the first of the creatures, its arms full of hollyhocks and lavender. It had not moved back at all in the face of Frank's furious advance, and now it just looked up at him as he raised the broom above his head. There was a blinding flash, and a rather nasty smell that she couldn't quite place but seemed familiar in some way, and when Margot looked again, Frank had gone. Well, not completely gone, just by the herbaceous border was a smouldering pile and sticking out at one angle Margot could see what was left of the broom. The smell she could now identify as a mixture of burnt overcoat and singed hair and something else which she didn't like to think about.

Margot was horrified. She galvanised herself into action, managed to slam the back door, turn the light off and take a firm grip on the frying pan back in her more secure position by the sink. She took another frightened peek from behind the curtains. There wasn't much left of the garden now, just a few plants lying on the path. One of them was finishing off the lawn by tearing up strips of turf and doing some kind of dance round the ornamental pond before jettisoning its load into the water, spraying the surrounding rockery with assorted pond weeds and goldfish. The others were all still, resting, waiting for the last one to finish. She noticed they all avoided going near the still smouldering pile in the corner, although occasionally pointing to it with the aerial things and then collapsing, squealing.

She could feel her heart beating faster and faster, soon they would be ready for something else. She knew, knew in her heart that then they would come for her. She thought of phoning the police but didn't dare leave the kitchen for an instant, anyway she probably wouldn't get a lot of response from the local station. The police were always too busy with other things these days, football hooligans and guarding royalty and suchlike. She had rung them up once about an intruder and they had told her it was probably the central heating making a noise. She didn't even have central heating, but fortunately it was just Frank climbing in the kitchen window, blind drunk after another night he had been 'kept late at the office'. If she told them about this, they'd probably sue her for wasting police time. So she stayed where she was, stomach in her throat, heart bursting out of her ribs, sweat creeping over each bony vertebrae, waiting.

When they were all together they turned and faced the house, seven wiry shadows against her. In fits and starts they advanced, like grandmother's footsteps they dashed forward, then back, then forward again until they were within a few yards of the back door. Then they stopped, waiting for her.

A few moments passed when a thousand thoughts went through Margot's mind. Her whole life did not pass before her in a flash or anything like that, but she certainly went through something of an identity crisis. At least that was what she decided to call it afterwards. She considered running out begging for mercy but was too afraid of ending up like Frank to risk that. She throught of just hiding in the cupboard under the sink but dismissed that when she considered being found there, and anway it really stank as she hadn't washed the bin out that week. She thought of running out into the street to get help, but knew that no one round their way was much into helping neighbours, except Frances who was off somewhere foreign. Anyone else would only go and call the welfare or something and get her carted off. But she had to do something, she could not spend the whole night in the kitchen, in the dark, waiting to be zapped or whatever, by some alien invasion. The fear began to ebb out of her and a certain acceptance of the situation took over. Just because these creatures had not appeared to be too fond of Frank did not mean they might not like her. After all she had not been that fond of Frank herself and he had never threatened her with the kitchen broom.

She replaced the frying pan carefully on the draining board and switched the light on. Opening the fridge, she took out two pints of milk. From the cupboard she fetched seven glasses, one cup and saucer and a plate. She poured seven glasses of milk out, took a packet of digestive biscuits and arranged them on the plate, put that lot on a tray, opened the back door and left it on the step. Back inside, she put a tea bag in her cup, switched the kettle on and sat down at the kitchen table to await her visitors.

They now moved steadily towards the back door, heads nodding from side to side, whirring and whooshing at each other, squealing in response to the whistle of the kettle. Margot poured the boiling water into her cup and whisked the tea bag round and out into the bin, amazed at how calm she felt inside. After all, it wasn't every day she had visitors from outer space, and especially after what they'd done to Frank. She stirred in a few drops of milk and sat back to enjoy it. That was the wonder of tea, she thought, it made anything you were doing seem normal if you had a cup. And now Frank was gone, she wouldn't even have to bother buying sugar. She looked out to see how her guests were getting on.

They had now reached the step and were examining the tray with great interest, bent over it in a huddle. One of them dipped his aerial in the milk and immediately fell over backwards. The others all touched the biscuits and smelt the milk gingerly, before one of them took one delicate sip of milk, then squealed to the others, who all grabbed a glass and glugged down the contents in one go. From then on it was free house, the biscuits went, as did Frank's cornflakes, a dozen eggs, the cheese, half a pound of bacon and all the jam sandwiches Margot could make. An hour later and they were all sitting round the table in the kitchen squealing and nudging each other. Margot was sitting in the middle of them with her third cup of tea suddenly feeling this was the most ordinary thing in the world.

And, thank heaven, they were nothing like that ugly ET. They were green, of course, with a covering of short smooth hair that felt like velvet when she touched it. They kept the aerial thing in a kind of ridge down the back of their skulls, only bringing it out when it was needed, though Margot had no idea when that might be. They had two eyes, in the usual place, but the iris was black, while the pupil was a deep green on some and red on others. Six fingers on each hand that were constantly moving, touching, examining. One of them started running its fingers through Margot's greying hair, squealing in panic to the others when some of the hair came away in its hands.

When they finally quietened down, Margot felt it was only right that she talk to them about Frank. It was all very well, and maybe she could get over the loss of Frank, but they really shouldn't go round blasting people all over the place. Some people might take it seriously amiss and just because Frank wasn't really very frightening didn't mean that there weren't human beings who could really zap them right back. She had no idea if they could understand her, but they all had their heads on one side and seemed to be listening and even looked out of the back door once or twice to where a pile of ashes was growing cold.

'And what on earth do you think I'm going to tell the neighbours when they ask where he is, and his boss, and his friends down at the gardening club? They're not going to believe all this now are they?

The visitors squealed attentively in response but Margot could see they weren't going to offer any solutions. The more she thought about it, the more she worried. The police might get involved, and what about all the papers, his pensions? She didn't know if there was money still to pay for the house; she couldn't move, not now. Surely she wouldn't have to move. Six green fingers pulling at her hand snapped her out of it. After all, she wasn't going to miss him, it would be hypocritical to say she was, and as for the rest she would just have to sort it out. She would go down to the Citizens Advice, you could trust them, they weren't really like the welfare.

The creatures wanted, and got, a tour of the house before finally settling down in front of the television in the front room. Only black and white, but they seemed to love it. Maybe it reminded them of wherever they had come from, Margot wondered, and relaxed with them for the last half of *Minder* and *News at Ten*.

It was during the commercial break that Margot heard a kind of whooshing sound from the kitchen. Seven little green faces also heard the noise and started twitching nervously and squealing to each other. Perched in a row on the edge of the sofa, they all turned and stared at the door as the whooshing stopped and the door slowly opened.

The creature that came in was a bit like a bird and a bit like a bat. It seemed to have wings but it didn't have feathers or a beak. It wasn't green, but it wasn't really grey or black either, something in between, a kind of shimmering colour that changed every time Margot looked at it. But one thing she could tell about this creature was that it was very angry indeed, its one green eye and one red eye glowing brightly as it peered down at the sofa and its occupants. It started whooshing again and the little creatures grew even more agitated. The blast of air blew over Margot's vase of flowers which smashed onto the fireplace, sending the seven into a complete panic, tripping over each other to get across the room to the creature's feet. Margot felt no fear of this whooshing thing, simply annoyed to have to clear up yet another mess. Really, these aliens would have to learn better manners if they were going to come more often.

The creature turned to Margot and clucked at her, a mixture of greeting and apology, even, Margot felt, a request for understanding. She was impressed.

'Oh that's alright, it was only an old vase, Frank's sister gave it to us years ago and I never really liked it.' She stood facing the creature, its long wings (or were they arms?) now sheltering seven little figures.

'Ah!' she exclaimed, 'you must be their mother, yes, I suppose I can see a bit of a family likeness! Yes, well I know what children can be like, mine are grown up now but when they were young, ooh they were right terrors, I can tell you!'

The creature clucked back sympathetically, or so Margot thought anyway, and hustled her brood back out into the garden. There was now another round craft on the lawn that had joined itself to the first by a tunnel. With one loud whoosh the creature raised its wings (or were they arms?) and all seven visitors ran squealing into the open doorway. The creature turned and bowed again to Margot, nodding her head from side to side, indicating her distress as to the state of Margot's garden, and Margot's husband. Then she retreated into the space-craft, the door slid shut, the lights flashed out once more and they were gone.

It was nearly two o'clock in the morning when Margot finally collapsed into bed. Although she was exhausted from her efforts, she knew she would find it hard to sleep and so had come upstairs armed with a fresh cup of tea and half a packet of biscuits that her visitors had overlooked. She had managed to get the garden into some semblance of order, and in fact once the mess had been cleared away it didn't look too bad. She could always go down to the nurseries and get some more plants before anyone came and saw.

As for Frank there was not a lot she could do about a burial, given the circumstances, so she had carefully dug a hole where the floribundas used to be and gingerly shovelled the ashes into it. She would plant a new rose tree on the spot, she promised herself, and that would be as good a memorial as any. Until then, she had put one of the garden gnomes from the front path on top so she wouldn't forget where he was. Really it was quite suitable, one of those that was carrying a pick. Looked a bit like him too, though hardly dressed for the part. She smiled at the thought of Frank parading around dressed as a gnome. She smiled at the thought of Frank doing anything now that he was gone.

She would just tell everyone that he had left her. She crunched on a ginger biscuit. She knew no one would have much trouble believing her, she had wondered why he hadn't done it years ago. Her children would help her out until she got herself straight and then, well, she might get a job, travel, have some fun.

And one thing she would do was throw a party for the children next door, inviting all her friends.

TRANSPLANT

She lay in the bed and wondered. They had not told her why she was there, lying between crisp hospital sheets. She had asked over and over, but they wouldn't tell her why. And now she was frightened of the doctors and nurses who only smiled at her and squeezed her hand sometimes if she cried. When her husband came, she asked him why, asked him to take her home now. She felt no pain, no sickness, she wanted to go home. He kissed her, told her that she would be coming home very soon now, it was just a few tests, that was all.

They gave her drugs that made her feel sleepy. She complained, so they gave her drugs that made her feel uncomplaining and sleepy. And she thought she felt better, just rather tired. Maybe when the tests were finished she would stop feeling sleepy. She didn't know what the tests were. Sometimes no one came near her cubicle all day, only at night they always came; the nurse, to give her pills and squeeze her hand because she was crying, and her husband who sat by the bed and said nothing. Sometimes they took her blood away inside needles that pricked her arm and she could see the red colour through the glass. She didn't know why they took it away, they never told her. She had forgotten how long she had been in this place. They told her not to worry when she told them she had forgotten where she lived.

They told her it was just the tests, everything would be alright. She wished she could remember where she lived, it made her feel frightened when she knew she had forgotten.

There were other patients. She had heard them sometimes but she never saw them, they never let her go out of her room to see the other patients. She asked the nurses if they were having tests as well but they only smiled and squeezed her hand in case she was going to cry when they wouldn't tell her.

This morning was special. They did not tell her about it but she knew anyway. She had heard the ambulance screaming in the early morning, and now the nurses and doctors all seemed to be running around. But they wouldn't tell her anything. Her husband came in and sat by the bed and talked to her, though he did not tell her why he had come in the morning and not in the evening. When he left he kissed her and squeezed her hand even though she was not crying. The nurse came and gave her an injection that made her feel sleepy. They lifted her off the bed and put her on a long white trolley. She asked them if she was going home but they only smiled. She asked them if the tests were over and they nodded. She was not frightened when they steered her out of the ward and down the corridor and into the lift. The nuse stroked her forehead and she liked that. The lift doors opened and they came out into another corridor. From the corner of her eye she thought she could see her husband talking to someone at the desk. She thought she saw him take something from the other man and put it in his pocket. She tried to wave to him but he had gone out of the door.

The trolley went through more swing doors and she saw only the lights above her head. She could hear the noise of the pump but she did not know what it was. And of course they would not tell her.

Elizabeth dragged the old wood-cart down the street, feeling the March winds pulling at her coat. At seventy-eight, or thereabouts, she was never quite sure of her age, she knew she was getting too old and slow for this kind of thing. But she liked to help, to do her bit for the group of women she had come to see as her family. Spring was slowly fighting its way in and today was the first day the sun had shone strong enough to warm her. As she reached the top of the street she was met by a group of children, the eldest only ten years old. They clustered round her, fascinated by her age.

'Can we help you with the wood?' asked the eldest. 'We'll be very careful and we'll collect lots for you!'

'Well, dears, if you promise not to be too long.'

'Yes, yes, we promise!' they cried and within a minute they were off, down towards the park, pulling the cart along at top speed.

Ahh well, she thought, I'm getting on a bit, it does the children no harm to help. After all, they never seemed to do much in the way of school learning these days. She shook her head, things had certainly changed since she was a girl.

She wrapped her scarf more tightly round her head and buttoned up the top cardigan of the collection that she wore. She made her way to the bench at the entrance to the park and sat down to wait for the return of the firewood. She tucked a loose white strand of hair under her scarf as the wind picked up, whistling through the streets, making the old tin rattle and crumbling bricks fall. Through her sharp blue eyes she saw the streets of her childhood slowly vanishing, every year a little more.

She tried to remember the Broadway Market of her youth, full of people bustling about, talking and laughing. She remembered Saturday mornings, market day, when you couldn't drive down the street at all, when all the shops spilled out onto the pavement and second-hand dealers moved in for the day. She remembered her mother pulling her around by one hand as she did all her shopping for the week. Elizabeth had always wanted to stop and look at all the different stalls, especially the ones that sold toys, the cheap Japanese kind. But her mother's hand always yanked her on, into the boring supermarket where she wasn't interested in anything. And when the shopping was done there was always the hour spent sitting on the step outside the *Cat and Mutton* while her mother drank halves of bitter, surrounded by her mates and piles of shopping. She got a bottle of orange or coke and a packet of crisps and a lecture on good behaviour. She didn't mind, especially in summer when lots of kids would gather around the pub and play games.

It was all so long ago, she must have been about six or seven then, she thought. Everything was different now, even the air smelt different. Gone were the petrol fumes, the factory smells. She looked up to a clear sky, blue with fat white clouds blown across it. She smelt the fresh air and tried to imagine the days when the smog got so bad she had to wear a mask and she couldn't see across the street. Sometimes she felt like a different person altogether than the child and young woman who had lived in Albion Drive all those years ago. She watched the women at work in the park, tending the rows of sturdy spring vegetables and preparing the soil for the new seedlings. London Fields had finally become fields after all this time. There was a small bit near the market the children called the Park because it still had a few trees left and grass and it reminded them of the big parks in the city. Otherwise London Fields had been harnessed to produce enough vegetables and fruit and pasture for the few cows and sheep needed to keep the small community alive.

The women paused from their work to wave at her. They seemed so young to Elizabeth, so innocent, so idealistic, she felt she couldn't understand half the things they went on about. But she had to admit they were always polite to her. In fact, some of the younger ones treated her with a kind of awed reverence which she found a trifle irritating and quite the opposite of what she was used to.

It was funny. When she was a girl she never had any respect for old people. She used to make fun of them with her friends if they saw one in the street alone. When she was taken to her grandparents she only wanted to go for the presents, she thought they were old fuddy-duddys and didn't know anything about anything. And now it was all different. The children were very polite to her and all the women listened to her and treated her as someone who was very experienced and who knew a lot. She was glad, of course. She used to feel she had got away with something. Her mother used to tell her that if she was horrible to the old people, then she would be lonely and miserable when she too, got old. It hadn't worked and Elizabeth had spent only a few sleepless moments worrying about her lonely old age, and now here she was and everyone was as nice as pie to her!

They said it was because of what she had been through during the bad years, the bravery and courage she, and women like her, had faced in order to save a future for their daughters. What they could never understand was that there had been no real choice, it was not a matter of bravery, but survival. The war that was happening did not allow for traitors or collaborators, so you either fought or died. Elizabeth had tried to explain this to some of the younger ones but to no avail, so she had given up. Over the last few years she had grown to enjoy basking in their hero-worship to the point that some of her stories had begun to sound a little far-fetched to the older women.

Sitting on the park bench, bathed by the warm, spring sunshine, Elizabeth could feel her eyes start to close, her memories blurring into each other as she drifted off to sleep, a tiny hunched figure on the seat. She was one of the few, the ones who had lived through it all and come out with both healthy bodies and their sanity. She had wandered into the community a few years before, pushing her hand-cart in front of her. She had been found by the children. Many of them had never seen an old woman before and the little wrinkled figure was a source of huge interest to them. The community had made a home for her and tried to look after her, as much as Elizabeth would let them. So many years of self-sufficiency and solitary life had made her wary and untrusting and at the beginning she had resented any help. For the first two years she had kept up the pretence that she was only staying for a little while. 'Just until me legs feel a little stronger', 'I'll stop till the weather's a little warmer' — she had an excuse for every season. But finally she had admitted to herself, and to them, that she would never leave, that she no longer wanted to leave. 'The children need me here, to give them a bit of discipline', she said, knowing that she had grown too fond of the children, too fond of playing the role of grandmother to give it up. So she had stayed, she grumbled incessantly, but she stayed.

She snored softly in her sleep, the lines on her face giving evidence to the years of chaos she had lived through. Years when mankind was struggling in its death throes.

It was during the 1980s that the first mutants had been born. Always boys; baby girls continued to gurgle and chuckle in their mothers' arms while their tiny brothers wasted and died, often within only a few months of being born. At first, the outbreak was limited to the industrial centres of Europe and the United States, but, as the years went by, the plague illness spread out until it reached into the heart of every continent.

The scientists researched every known gas and chemical for either a cause or a cure. The politicians struggled to control the mounting tide of panic by making endless promises while no solution came. The anti-nuclear faction, the conservationists, even the vegetarian societies put forward their solutions and their membership quadrupled overnight. But there was no conclusive evidence as to the cause of the deformities. Some subtle blend of poisons had caused the Y chromosome to mutate and the change was irreversible. The XX combination was still a winner, but for mankind it was the end.

Of course, it took years for people to believe it. At first, it lay deep in their hearts, an unspoken fear, the beginning of a doubt that the technocrats and scientists could get them out of this catastrophe. But, like the disease itself, the desperation grew stronger as there were fewer and fewer young men to take the reins of power from their fathers.

Women turned away, afraid of giving birth to one of the pathetic results of the mutation. They stayed in their homes trying to preserve some semblance of an ordered life for their healthy children while outside anarchy set in. The churches preached hysterically about the sins of the fathers and the need for constant prayer in the hope that God would forgive and would stop his vengeful purge. Like a return to the Middle Ages, the world closed in on itself, obscure sects flourished in a desperate bid to find some meaning to it all as the chaos deepened.

Elizabeth stirred, she opened her eyes and looked around to find the cart had been quietly returned to her, loaded full of firewood, while she slept. She felt a pang of fear for a second. Fancy going to sleep like that, right out in the open, anything could have happened. She knew that it was alright to do so now, but she would never get used to it, the safety. 'You can't teach an old dog . . .' she thought as she pushed the cart back through the park and down the market. As she turned into Brougham Road, she remembered that tonight was the night of the street meeting, and it was to be held at her house. 'Too many people, all that noise and nowhere for me to sit,' she grumbled to herself though she knew that her favourite chair was always kept empty for her. But there was noise, and she could hear it from halfway up the street. Clearly some kind of heated argument was going on and Elizabeth quickened her step. She might complain, but she could not bear for anything to go on without her knowing all about it.

She loaded the wood into the shelter and put away the car before hurriedly making her way inside No. 98 and into the living room where a group of about twenty women were in the middle of a heated discussion.

The room was long and narrow, divided by

double doors that were folded back for the meetings. Women sat everywhere, squashed on to ancient sofas, perched on the edges of tables, huddled by the fireplace. Their ages ranged from the early twenties to forties and fifties and they all bore the scars of their past on their faces. Deep lines etched into young faces, fingers that constantly pulled at each other and eyes that constantly flashed from side to side as though waiting for the attack that might come at any minute.

They stopped as Elizabeth entered and one of the younger ones leapt out of the fireside chair so that she could sit down. Elizabeth smiled her thanks and settled herself by the fire, ready to pick up on what was happening.

Julie started speaking again. Strong, handsome Julie. Forty years old with iron grey hair, she was one of the toughest women in the street. Many of the others had been frightened of her in the beginning, but with time it was easy to see that her hardness was only a shell, and not a very durable one at that. Her voice was urgent.

'We must start now. We have already waited too long. The streets are getting dangerous and, if nothing is done before next autumn, it may be too late!'

'But there is so much else to do. We've survived this winter without a famine, but if we don't go on working full-time on food production all our efforts will be wasted!' This was Cathy, just turned twenty, she belonged to a new generation of women, energetic and idealistic but sometimes lacking the determination and endurance of the older women who had already survived so much. 'There are so few of us in Hackney, and we don't have the tools for such a big job.'

She voiced a general fear, the problems of dealing with such a harsh environment were enormous. Many of the women had gone to the countryside, leaving London to the rats, a dangerous and desolate place full of falling buildings, disease and waste. But a few groups had stayed, determined to make something of the huge city they had inherited, but often the difficulties seemed insurmountable.

'Well, what do you suggest then? That we all simply pack our bags and go somehwere else! Because if we don't do something about that block, that's what we're going to have to do. It simply won't be safe to live round here anymore until the block has fallen of its own accord!'

Cathy sat quiet, twisting her fingers together and gazing into the fire. Much as she loved Julie, these outbursts upset her. She felt Julie treated her like a child, and she feared the humiliation she could feel in front of so many people.

'Okay, okay,' said Julie, 'that's putting it a bit strong, but I do think we've put off the job for long enough. The cracks in the walls are getting wider and wider and I honestly think it won't last much longer. We've got to do something about it before it gets too dangerous to work on.'

'Couldn't we at least start on it?' suggested Sandy. She seldom spoke at meetings, but last year her daughter had been killed by falling masonry and she had come to this meeting to support Julie in her efforts to get the old tower block pulled down. 'Even if we just demolished the top few floors, it would at least make the houses in Brougham Road safe, then we could finish the job next year, so we could still spend a lot of the time on the farm.'

There was a general mutter of agreement from the group. Many wanted to agree with Sandy because of what had happened to her child. Julie felt infuriated by the compromise. It enraged her that it never seemed possible to get anything done completely.

Although there were further objections made, the basic principle of doing the work that year was accepted. Over the hours the mechanics of the operation were worked out. One group of women would start on the block straight away, while another would travel round to the other groups in London to get advice and borrow tools and hopefully some helpers. There was plenty of old scaffolding lying around, and Barbara, their resident historian, was a valuable source of information when it came to mediaeval techniques of building. She spent hours wrapped up in old books salvaged from the museums, and had become an expert on the more practical aspects of life before the industrial revolution. With a small team of young admirers she hammered and tinkered away, far into the night. This produced efficient farm implements and ploughs out of a weird collection of iron machinery scavenged from many of the factories out towards Dagenham. The prospect of designing and constructing equipment for demolishing a fifteen floor block made her eyes sparkle, and she hurried off, jamming her glasses on her nose and muttering to herself about angles and tangents and winches.

The other women started drifting off back to their own houses. It was getting late. A few stayed up to discuss the meeting among themselves, to play music or just sit and talk. At No. 98 there was a period of silence as the remaining three women sat round the fire appreciating the peace now that the others had gone. It was always a bit of a strain having the meeting at their house, even though it only happened once a month.

After a few minutes Julie went and sat by Cathy and put her arm round her, twisting her fingers in Cathy's long brown hair.

'I'm sorry, love, if I snapped at you in the

meeting, you know what I'm like when I've got a bee in my bonnet about something.'

'I know, I just wish you didn't let it come out like that, it makes me feel such a fool, especially when everyone is here. I know you don't mean it, but sometimes I think you forget that I'm just as much a part of this community as you are. I'm not a child, and I've worked as hard as anyone to set it up. For you to think that I'd consider leaving for any reason just makes me mad.'

Cathy turned her head and looked at Julie. On each cheek Julie could see a faint red spot of anger.

'Oh, I'm sorry, Cath, I don't mean it, you know that!' Julie was tired. Unwilling to get involved in a full scale row, she wanted to appease Cathy. Unwilling to take responsibility for what she saw as the other woman's touchiness, her effort at appeasement carried a tone of irritation in it that Cathy couldn't miss.

'That's hardly the point. If you don't mean it, then don't do it!' Cathy crouched by the fire, staring resolutely at the glowing coals.

'I'll try Cathy, what more can I say. You know me well enough to understand. You shouldn't let it upset you so much. It's hard for me to change my spots now!'

'I see, I'm the one who has to change. You're the one who makes me feel an idiot but I'm the one who has to change!'

'No, I don't mean it like that. Oh Cathy, I really don't want to fight about it. I expect we both have to change, or something, it always seems to come down to that in the end. Maybe just being here a little longer, feeling this security in Hackney will make it easier. But I just don't want to fight about it now.'

Cathy turned to see Julie's face, tired and

vulnerable, looking for some comfort. It was so easy
to let it go again, to smile and move over, to sit on
the floor beneath the older woman's knees. Julie
wrapped her arms round her and buried her face in
Cathy's neck. The tiny kisses made Cathy giggle and
she pulled away.

'Come on, let's go and make the dinner.' She got
up and took Julie's hand and they disappeared into
the kitchen.

Elizabeth chuckled to herself. 'These young
people,' she thought, 'always up one minute and
down the next!' She was glad that she no longer felt
the need for such a single-minded relationship. There
had been a time, she could remember, when she had
felt her heart pulled in two just that way, but she
had learnt to trust only herself. Now, although she
loved the women she lived with, she still preserved
that sense of independence. Or she certainly thought
she did.

The door banged open and shut as Sue burst into
the room, laden down with a motley collection of
junk she'd picked up in the city.

'Sorry I missed the meeting, I went further than
I meant to, and there was so much stuff, I couldn't
resist having a good look.'

Sue was forever foraging. She went off for days
on her own and always returned with armfuls of
things they didn't know what to do with; ornaments
that had escaped the looters, pictures, crazy clothes
out of old boutiques, her room was full of them.
But every now and then she had brought something
home that was really valuable to the community, like
a pile of old clocks, or some butchers' knives. So
she could still justify her wanderings to the rest of
Hackney when she was continually absent from
meetings and rarely did any work in the fields.

'Just look what I found!' From the depths of her

enormous coat she produced a tiny silver fox. 'I found it in Bond Street. It's amazing, you wouldn't think there was anything left after all this time!'

'Let me see, dear,' asked Elizabeth. She took the tiny figure and turned it over and over in her hands as she looked at it. 'It's very beautiful, must have been made for some rich people to buy, we never had anything like this.'

Sue's enthusiasm to show the silver animal to the others would not allow her to let Elizabeth launch into one of her stories of her childhood. She took it back and hurried off to the kitchen to show the others.

'It's lovely!' said Cathy. 'Isn't it Julie?'

'It certainly is Sue, I don't know how you manage to find all these things.'

Sue almost glowed with pride. For a woman of over thirty, she still seemed very childlike sometimes. She never spoke of the past. Julie had tried to talk to her about it but it did no good, Sue simply refused to answer her questions, and had got very angry when Julie persisted. Julie worried about it sometimes, but there was never enough time to help and Sue always seemed okay, the children loved her. It was easy to do nothing about it.

'Go and tell Elizabeth and Caroline that dinner is ready, please Cath, we can eat now that Sue is back.'

The kitchen and dining area were in fact in the next house. An archway had been knocked through to allow for more room, not only for the women living there, but also so that big meetings were not all squashed into a tiny living room. Cath returned, followed by Elizabeth, and the four women sat down at the table and started serving.

'Did you call for Caroline?' asked Julie.

'Yes, she's down the street, but she said she was

coming straight away,' replied Cathy.

As Julie rose to make sure her daughter was coming, a slim dark figure slipped into the kitchen.

'Sorry I'm late, what's for dinner, I'm starving!' At fourteen years old Caroline was slowly moving into adulthood. She was still treated much as a child and enjoyed the freedom from responsibility that allowed her. She hadn't had much of a childhood until she'd come to Hackney and Julie was trying to make up for the years of isolation and fear. Caroline still wore a trace of the hunted look of her mother, but every day she relaxed more as a new-found sense of security built up in her.

The meal over and cleared away, the women drifted off to bed. Outside the night was chilly, with a slow drizzle that soaked the city, eating a little more of its structure away. Julie and Cathy slept tightly wrapped in each other's arms, feeling the warmth soak through to comfort each one through troubled dreams. Elizabeth snored under a pile of blankets while Caroline whimpered in a tight curled ball. At the top of the house, Sue lay awake in silence for hours before her brain finally let her sink into a sleep full of anxious mutterings and grumblings.

The next day it rained, a slow continuous rain that made any work on the block impossible. In a way Julie was glad. She was trying to write an account of the collapse before it was all forgotten and became part of the new mythology. But she always felt guilty about spending time on it when there were so many other things to be done. Only when the weather was bad could she settle down to a day's work on, the history without any twinges of guilt.

It was certainly a day for staying indoors for everyone. Elizabeth sat and darned socks and jerseys by the fire while Cathy and Caroline painted the kitchen. Sue was in her room all day surrounded by a wide-eyed group of children, telling them stories about brave princesses and handsome dragons and showing them her collection of treasures.

Outside the rain went on, the whole of London was grey, wet and cold. Over in the centre of the city the rain drenched the old buildings, trickling down through every crack and niche, slowly, slowly wearing away the mortar until, with an agonising crack and roar, the building would fall, crashing down onto the roadway below. No one lived there, it was just too dangerous. Julie had taken Caroline on a tour of the city one summer's day soon after they settled in Hackney. She had shown her Buckingham Palace, the Tower of London and what was left of the Houses of Parliament. But it was hard for Caroline to understand these buildings. Empty, looted and often nearly completely destroyed, they were just shells, and Caroline had got bored and whined to be taken home. It was only the older women who could remember what London used to be like, who still went back now and wandered round the streets, filled with a weird sense of loss and pride. The loss of the vitality of London, the hustle and bustle of millions that made it such a glittering metropolis, but pride that it was theirs at last. No longer would men control it and its wealth, and maybe one day there would be time to repair the old buildings and let life flow back into its ancient streets. Julie had lived in London all her life, except just before and just after her daughter was born. Then she'd fled to the countryside to escape the vengeance of the last few men, who would watch pregnant women and kill those that bore healthy daughters, such was their dying hatred. But she knew she could never leave London for good and as soon as Caroline could walk she had returned. She loved the old city and dreamt of the day when they could make it habitable again, hearing the noise of London life as she had done so many years before.

Only of course, all these new people would be women. Julie had difficulty in believing it herself sometimes, that the men were really gone for ever. Whenever she left the immediate safety of Hackney, and went into the city, she was afraid she would meet them, skulking round corners like they used to. Waiting to pounce and wreak their frustrated rage on any woman unfortunate enough to be alone. She used to worry a lot when Sue went off for days on her own, always a doubt in her mind that Sue would not come back, like so many others she had known in the past. She got up from her desk and went over to the window that looked out on the street. She could see a group of children playing in the rain, all girls. From the kitchen came the sound of hysterical laughter as Cathy and Caroline went on with their painting; Elizabeth was gossiping away with Barbara in the front room, and from Sue's room Julie could hear the oohs and ahhs of Sue's young audience. Everywhere the sound was female, old or young, happy or sad, always female.

She went back to the typewriter and went on with her work, unwilling to let this opportunity go by. She had already covered the discovery of the mutation and the realisation that it could not be stopped. She had written about the mass rapes and the beginnings of organised women's resistance. She herself could remember when she was fifteen and of obviously child-bearing age, how she had had to live hidden away in an old warehouse down by the docks, for fear she would be found by any of the men left. Night time forays for food were all she saw of the city for those fear-ridden years, till the number of men grew less and less and the women could start taking over the streets for themselves. She had learnt to fight, to use a knife, everyone did, there was no room for the squeamish. Only once had she killed a man, but the memory still woke her up shaking. He had come at her from behind as she was going through the contents of a dustbin, his eyes crazed, he spun her round to face him and then pushed her down onto the ground. She went easily but her knife was already out and he fell heavily onto it and her. She could see his face twisted with pain and fury, his hands still grabbing at her as he died. It was the only time she had truly wanted to leave London for ever, wanted to run to the comparative safety of the countryside and try to bury her memories in a communion with nature. She did go, for the week-end. She went to a safe house down in Kent, the birds woke her up every morning and she was afraid of the cows. By the next night she was back in London.

Gradually the men seemed to disappear. Often they were killed by women in self-defence or out of just plain revenge, often they killed each other, sometimes they killed themselves. As they realised that their overwhelming drive to sire sons to take over from them was no longer a viable philosophy to live by, their grip on their own lives started slipping. An almost masochistic hedonism took over, resulting in a huge increase in deaths from drink and drugs. Men succumbed to all the great killers like cancer, heart disease, as well as the great parasitic killers of the hot countries. In their madness it was as though they embraced death with enthusiasm, to see who could first achieve the end of their own insane race.

Rumours abounded about how there were still groups of very old men left living up north, but it was over four years since Julie or the others had seen a man and many of the children had forgotten what they looked like.

And it had been the children who had broken the male spell for good. In the middle of all the madness and breakdown, an old power had been rediscovered, the power of women to control their fertility. It was still rare, and not really understood, but pregnancies occurred in women who really wanted them, and there seemed to be no sign of weakness or defect caused by the absence of a father. Of course, it had taken years for women to believe in it. Scepticism abounded and many women suffered when they announced their state and their own friends accused them of having sex with men. But in time they saw what it meant. Until then, they had seen themselves doomed along with the menfolk. But this discovery meant the beginning for them, their race was not going to die. When the men found out, their anger was multiplied, thousands of women died, thousands were permanently damaged both mentally and physically by the brutality of men. But women now had the will to survive.

By Wednesday the rain had died away and the work on the block could be started. Five women from Albion Drive headed off for South London where there was another community who had already dealt with the problem of tower blocks, to get advice, while the others started a preliminary survey of the block and the best way to go about pulling it down.

'It's a pity we can't get hold of some dynamite or something. That would certainly help matters,' said Sue. 'It's going to be a hell of a job to knock it down by hand.'

'I think we can rig up a ball and chain on the

scaffolding which should help with the stronger bits. The main problem with the rest of it is to stop it falling down without control.' Barbara had come equipped with her plans and the group gathered round her to examine them.

'Well, I'd like to go into the block and have a look round to make sure there isn't anything worth saving before the whole thing comes down round our ears. You don't mind do you, it won't take more than a few hours?' Sue knew they wouldn't be too pleased with her, and she was right.

'Surely you've already been up the block, Sue,' said Julie, irritated. 'After all this discussion about when it should be done, we don't want to delay at this stage. I wouldn't think there'd be anything there anyway.'

'I know, and I'm sorry I left it so late, but I would like to do it. The blocks weren't as much looted as some of the other places, so there could be some tools in there worth having. I know I should have done it long ago but I suppose it's just that it was round the corner, so I kept putting it off for another day.'

'Oh let her go,' said Cathy, 'one more day won't make much difference and she'll only mope around and be impossible if she's not allowed!'

'Well, I suppose we can spend today finalising the plans and getting all the equipment ready. The others might get back from South in time too. But for heaven's sake don't be long Sue, and remember that the block is pretty unstable. If you're not out by nightfall make sure you put out a light to say you're okay.' Julie turned to go back to the house. Sometimes Sue nearly drove her round the bend. She always seemed so out of touch with everyone else, so insensitive to the mood of the group, and so persistent as to her own demands.

'Don't worry, I won't be long, and thanks.' Sue set off across the green to the block, carrying her bag of tools and a bag of lure in case of rats. The others watched her for a while, till her blonde curly head vanished inside the black doorway, and then followed Julie back to No. 98. Cathy caught up with her just as she was going into the house.

'You're doing it again Julie, trying to take the whole responsibility onto your own shoulders.'

'What do you mean?' Julie shrugged past her into the living room.

'No one else really minds losing one more day to let Sue go in, only you. Anyone would think she was doing it on purpose to spite you. There is a whole community of women here and you don't have to let every setback seem like a personal slur on your character.'

Julie sat down by the fire and looked up at the younger woman, 'I suppose you're right, old habits die hard with me, but, honestly, Sue can be impossible at times. The other day she was saying that the only stuff worth getting was always in the centre of town and now she's suddenly passionately interested in the contents of a decrepit old tower block!'

'Yes I know, she's always been like that. But still, you mustn't let it get to you so much. Come on in the kitchen and I'll make a cup of tea.'

They stayed up late that night, waiting for Sue, drinking endless cups of mint tea and talking while Elizabeth dozed in the corner. Outside the night was dark and starless and it was hard to make out the small figure that emerged from the back entrance of the block and made her way home, pulling a loaded handcart behind her.

Sue loved foraging and she had become quite an

expert at it. She loved going into old crumbling buildings and rescuing all kinds of treasures, although she knew that most of them were pretty useless. Mostly, she loved to be alone, away from the others and their demands. Away from their meetings, so full of emotions that she could not deal with, words she did not really understand. They never seemed to do anything else but argue and it made her head ache to listen to them. Out in the city it was always so quiet, great grey buildings standing silently as the years went by, occasionally losing a little of themselves, as the masonry slipped gracefully and then roared into the street below. Blind eyes staring across the street over her head as she climbed and clambered over their stone skeletons. She had had a few narrow shaves; once she had been trapped for several hours by a fallen beam, but she had always managed to get out in the end and get herself home, however battered. She had ceased to fear the old buildings, rather had grown to love them and to guard their secrets. Old-fashioned iron lift doors that clanged shut, echoing in empty department stores in Oxford Street, executive roof gardens complete with fountains and statues. Sue spent hours working her way through whole streets, playing on broken escalators, stretching her arms out as she felt the city become hers. No longer a place to fear every face, suspect every noise, now it was hers, and she loved it.

But now she was in a hurry and in no mood for meditation. She had upset Julie and she knew it, quite apart from the others who wanted to start work. Julie was right, she should have done it weeks ago, but the thought of investigating an old sixties tower block when she had the whole of London to play with had seemed tedious. It was only when she thought of them pulling it down before she could see inside it, that she realised how important it was for her to go. She was well equipped for these expeditions. She carried tools, a knife, rope and a lamp, along with a big sack and her coat with a thousand pockets for her finds. In addition, she took a bag of lure for the rats. Many of the rats had already left the high blocks in favour of the warmth and security of ground floor living, even rats couldn't take the pressures of living on the sixteenth floor, but there were still too many around to take the chance. The lure was made up of a mixture of herbs and grain and the rats loved it, though it sent them to sleep for hours. Sue always carried it with her, although she hated rats and tried to avoid places where she knew they'd be.

Inside the block it was dark and cold. Bare concrete daubed with slogans and obscenities, broken glass and brick. It was not an encouraging sight. She made her way up to the first floor and pushed back the broken door of the first flat. It was a mess.

Most of the flats she went into were stripped bare, everything of value stolen or packed up and taken by whoever lived there, all the furniture burnt, curtains and carpets taken for clothing and warmth elsewhere. Occasionally tramps, women hiding out, or men gone crazy came and lived in these flats, seeking the anonymity of tower block existence. Then, as in the flat, there was a semblance of order left, a mad parody of how the bureaucrats had intended people to live in these places. The windows were boarded, leaving just a chink as a lookout, and a small section that could be pulled aside to let in a little light. As Sue pulled the flap back, the morning sunshine caught on the rotting wallpaper, it was green, displaying a kind of wooden pergola with roses on it. Hanging from the ceiling, cracked deep on one side, an old lampshade dangled incongruously. The old sofa was still there, although the rats and

mice had pulled most of the stuffing out of it and
Sue didn't risk sitting on it for fear of what else might
have chosen it as a home. A formica table with
rusting legs stood in the corner. She went through
into the other rooms to check them out quickly
before she started a proper search. The bedroom
was bare, even the wiring had been pulled out. The
kitchen and bathroom were much the same, clearly
whoever had taken up residence in the flat had been
satisfied with one room. Dust lay thick everywhere
and Sue sneezed as it clogged up her nose. She went
back to the sitting room and started to work pains-
takingly through the flat, through every crack and
cubbyhole, behind the pipes, under the boards, she
had learnt all the hiding places.

And from that flat she worked her way through
the whole building till finally she emerged on the roof
as evening drew into night. She had not found much,
a few nails and screws, a mirror and a china jug were
the best, along with a few other bits of kitchen stuff
and some flower pots. Considering how much the
Hackney women already had of all that kind of thing,
they would not be too impressed by this haul. Sue
could imagine Julie's face, the sarcasm as she asked
after the success of her operation. Sue did not relish
the thought. She sat up on the roof, looking down
from sixteen floors and decided to have a rest and a
smoke before she returned to the others.

The smoke of her cigarette curled up round her
head in the still night air, as she leaned against the
air vent and watched the pigeons flying into the city
to roost on the high window ledges for the night.
Below, the streets of Hackney fanned out, to the
north ran Brougham Road, leading into Shrubland
Road and Albion Drive. The rows of terraced houses
in Brougham Road giving way to the semis of the
other two. Across from the block lay a wasteland of

rubbish and half-built houses. It had been planned as a new estate, but with The Death no one planned much for the future. The rain had filled in the foundations and eaten away at the unprotected woodwork, while the new bricks disappeared by the wheelbarrow as they were used for repair jobs elsewhere. Along one side of the block ran Broadway Market itself. Wide one end and gradually getting narrow at the other, it ran for about two hundred yards. On each side, the old shops were still fairly intact, there was not much profitable to loot in the market, so the buildings had been unmolested. A few of them were lived in now, although most of the women preferred the streets with gardens. Sue could see a light from Gillian's house halfway down, the old photographer's shop and opposite Beth and Vivian in the gardeners' shop. Sue had only vague memories of days when people had filled the streets and she found it hard to imagine such a thing being enjoyable. She was glad she didn't live in the market. with all those memories round her, and yet she knew she could never leave the city itself. She had tried once, Julie had suggested she might be happier away in the countryside and she had gone to live with a community down on the Thames. But she was homesick for her dirty old buildings and she couldn't cope with the problems of nature on such a big scale. A few park trees was what she was used to and she had to come back to it in the end.

To the south lay the river, a shining band in the moonlight, threading its way through the blackness of the city. She had crossed it many times and, now that the fish had returned, she sometimes took the children fishing for the day in an old punt she had rescued from London University. To the east was the true wasteland of industrial London. There were no communities out there that they knew of, only broken down houses and rusting machinery. Dagenham, with its huge car works, was slowly being taken over by creeping botanical strands as nature pushed back into the town, reclaiming her own once more.

Sue rose stiffly from her place and wandered round the top of the block, almost feeling it creak beneath her feet, feeling the urgency in its structure. Yes it would fall soon if something were not done about it. From the other side she could see out to the black silhouette of St Pauls, gutted by fire but still standing, the Tower of London, actually used again as a refuge during the excesses of The Death. And further into the heart of London she could see where the ruins of Westminster blocked the streets. Sue shook her head, she could not imagine what all this had been like when Elizabeth was born. She had known men, to her cost, but so many, so many men and women in a city like this . . . no she could not imagine that.

She took the last suck on her cigarette, stubbed out the remains on the concrete and made her way to the stairs, stopping to light the lamp for her descent. As she stepped down she banged her head on the ceiling inside the stair head, and, rubbing her head, she looked up and saw that there was a gap between the roof outside and the ceiling inside. A false ceiling had been put in. At one stage it must have been very hard to spot, but now the weather had taken its toll and the hardboard was beginning to come away. It did not take long to prise her crowbar into the crack and start pulling the rest of it away. As the hardboard came away she could hear something sliding toward the growing hole, she listened for the telltale scratching of rats or mice, but there were none, and, as soon as she stopped tugging at the board, the noise stopped. Carefully she held up the lamp to the crack and pushed a bit harder on the crowbar. The light caught on metal, black metal. She worked quickly and efficiently, and as she pulled the first section of hardboard down, so the first machine gun fell into her arms.

Altogether, it took an hour to finish the job. At her feet lay three machine guns, two pistols of some sort and two rifles complete with telescopic sights. Also, there was a silencer and several boxes of different kinds of ammunition and eight long bands of bullets for the machine guns. Sue sat on the stairs and gazed at them. She hadn't seen anything like it for years. They seemed to have a power all of their own and she had to force herself not to be frightened of them. Who could have stashed them here? Maybe it had been the occupier of that first floor flat. Whoever it was must have had to leave in a hurry so they couldn't get them after hiding them so carefully.

They were very dusty, but apart from that, seemed to be in good order. She loaded them carefully into her sack and, collecting the rest of her tools and the few other things she had found, started back down the stairs of the block. In the dark it seemed to take hours and the sack bit hard into her shoulder and jarred against her every time she clunked into the wall. Finally she was down and outside, gulping lungs full of fresh air after the musty, decaying smell of the block. Outside she loaded everything onto her handcart and dragged it off up the road to No. 98, running nearly all the way, impatient to get to the others and show them the guns.

Julie and Cathy had spent the day together, enjoying a rare time when they could relax without feeling they were letting down the community, after all, this time it was Sue's fault. By the time evening came round, a few others had joined them, Elizabeth was in her usual place by the fire knitting, while the others played cards and talked. Julie worried as soon as it got dark, but after her outburst of the morning, decided it was better not to go on about Sue again. All they could do was wait. She looked over to where Caroline had her head in a book in the corner, twining her long hair round her fingers, a habit she had picked up from her mother. Caroline was nearly fifteen now, not really a child anymore, she was already beginning to pull away from Julie, and Julie felt the tug intensely. She knew it had to happen, but she had fought so hard to care for Caroline and protect her in this new and unwelcoming world that the bond between them had been tied very tight. Caroline looked up, sensing her mother's eyes on her and smiled. To her, Julie was a rock, one that might cry sometimes or get angry, but a rock all the same. She felt like venturing a little further away from the rock sometimes and she dreaded the scenes that ensued. It was so hard to be neither child nor adult, no one treated her ideas as real, not even Cathy, who seemed more like her sister than her mother's lover. She wanted responsibility and yet she knew she still wanted to run and hide in Julie's room when things went wrong, like she'd always done.

When Sue finally arrived, it took some time to work out what she was saying through all the excitement and breathlessness. When they'd got the sack in the room and laid its contents out on the carpet, there was a stunned silence.

'Well, now what do we do with them?' asked Vivian. Vivian of the gardener's shop. 'Isn't it a bit dangerous to keep them, with the children around, it's not as though we need them anymore.'

Vivian wasn't the only woman disturbed to see the guns. To many of them they brought memories of the past they would rather forget. Now they only kept a couple of air rifles which were used very sparingly to deal with the occasional fox that became too troublesome. But they hadn't been used for months on end and the sight of such a formidable armoury was unnerving.

'But we've got to!' cried Sue. 'We don't know that we really are safe yet, surely we should keep the guns in case we need to defend ourselves. It would only be if we were attacked or something, just for security!'

'Yes Sue, I know what you mean but you don't see the danger of it. Who will be the enemy? I know at the moment you'd say men, but what about in ten years time, or twenty years, when there really are no men left? If we still have these guns, isn't there a danger we might use them for something else. They would give us so much power.'

'Surely you can't mean we'd use the guns on other communities of women!' Caroline was shocked at her mother's attitude. 'We aren't like men, we could look after them safely so they wouldn't be a danger!'

Julie knew she had upset Caroline again, at the moment she seemed to be upsetting everyone. And maybe Caroline and Sue were right. Maybe she should have more faith in the new women and learn to trust them. She scratched her head and looked over to see what Cathy was thinking, but only got a brief smile from that direction. Elizabeth would understand, she knew, but Elizabeth had long given up intervening in group meetings, she took their decisions with a quiet smile and often it was impossible to know what she thought of them. Julie watched her as she sat staring sadly at the pile of guns, lost in a thousand memories.

'I know I don't trust people as much as I should,

and I don't think we would behave like men or anything like that. It's just, well, I just don't like to see these things that are so male, so much a part of what they did to us, back in our community, I just don't think we should keep them.'

'I agree with Julie,' said Vivian. 'We haven't needed them up to now, so why start? If men did turn up they'd be so old I don't think we'd need all that to deal with them and in a few years we shouldn't ever need them again. They're so ugly, I don't like to be in the same room with them!'

'You mustn't let your decisions now be made just because of past history!' replied Sue. 'We all have bitter memories about guns and men and all that, but those days are past and we're faced with different problems. I don't think men are the only ones. We don't know much about what's going on in the countryside, they might need them for protection from animals or something like that. It doesn't all have to be about the men thing, you know, just because they used to use them!'

'What do you think Cathy? You seem very engrossed sitting there, have you got any ideas what to do?'

Cathy could sense the implied request for support in Julie's voice and she felt her muscles tense for the friction that would invariably follow her 'betrayal'.

'I know it's very hard, but really I think we should keep the guns. I wish Sue had never found them, I wish the whole block was down and destroyed, it seems to bring nothing but trouble. But now she has found them, I can't see that it's possible to just throw them away. As Sue says, there may well be a use for them in another group, we don't have to keep them here for good. Maybe we'll be threatened by animals, wolves or something. If that happens, and we've destroyed the only means of properly protecting ourselves, I think it'll breed nothing but trouble in the community, let alone actual damage to ourselves and our children.'

'So we are to raise another generation of children to know machine guns!' Julie was bitter, knowing by the looks on the women around her that she was going to lose out. 'Will it ever end, I wonder? Perhaps we should start lessons next week so we can all have the pleasure of learning to use one!'

'Oh come on Julie, it's not as bad as that!' Sue cried. 'You and I know how to use them for a start, so there would be no need to teach anyone else and if *we* didn't use them we could safely reckon we didn't have to keep them anymore.'

'Oh thanks, now I'm the one who has to fire the fucking things, well you can forget that, I've had enough of all that to last a lifetime!'

'Okay, okay, stop all this, it's not making the decision any easier!' Cathy stared round at Sue and Julie. Always these confrontations happened; why, she could never work out. Both women were devoted to each other and yet they clashed on nearly everything. Julie said it was because they'd both spent so much time alone and were so untrusting, but Cathy was not convinced.

'It's just because Julie can see the decision isn't going to go her way. Well, you're right Julie, look round you and see. These women are prepared to take the risk to make sure their community is safe, you weren't the only one who suffered you know!'

'That's not fair!' Caroline rushed to her mother's defence despite her disagreement with her moments before. 'Julie's just saying what she thinks, and she's right as well, it's only that we don't think all that from the past is so important anymore!'

'Thank you dear, but I think Sue is right in a way. I don't have the faith in women that you do, maybe I never will. If the group wants to keep the guns when it's discussed at the big meeting, then I shall go along with that decision, but I can never agree with it. As for tonight, I think I'll just go to bed, tomorrow's going to be a long day, what with starting work on the block, and I'm very tired.' Julie rose and, stepping over several women, she got to the door. Turning to say goodnight, she squeezed Sue's shoulder and blew Cathy a kiss.

After she had gone the mood of the evening relaxed. The guns were stored away until a final decision could be made with all the other women. Soon everyone had left for their beds till only Sue and Cathy were still sitting by the fire talking.

'I don't trust Julie when she gives in like that, all of a sudden,' said Sue.

'I know what you mean, I'll probably get a basinful when I go to bed, I normally do. I can't stand it when you and her cross swords, it makes her bad-tempered for days.'

'I'm sorry, I know I don't handle it very well when she starts, and I should know better than to be upset by that sharp tongue of hers after all this time. I'll try to be nice to her in the morning, give her breakfast in bed or something. What do you reckon?'

'Oh I don't know, Sue! If you like. I'm just fed up with being the intermediary between you two; sometimes I feel I don't exist at all in this house when you two start going. God knows what it's going to be like when Caroline starts pushing too; I'll have to be off with Elizabeth, I think, and opt out of the whole thing!'

'Are we really as bad as that? Why do you think it is?'

'I don't know, and I don't know if it matters. Don't mind me Sue, I'm in a funny mood at the moment. You'd better go off to bed. After all you've done today you must be exhausted. Don't worry about Julie, she'll get over it, she always does.'

With Sue gone to bed, Cathy sank back in Elizabeth's chair, luxuriating in the pleasure of being alone. So little time was left for this, so much that needed to be done with others. Sue was the only one whose work was solitary. Not that she'd like to do what Sue did. The thought of those empty, rotting buildings made her shiver. Sometimes she longed for the country, where she was born. Way up north she had lived, just outside Lancaster, until her mother had come south in search of old friends and family who would look after her and the children. And she had stayed in London, when her mother had finally found better contacts on the south coast, stayed because of Julie, because of falling in love. Now she felt part of the place and knew she would never leave, whatever happened between her and Julie, but there were still times when she missed the tranquility of the countryside. She rose stiffly, put out the lamp, and climbed the stairs to her bedroom. She could hear Julie's breathing and knew she was still awake, waiting for her, the stillness of the mound in the bed a deception. She smiled, Julie behaved like a child sometimes. She slipped her clothes off and slid into bed beside the older woman, taking the pouch of tobacco, cigarette papers, flints, water and an ash tray in preparation for the talk that would invariably follow such a night.

They kept the guns in the end. They were taken to pieces and distributed amongst the houses so that no one house had total responsibility for them. For a week or so it was a great talking point and there were quite a few repetitions of the disagreements of the first night. But once the decision had been made, there were too many other things to worry about to go on being concerned with that issue. The demolition of the block got well under way as the summer progressed. The women who had gone to South London returned with a store of advice and two more women, who had volunteered to come and help since they'd done it before. It was a difficult job and hard work for the women, who also had to make sure the fields were kept properly and the animals cared for. The children were often the ones to be neglected, and Elizabeth was overworked in her baby-sitting duties and was rarely seen without a posse of small children behind her. Even Sue's scavenging had to be curtailed until all the work was done. Once this scaffolding was put up, and the theory of how they were going to do it worked out, the job went ahead quite steadily. By the end of June they had demolished the top ten storeys and were happy to rest for a while. The block was no longer a danger to them or their children and, although they would finish the job, it was no longer essential. The children had become impossible because no one had time to deal with them and everyone needed a break before social life ceased to exist altogether. It was a time to rest and enjoy the summer sun. The women were proud of what they had achieved and the frayed tempers of the past months soon healed, rows were resolved and the children stopped complaining.

Julie loved sitting out in the street in her old deck-chair long into the night in the summer. With a box full of tobacco and her wonderful pipe, foraged for her by Sue from Harrods, she could sit for hours soaking up the sun, as the lines of worry lifted off her face. They would leave the rest of the job until next year, she thought. Now that it was safe, the pressure was off and she wanted to spend more time with Cathy and Caroline, especially Caroline, whom she felt she'd been neglecting recently. The block had been a challenge and she had enjoyed dealing with it, the community was the stronger for it, but now it was time for something else, for some attention to more personal things, and for enjoying life. .

Julie had been right in her worries about Caroline. During the last months, since the whole issue of the tower block had first come up, she had had very little time to spend with her daughter. She always seemed to be busy when Caroline wanted to see her, working on the demolition site, going to meetings, helping organise the farm work. What little time she had left over, she spent catching up on her writing, not wanting all their efforts to go unrecorded. She knew she was doing this, but felt unable to answer Caroline's demands. She thought it would be all right, just for a while, till the block was safe.

And yet, even in that short time, things had changed so that Julie felt out of touch with one of the two people closest to her heart. Caroline had suddenly ceased to be a child, almost overnight, it seemed to Julie. Sue had given her a haircut and, after years of having long hair, the new short, sharp cut made her look years older. Her body was beginning to fill out, though she would always stay on the thin side like her mother. But adolescence had given her face a secret depth and now, when Julie looked into the deep brown eyes facing her, she could no longer see the gawky, shy little girl she had pulled round with her for so long.

'I want to join the meetings, Julie. I'm sick of being left out of all the decisions you make. Surely I'm old enough now to come as well, I'm nearly fifteen you know!' Caroline had found her mother up in her study writing. She had sat down opposite, staring at her until Julie knew that she was not to be put off this time and folded her work away.

'I know how old you are dear, but are you sure

you want to start all that yet? It's not really much fun you know, sitting in meetings for hours and trying to work out all the arguments that crop up. I'm sure you'd have a better time out with your friends.' Julie hated to see her daughter's face so serious.

'It's not just a matter of having fun, Mother. I want to take part, I want to really belong.'

'But you do! Of course you do, you must never think otherwise!'

'Yes I know I do, as your daughter and all that, and I know everyone wants me to stay. But I want to be a part of it for what *I* want to say, my ideas, not yours! I know you want me to have a good time, but there are more things to life than that, and anyway I would be having a good time if I felt like I was contributing to the place.'

'Are you sure you know what you would be committing yourself to? It's not just a matter of going to meetings. We have to make decisions and then try to carry them out, often they're the wrong decisions because so many things are new to us.'

'Exactly!' interrupted Caroline. 'Everything is new since all the men went, and so all the old ideas don't count anymore. What the meetings need is young people like me to try and give our ideas, this is a time for us!'

'Yes I know.' Julie felt exhausted already. Her efforts to bring Caroline up to be self-sufficient and confident had finally triumphed with a vengeance. Her daughter had developed an impossibly stubborn streak when she finally decided what she wanted, and Julie knew already she was going to give in once again. 'The thing is Caroline, that although the old solutions may not seem much use at the moment, there are still lots of things to be learnt from the experience that all these women have been through.

Think about Elizabeth and what she has survived
before you go dismissing us old ones so quickly.'

'I know that, I didn't mean it to sound like that.
It's just that there is our side as well and we never
get a chance to say our piece. I know a lot of the
other kids think the same as me and it's just so frus-
trating never to get the chance to do things!'

Julie sat back in her chair and looked at her
daughter. In many ways she was so like herself. Her
cornflower blue eyes sparkled with animation as she
talked, constantly flicking back the fringe Sue had
given her. Although she was a bit thin, she was tough,
and the muscles in her arms flexed as she spoke.

'Please Julie, try to understand. I told the other
girls I was sure that you would be okay about it!
I promised them!'

'Well, that was foolish wasn't it, to promise them
before you asked me. Suppose I say I won't introduce
you?'

'Well, I suppose I'll have to ask Cathy then, or
Sue, but I did want to ask you, and you won't say
no will you?'

Caroline's voice was now hitting that emotional
point that Julie could not resist, and Caroline knew
it. Already she was hugging Julie and bouncing about
the room, upsetting all Julie's papers on the floor.

'Careful, Caroline, you are supposed to be
behaving with more responsibility now, remember!
Tell me, what are the other children, or should I
say young adults, going to do when they hear the
news?'

'Well, then they can ask their parents and say that
you've let me go to meetings and then hopefully
there will be more of us to say our point of view!'

For a minute Julie's eyes were filled with a
horrific vision of the Hackney Meetings being taken
over by a bunch of irresponsible fifteen-year-olds.

112

It had taken a long time to establish a format for the meetings that made them work, a system of introductions for the young women when they joined. Until two years ago the youngest had been Lynne at twenty, but as their lives stabilised, the children's demands had become more sophisticated, they wanted a closer involvement. Now Julie was facing a situation where her own daughter, and daughter's friends, might be on the verge of challenging and destroying all those old values that had worked so well up until now. She shook her head, knowing how unfair and mistrustful she was being.

'You must remember that it is a commitment, and one that we will hold you to if you do come. Some of the women here don't come to meetings, or come only rarely and take little part because they either cannot make the commitment to the community after what they've been through, or because they're happier to trust the others to make the decisions for them. There are many women here who have been badly damaged mentally by what happened to them, and we must be careful to look after their interests, even though they can't argue well for themselves. The meetings are a way of helping the community, like any other way, they are not the way we rule the community. You must always understand that.'

'I do, but it's the decision-making that's the important thing really, isn't it? I mean that's where the big things get decided, that's where the power of the community is.'

'You like the idea of that don't you, my love, well be careful. You'll find the women here are very suspicious of anyone they think has too much power. They go on at me sometimes because I've got such a big mouth at meetings. Remember that all the women have survived pretty well on their own, we all drifted together from scattered backgrounds, some, like Sue's, we don't even know about. All those women could go off and live alone again. If they could before, with the threat of men still alive, to do it now would be easy. So if you go around making a whole lot of decisions they don't like, and try to enforce them with your friends, you might find you didn't have a community left to control!'

'You really don't trust anyone do you, Julie!' Those eyes cut into her heart.

'I'm sorry Caroline, I probably shouldn't have said that. I'm sure you won't behave like that, nor the other girls. It's just a reaction to change I suppose. We've been trying to stabilise things for so long that new ideas can be difficult to take.' Julie reached across the table and took Caroline's hand. 'Just be careful and you'll be fine, I know you will.' Caroline smiled and the tension was suddenly broken.

'I won't let you down, Julie, I promise!' She put her arms round her mother, 'I know how important everything here is to you after what we came from. I remember some of those old times too, and all that lonely time when we couldn't find anyone and I was sick. I wouldn't do anything to spoil things now.'

'Alright love, you come along to the next meeting with me and we'll see how it goes. If you don't like it, you can always do something else. Just give it a chance before you jump down all our throats for being so old-fashioned or whatever!'

Caroline laughed, kissed her mother and was gone. Julie could hear her thumping down the stairs and banging the front door as she ran off to tell all her friends. Julie had the feeling she was stirring up a hornet's nest, but she knew that it would have happened sooner or later. She just wished, in a tired kind of way, that it had not been her daughter who was going to trigger off this new rush of young women wanting their way in the community. As it was, she got into trouble in meetings for taking too much control, often justly, and now she seemed to have passed on that same characteristic to her daughter. She sighed and started to gather up her papers and tried to restore them to some order. In writing she found a release from the worries of her life, though today even the papers seemed to have a will of their own, as they slipped from her hands again and fluttered across the table.

'Damn!' She stomped out of the room and finally found solace in a cup of tea with Elizabeth, sitting out in the back garden.

'It seems to be a day for moods, today,' commented Elizabeth, fixing a beady eye on Julie's scowling face. 'What's upset you my dear, or can I guess that it's that young lady who's just gone prancing out of the house like she's won the pools?'

There were expressions of Elizabeth's that no one understood, but Julie had stopped asking about them since she rarely grasped the explanation and it often lasted for hours.

'If you mean Caroline, yes I suppose it is her, but I feel pretty out of sorts anyway.'

'What's she done, Julie? Whatever it is, she obviously isn't sorry about it.'

'Oh it's nothing wrong, it's just that she wants to join the meetings, and I suppose it feels a bit strange to see her as an adult. She still seems so young to me, she's a good kid but I can't yet believe she's old enough to be taking on that kind of responsibility.' Julie sat forward in her chair, with her hands clasped round the warm mug, digging her heels into the edge of the lawn.

'Well, she is very young, but she seems to have her head pretty well screwed onto her shoulders.

She is a bit over enthusiastic at times, but she'll grow out of that I should think. These young ones now, all seem full of bright ideas to me, perhaps it's a good thing to let them have a bit more say.' Elizabeth tried to steer clear of these discussions. She loved Julie and the others, who had taken the place of the family she could only dimly remember, but she was too tired these days to want to take any active part in things. Her bones creaked when she moved now, and her hearing was fading. She just wanted to rest. She felt she had earned that and although she liked to help, to look after the children and work in the house, she no longer cared very much about how things were run. After all, someone else had always done it, and she had still survived, what could these women do that would be so bad as to upset her after all those years?

She leaned over and took Julie's large brown hand in her small wrinkled one. 'What you need my dear, is a holiday. I can remember going on one, oh so long ago. We went to the seaside, me and my mother and my two little brothers. I can remember the beach, we collected shells and built a sandcastle. Do you know, we waited for ages to watch the tide come in and wash it away, we even put little paper flags on it!'

Julie smiled and stroked the small hand in hers as Elizabeth's voice murmured on, recounting a lost past; Punch and Judy shows, ice cream and candyfloss, the fairground and the piers. Sometimes she laughed as she recalled an incident, sometimes she just stared out at the bed of foxgloves, letting the thoughts flood through her head.

'Oh and the ride home on the train! We were all so tired, so stuffed full of sweets and lollies, but we still wanted to play out in the corridor and mother was tired and made us stay in our seats all the way home! Yes, that's what you need, a holiday!'

Julie had forgotten the point of it all, after the first few sentences, and had been lost in her own world of the past, when Elizabeth's statement brought her back.

'I'm sure you're right, but when am I supposed to have one, and where do you go now? We can hardly go off for a day trip by the seaside.'

'I suppose not. You always seem to be rushing around, too busy to do anything. Surely you women should take holidays sometimes. I always had three weeks a year when I worked, before everything was different.' Different was as near as Elizabeth could get to discussing the enormous changes that had been wrought in her life.

'Anyway, you must see to Caroline if you are going to introduce her to the meetings, so I suppose you would have to wait till the autumn to go away. She'll need you, you know, even if she pretends she doesn't at the moment. They're all the same, all that confidence and big talk to their mothers, but when it comes to the rest, they'll suddenly feel very young and insecure again.'

Julie stretched out, feeling the ache across her shoulders. Elizabeth was right. She should try to get away sometime, they had always agreed that they were entitled to a break from things during the year, she had just never taken it. Maybe she would go when Caroline was more settled. Cathy was always moaning on about the countryside, well maybe she would take her there for a while. It would be beautiful in the autumn.

The week passed quickly, full of uncompleted projects for Julie and Cathy, as the hot summer weather took them away from their work and off for swims in the river. By the time the next meeting came round, Julie had become accustomed to the idea of Caroline joining. She felt good as she, Cathy and Caroline went down to the market, to Vivian's house where the meeting was to be held that week. Sue was not there, she had hung around for a while after the tower block work was finished, but had now been gone for several days on a major expedition across London to investigate the state of the Kensington museums and Knightsbridge. Julie had tried to talk to her again, after the business with the guns, but had got the same rebuff as before. There seemed to be no way she could get through Sue's defences.

The evening was dark and windy as they made their way down the street. Cathy held up the lamp ahead of them on a long stick and it swayed dangerously as the wind caught it. In the dark Caroline felt for Julie's hand, suddenly the idea of attending the meetings did not seem such a good one. If she had not come, she could have been out in the streets with her friends from Albion Drive; all their mothers had persuaded them to wait another year before they gave up the luxury of childhood. But she felt that she could not back down, especially when she had started the whole thing. It seemed to take an hour to get to Vivian's house and, as every minute passed, she felt her confidence slipping away.

There were already over fifteen women in the living room when they came in, and they could hear women's voices floating on the wind as more arrived behind them.

'There are quite a few women here tonight,' said Vivian, as she led them through into the main room.

'That's good, though I'm a bit surprised, what with the weather being so bad.'

Julie was surprised, though she suspected that the

information about Caroline and the other young ones had been received with some interest and quite a few had turned up to see the outcome. Julie looked around and was glad to see that not all Caroline's youthful supporters had fallen by the wayside. In the corner sat Allison and Jenny, at fifteen and sixteen, they were Caroline's closest allies and Julie watched as Caroline hurried over and started whispering excitedly to them. By the fireplace was another group that Julie didn't recognise. One of them looked vaguely like an old friend of Julie's from her fighting days and Julie felt her stomach turn over as she caught the woman's eye, rose and went over to her.

'Hello. You're Julie aren't you?'

'Yes, that's right. How did you know?'

'I've seen a picture of you, my mother had it. She said you and her used to patrol together sometimes.'

'What was her name?' Julie knew, but still had to ask.

'Bonnie. Do you remember her?'

'Oh yes, I remember. She had a little girl and went off to Wales, that was the last I heard of her though.'

'That was my sister. I was born in Wales. We were fine for years but even there she couldn't find real safety. Some men found us when I was ten. They had guns and everything and we were out in the hills alone, there was nothing I could do except run away and avoid being caught myself. We never heard from Bonnie again. I went to Cornwall and settled there.'

Julie stared at the young woman, her head in a swirl of memories as the room continued to fill up with women, all talking and settling themselves down onto the collection of cushions and mattresses that covered the floor. She had loved Bonnie so dearly, for so long. It had been like a pain inside, something she never talked about, never told anyone about and had hoped would go away. She remembered the patrols. Dangerous exercises they were, out in the streets looking for signs of trouble, watching for the gangs of men, following them and protecting any women they came across. And yet she was always in seventh heaven when she went with Bonnie. Sometimes they stayed out several days and had to sleep wrapped tight in each other's arms in old sleeping bags to keep out the cold, Julie would stay awake for hours, intoxicated by the feel of the other woman's body beside her.

'Did you know her well?' The girl's voice caught Julie by surprise.

'Well, yes and no really. It was different then, you made friends very quickly, in case you might lose them. But I knew her for a while. I thought she went away with her sister.'

'She did, but they split up in Wales. Grace wanted to go down south to Cardiff, she was a city woman like you. So they parted.'

At the front of the room, Vivian was calling out to the others to be quiet. Her voice made Julie look away from the young woman and re-focus on the present. She felt at a loss, unsure of herself again. The memories of Bonnie, of those years, were normally so far buried and suddenly they had been exposed like an unhealed wound. Julie rose and went back to her place in the corner next to Cathy, sensing the relief on the girl's face that she had come back. It must be strange for these new young ones, faced with the terrible memories of their mothers and grandmothers, so much suffering and hatred to take on.

'Are you alright Julie? You look a bit pale.' Cathy put her arm round her.

'I'm fine, I've just had a bit of a shock, meeting the daughter of one of my patrol from the old days.'

'Which one is she?'

'There, over by the fireplace. Don't stare for heaven's sake, I think she's had enough of me staring as it is!'

Cathy watched the other woman curiously and carefully so that she would not see. For her anything that came out of Julie's past was of interest, she knew so little of it. Julie would never talk to her about it, although she talked at length about history. She knew that Julie had been through a lot, had picked up the odd crumb here and there, about the patrols and the men and how Julie had lived through those days. But she had heard little of her friends and lovers. She knew there had been problems, not all the women wanted to have relationships with other women. Even though they hated the men so much, they preferred to stay celibate. Her mother had been one of these, avoiding any sexual encounters, although she could not avoid the one that brought her child into existence. Cathy had heard of Bonnie in this context, though she had her suspicions about the relationship between Bonnie and Julie.

Finally silence fell over the group of women and Vivian stood up again to welcome them all. As the unofficial hostess, it fell to her to run the meeting and she sat down nervously in front of them. The meetings followed a traditional course, loosely based on business meetings of the old days, vaguely remembered by the women who had had to take notes and make coffee rather than take part in the decision making. After a report from the last meeting, discussing plans for the harvest and food storage for the winter, and a progress report on an information centre some of the women were trying to organise, the meeting was open to new issues and general

121

discussion. There was the inevitable silence following the end of the formal discussion and to Caroline it seemed all eyes were on her. She felt her hands go clammy and stick together as she rose from her seat next to Allison and Jenny and turned to where Julie was already standing, waiting for her. It was Julie who spoke first.

'I would like the meeting to consider the application from a prospective new member, my daughter Caroline. I have discussed the matter with her, the responsibilities that belonging to this meeting entail, and the problems that her undoubted youth may well bring with her. Despite my words, she's still very keen to join us and I have decided to show my support of her application by introducing her tonight. If any women have any objections, please will they make them known to us now.'

A murmur of voices started up as Julie sat down, leaving Caroline to face the meeting. The room quieted again as there were clearly going to be no immediate objections. For all the criticisms thrown at her, Julie was a respected member, and for many of the women her word was good enough. Now they waited for Caroline to speak.

'I'd like to thank Julie for introducing me tonight and all of you for listening to me now. I've been feeling for some time that I'd like to play more of a part in helping this community and joining the meetings seemed like a good place to start.'

As she paused there was a muffled applause. It was usually expected that new members made some kind of brief speech to accept membership and the one Caroline gave was quite in order. However, when the applause had stopped and the expectant faces of the women looked round to see who was to speak next, they saw that Caroline was still on her feet, waiting for them to be quiet so she could continue. Some of the older women looked askance. It seemed a little presumptuous for such a young woman, at her first meeting, to take up any more of their time.

'I just wanted to say a bit more about how we young women feel about the community and all that.' Caroline could feel the tension in the room, could hear the whispers. She looked down to where her mother sat and received an encouraging, if worried, grin. 'It's just that we feel that we don't get enough say in things, that we are treated as children far too long!' She paused and looked round, flicking her fringe back nervously, hands clenched deep in her pockets. Quite a few of her friends were applauding her and nodding in agreement, many of the other women also looked as though they were not really that surprised. But here and there was a face that was filled with doubt and worry. One woman had risen to her feet, looking to Vivian for permission to speak. Vivian nodded, wishing all this had not happened when the meeting was at her house.

'My name is Belinda. I can understand how young Caroline feels, but surely she must learn the value of patience, the value of mature judgement, that only comes with a greater experience of life than fifteen years or so can have.'

'But surely, if we are to get all this experience, what better way than through our own community, through the meetings.'

'Yes indeed, and that is why we have the system of introductions, so that you can learn how things are run here, how to take over the organisation when it is your turn!'

'But that's the point. We don't necessarily want to take things over just as you have them! We think there are things that should be changed, things that,

as young people, we know more about than you!'
Caroline was beginning to lose her fiery young temper
and her self-control. 'Sometimes all you can see is
the past, the horror that you all had to go through
in some way or another. I know that's why Julie
didn't want me to come to the meetings, she wants
me to go on being a child for ever, because she feels
so guilty about what's happened in my life, how I
never had a decent childhood! But it's too late for
that, we've got to go on, not look back all the time,
not just count our blessings, be glad we're still alive;
we've got to make things really better!'

Julie sighed. She had not expected the guilt thing,
but the rest of Caroline's speech was predictable.
She knew how the others would react to it and she
was not disappointed.

A tall woman with a baby in her arms, had sprung
to her feet on the other side of the room.

'Listen young woman, you may have been luckier
than some, and so more ready to forget the past and
all that holds for us, but you must surely realise that
we cannot forget so easily. We must learn from what's
happened, learn to care more for our world, without
constant reference to the past, we would soon forget.
You and your young friends want to come and sweep
us all away with your spanking new brooms! How
will you ever know your own past, your own
history?'

Caroline knew she'd made a mess of things. She
hadn't meant to sound like that, to make out they
had nothing of value to teach. But they seemed so
sensitive, she couldn't understand it. Whenever the
past was mentioned they just couldn't take any
criticism. She sat down again, feeling mortified and
defeated.

Jenny squeezed her hand and murmured, 'Well
you tried anyway, and it's a start.' Caroline shrugged

her shoulders and turned away. Why hadn't they spoken up for her when the other women had started on her? They just sat there, the two of them, full of love and support but no action. It must be because they were in love, she thought scornfully, though Julie and Cathy had never seemed to behave like that. She looked over at her mother, but Julie seemed to be in a world of her own that night. Apart from one hurried smile, she had felt no contact with her at all.

Julie was lost in her memories. She had continued to watch the young woman, though she knew she shouldn't, and from the memory of Bonnie a thousand other memories had come. Her hand reached up to touch the scar running down her neck and shoulder, that had been touch and and go for a while, especially with the fear of tetanus and gangrene always present. She could picture the camp as clearly as though it were yesterday, the old warehouse down by the river. At night you could hear the water lapping against the walls and the roof would be covered with seabirds whenever the weather drove them inland. She had spent eight years of her life in that great dark building, and though it was only a short time, nothing had ever seemed as important. Even now, in the new security of the Hackney community, she never had that same electric feeling that she was truly alive. But then there was Bonnie to make every simple operation seem like a treat.

She laughed to herself at her own infatuation. Yet they never had had a relationship, apart from that of sisters, a fact she knew Cathy never believed. She had had relationships with other women, but they never lasted for some reason, and she had landed up back with Bonnie again. When Bonnie was raped she wanted to go out and kill every man in London. For two days the others had to keep her locked up to prevent her from going on the rampage, and probably getting herself killed for her trouble. When Bonnie was pregnant, she had felt an insane jealousy for the child that was going to take Bonnie away from her, stop her going on patrol, stop her squeezing into Julie's sleeping bag and wrapping her soft body round her.

She even had to admit to herself that sometimes she hoped the baby would be a boy, then it would die and Bonnie would be returned to her, looking like herself. Not that blown-up woman who could no longer swing in and out of the old buildings, dodge down alleyways and shin up drainpipes. When Bonnie moved away to Wales with the healthy little girl that she bore, Julie thought the world had come to an end. She had cried for days, on her own away from the others, she thought they would not understand. And yet she had not gone with Bonnie, she could not bear to leave, to give up on the city just when some kind of an end was in sight. She could remember standing by the river watching the small boat heading upstream, slowly disappearing from sight. Wishing she was there to row, but still standing fixed, on the bank. She had vowed to go and visit her, but there had been so much to do, and over the months the urgency of the visit grew less. It became something she talked about always in the future, never something she did.

A voice interrupted her dreamings.

'Julie, I would like to ask you what you think of your daughter's outburst!'

The speaker was Angela, never a great fan of hers, Julie thought. She got to her feet, feeling disoriented, too much rooted in the past.

'I'm not sure myself. Caroline and I have talked about it and to begin with, I was against the idea. I felt she was being too rash, wanting things to change too quickly. But after a while, I began to think that maybe it was me not wanting things to change at all. We have seen so much change in our lives that now we have some stability, it's very hard to give it up and trust the ideals of women who are so young and, to us, so inexperienced. Maybe we've held them back. I seem to remember that when I was fourteen and fifteen I was out on the streets learning how to use a machine gun and spending hours on rooftops with a rifle waiting for the men to come. Just because we feel we need the rest now, does not mean that our children are any different from how we were then. I think we should give them a chance, let them come, and let them have more say. The introduction system is too cumbersome, makes them wait too long. Hopefully they can't do much damage, and we'll always be around to watch them after all.'

Caroline stared as her mother sat down again. She was amazed at the change of heart in her. Only yesterday Julie had been going on about how irresponsible most of Caroline's friends were, and now here she was, defending them and even suggesting the introduction idea should be dropped. She felt she should say something but didn't really know what to say. Fortunately someone else had got to her feet in the meantime and was waiting to speak. It was Bonnie's daughter.

'My name is Robin. I don't come from this community, but I would like to say something if you don't mind.' There was no objection so she continued. 'I come from a country community in Cornwall. We have learnt the hard way that you can't run away to the countryside, that the struggle is everywhere. Now that we are at peace finally, and have established ourselves, we too have had to learn to deal with new problems. There's been so much time and energy spent on survival, now we

127

have that in our grasp, we must try to shape our community for the future, not just for the past. There was a struggle in our village very similar to the one that is happening tonight and many women were made very hurt and angry by it. But we realised one thing, one thing that made our understanding of our mothers much clearer, one thing which, once they admitted it to themselves, made them less sensitive, more willing to listen to new ideas.'

The room had quieted completely, all eyes on the young woman as she stood with one hand on her hip, her cropped blonde hair picking up flashes of light from the lamp in the corner.

'The women in the village who had survived, who could remember, however faintly, the old life, whose mothers had told them stories of how things used to be. Those who could remember men, healthy men, men that they thought they loved, that they shared their lives with and whose children they bore willingly. All these and more, felt a terrible guilt. A guilt that it was their inaction for so long that had caused the catastrophe of The Death. They saw themselves as having supported the rule of men which had led to such destruction, even of the race itself. The women felt they had betrayed their children and themselves by their weakness. And, as a result, their whole desire was for atonement and self-punishment. They wanted to shoulder all the work, wanted their daughters to have total freedom, anything to avoid that finger of accusation pointed at them. Among all of us are women who were married to men of power, who might have done something but did not, an inheritance of inaction over so many years. So much fear for so long.'

Robin turned her head toward Julie, her gaze fixed on her. Julie sat numb. 'There were some who always despised the men, but even they did not let their love for women overcome their fear, their guilt. But they must know that it is finally all over. That we have our world back, not as good as before, but we can make it work in time. We feel no resentment for the older women, the way things have happened is beyond us now and you mustn't burden us with your guilt.'

She sat down and for a minute there was silence, then a babble of voices broke out. The shock of what Robin had said cut deep into more than one memory. Julie felt she could never move again, she hugged her knees with her arms and, as her eyes roved the room, they kept coming back to Robin's. She felt like a butterfly pinned down, and as the woman moved over to join her, she could feel the sweat break out on her body, the slight trickle making its way down her back. She felt removed from the discussion again. She knew there would be no practical decisions made that night, that was not the way of the meetings and she could not face entering the fury of discussion that had now built up. Robin sat beside her also lost in thought, rolling long thin cigarettes between her fingers. Julie looked sideways at her hands. Like Bonnie's they were stubby with square fingernails, but strong. She looked at her own, worn, large, with the tiny age spots that had begun to appear on her skin. For some reason she suddenly felt ashamed of them and tucked her hands under her knees. It seemed like hours passed without either of them acknowledging the other's presence. Not until the meeting had finally died down. Only then, as Vivian closed the discussion and women started drifting off, or chatting amongst themselves in corners, did Robin lean over with her tin of herbal tobacco in her hand.

'Would you like one of these?'

'Thanks.' Julie took the tin and carefully packed

the tobacco in her pipe, lit it, leaned back and and watched the smoke rise up, blurring her view of the other woman's face.

'How long are you staying?'

'Just tonight. It's a long way back and I must be home for the harvest. I've been away a few weeks as it is.'

'Why did you leave?'

'I don't know, just curiosity I think. We've been hearing a lot about the London women and after all the stories I'd heard mother tell me, I wanted to see for myself.'

'Do you think you'll come back?'

'No. I'm a real country girl now, I'm afraid!' She smiled, the first time Julie had seen her looking relaxed. 'It's so beautiful where we are, I just couldn't leave all that for your dirty old city.'

'It's not that bad, you know. We've begun to clear up bits of it and one day it'll be beautiful too, in its own way.'

Robin laughed, 'Yes, "in its own way", but not like the country. Not enough green! But I can see what you mean. Maybe we shouldn't talk about it, I don't think either one of us is going to change her mind somehow!'

Silence again. Julie could feel her heart thumping loudly. By chance Robin dropped her cigarette and leaned over Julie to pick it up, her hand brushing against Julie's leg. Julie felt confused and excited, she had not felt like this for a long time. She was frightened and looked up to try and find Cathy, so she could go home, escape from all the emotion she was feeling. Cathy was there, talking to Vivian and Allison over by the window but watching Julie with half an eye. When she saw Julie looking for her, she made her way over and squatted in front of them.

'What are you doing love? I thought I'd go

home soon, all this has made me really tired and I know Caroline wants to go, as she's feeling a bit freaked by everything.'

'Yes, I'll come now as well.' Julie scrambled to her feet, collecting her coat and bag in a hurry, Cathy stopped her outside in the corridor.

'You know you don't have to come if you don't want to.'

'What do you mean?'

'You know. You and that Robin, you seem to be getting on very well and she's going back to Cornwall tomorrow. If you want to stay longer with her I don't mind.'

Julie knew Cathy meant 'stay the night' but couldn't manage saying it. She felt helpless, they all spent so much time on practical things, there never seemed any time left to sort out their feelings for each other. She gazed at Cathy, loving her young, serious face, loving how her brown hair fell in such untidy tangles round her shoulders, wanting to touch her and be near her. But also wanting the excitement of being with Robin.

'I don't know, I just don't know how I feel Cathy. I don't want to hurt you, or her, or me for that matter!'

'Look, why don't you stay for a while anyway. Mary is away so you could always stay in her room if you wanted and, if not, just come home. I don't mind, but I do want to go now.'

Julie hugged her; but she stayed. Caroline looked at Julie oddly as she left with Cathy.

'I'll see you tomorrow love and we'll talk about the meeting then, eh!'

'Yes, okay, if that's what you want.' Caroline turned and followed Cathy out into the darkness.

Julie and Robin sat talking for hours, throwing on

log after log to keep the fire going. When all the others had gone, Julie suddenly felt free to talk openly and had fired questions at the young woman about Bonnie, about Cornwall, about the upside-down world they had inherited. They laughed and smoked cigarettes until, when Julie thought it would never happen, Robin leaned over and kissed her. Later she couldn't remember how they got from sitting by the fire, to being wrapped in each other's arms in Mary's bed. The tall, lean body of the younger woman felt strange after the softness of Cathy. They made love for hours, stopping for more jokes, cigarettes and conversations. The night seemed to go on forever. But finally daylight fought its way through the chinks in the curtain. Downstairs they could hear Vivian tidying up the living room and singing to herself. Julie giggled, 'Do you think she knows we're up here? I never asked her you know.'

'Well if she doesn't, she's a lot dimmer than I took her for. I think everyone had a pretty good idea of what was going on, don't you?'

'I suppose so. It was all so surprising, I get the feeling I was the last one to realise it.'

Julie sat up and, as the sheet fell away, she suddenly felt embarassed by her body. She really felt she was getting old. She pulled the sheets back up over her and Robin laughed.

'There's no need for that, you know. There's nothing wrong with your body that I noticed.' She leaned over Julie and got her tobacco tin from the table. 'One last smoke and then I must get up. I have to be going soon, otherwise I won't reach Windsor before dark.'

'How are you travelling?'

'I've got the horse, a special loan, as long as I promised to be back by the beginning of September.'

Julie slipped out of bed and drew the curtains

back, letting the sunshine stream in.

'Well at least the weather's a lot better for you.' She didn't really want to think about Robin going, although she knew she wouldn't know what to do if she stayed. They didn't talk about what had happened and why, it didn't seem so important really. There was not much chance they'd see each other again for a long time. Outside it was still very windy, rippling Robin's hair as she packed her things into the saddle bags and finally turned to say goodbye.

'Give Caroline and the others their chance, Julie. After all, someone gave me a chance. They'll make mistakes and all that but it will be better. You can't hold them away from things for much longer anyway.'

Julie nodded, 'I think it will be okay. The women were pretty shocked by what you said last night but I think it went home for a lot of them. It's just a matter of time!'

'I thought you'd like this. Something to remember me by.' Robin pressed an envelope into her hand, mounted the horse and rode off so suddenly Julie was barely aware she'd gone. She didn't open the envelope till she was home in her room. It was a picture of Bonnie.

Cathy was out all day on the farm and Caroline was off with Jenny and Allison, trying to work out a program of ideas to take to the next Meeting. Julie lay on her bed, trying to work out how she felt about everything. So many emotions, they didn't seem to conflict, but each wanted to be thought of ... Cathy, Robin, Bonnie, her friends and the community, out on patrols. She wanted Cathy to come home and talk to her. Even Elizabeth was out, off sampling Barbara's home-made wine. She'd be coming home a bit tipsy tonight and rambling on even more about the old times.

When Cathy finally did come, Julie felt shy, just like when she had first met her and fallen for her youthful charm and gentle body. She had learnt since then that Cathy was not as sweet and innocent as she seemed and there had been times she was afraid of her. But that evening she felt relaxed and unafraid. Just shy, not knowing what to say.

In fact she hardly said anything. Cathy slumped down on the bed beside her and gave her a kiss.

'For one moment I thought you might run off to Cornwall!'

'And leave my beloved daughter to your tender mercies, you must be joking! Besides, I never could ride a horse!'

Cathy sat on the bed beside her, lying back so her head fell into Julie's lap and she could talk without having to see Julie's face.

'So, was everything alright?'

Julie stiffened slightly, 'Yes, well I suppose so, there wasn't really a lot to be alright or not. She's gone off back to Cornwall.'

'And you don't wish she was still her?'

'No, I don't wish that. Oh I don't know, Cathy! That's an impossible question. I knew she was going to go, if she wasn't I doubt anything would have happened.'

They both lay still, each chewing over the contents of their own minds. Cathy knew she would get little more on the subject out of Julie, at least not then. She would just have to get herself back to normal so she could stop talking about it. Julie couldn't see what there was to talk about. It had been just that one night, just an interlude where she had felt some connection with her lost past. Cathy was here, her present, it was not the same thing at all.

Finally Cathy rolled over onto one elbow and stretched up to kiss Julie and let the older woman fold her arms round her body. The situation was not resolved, another chapter of misunderstanding that could mature into lingering resentment had been written. But for now they could carry on as before. A lifetime of having to put off such discussions for more urgent matters had left them both ill-prepared. Neither of them really wanted to have a full-blown talk about it, neither really knew what to say. A kiss and a cuddle would have to do to keep the worst of the insecurities at bay.

They lay on the bed together for hours, dozing off as dusk fell, till they were disturbed by the banging of the front door.

'Sounds like Sue's back', yawned Cathy and struggled off the bed. 'We'd better go down and see what she's been up to and bring her up to date on all this carry-on with Caroline. She really should be around for the next meeting you know. Caroline was pretty upset that she didn't bother to come back for the last one.'

'Well, you know Sue, hardly the most responsible woman in the world!' Julie put on a sweater over her tee-shirt and pulled on her boots. 'Right, let's go and eat, I'm really hungry now.'

They would talk about it all later she thought. When they were in bed again, but there was no hurry.

By the end of September most of the harvest work was done. It had been a good year and the women looked forward to a winter when they need not worry about shortages. There would also be more variety in their diet than previously. The group of women in charge of the storing operation had done a good job, the improvised barns and sheds were strong and dry. Supplies of wheat had been brought in from Kent in trade for a collection of manufactured goods from the city.

Cathy wandered up Brougham Road with two small children hanging on each arm, exhausted but satisfied with the day's work she had done fixing up the stables so the animals would withstand the winter storms. Altogether it was a time of resting. Julie had meant to go away, but Caroline still needed a lot of support and advice as she and her young friends took on a variety of tasks. They continually had to defend themselves against some of the more staid members of the collective, and Julie didn't think she should leave her.

Cathy sighed, that was always the problem with Julie, so many other commitments. When Cathy had first met her, out in the countryside, it had seemed very different. Julie had been on her own with one small child, trying to fend for herself. When Julie had insisted on coming back to London as soon as it was safe, Cathy had objected. She felt she belonged in the countryside, and yet she had come to London and now she could not imagine living anywhere else. She had wondered about that when Robin came. Robin was so much a country woman, like Cathy had been as a child, and yet Cathy had felt no desire to follow her back to her green fields in Cornwall. It was more than just being with Julie, the city had become a part of her. She couldn't behave like Sue, but she loved to wander round the beautiful old streets and admire the buildings which had withstood so much and refused to crumble and decay. She could feel Julie's dream come alive then, see the streets again in their best, thronging with women.

'Cathy, my dear!'

Cathy jumped as Elizabeth called out to her from the doorway of the house where she was sunning herself in the evening light.

'Yes Elizabeth, what can I do for you?'

'Oh nothing, just an old lady wanting to have a bit of a chat if you're not too busy!'

'Of course I'm not!' Cathy sent the two little ones off home and pulled out another chair to sit beside Elizabeth on the porch.

'I hear it's been a good harvest this year.'

'It certainly has, I don't think we're going to have to worry about the winter this year.'

'Ah well, I hope not. It's bad enough all that cold getting into me bones, I'm not as young as I was you know!'

'Yes, I think we all know that, Elizabeth!' Cathy laughed, the "I'm not as young as I was" line had become one of Elizabeth's favourites. 'But you needn't worry too much about the cold. Your room's quite warm and dry now isn't it? I thought Sue did some work on it in the spring.'

'Oh yes, young Sue was a great help. It's made such a difference to me. But you won't be interested in all this, just an old woman's problems. How are you and Julie? She never has time to talk to me these days.'

'Julie's fine, it's just we've been so busy these last few weeks, and then there was all the thing about Caroline joining the meetings.'

'Oh yes, I heard about that. Mind you, it's better to let the young ones have their chance. After all, we old ones didn't make such a good job of things did we? Look where we've all ended up!'

Cathy stared at Elizabeth. She came out with such amazing things at times. Maybe it was just that she was the only really old person Cathy had known, maybe all old people were like her. Cathy wondered what Julie would be like in another thirty years and laughed.

'What are you laughing at, my dear?'

'Oh nothing, Elizabeth, just something that flashed through my mind.'

'By the way, what happened to that Robin who was here?' Elizabeth eyed Cathy and leaned forward in a conspiratorial way.

'You old gossip Elizabeth, why do you want to know about that?'

'Oh I don't know. You young ones are always telling me it's good to show your feelings and talk about things, and now here I am trying to do it right and I'm accused of being a gossip!' Elizabeth turned away from Cathy in mock anger and sulked.

'Don't be silly, I don't mean it like that. It's just that no one else has asked me so outright about it. There isn't really much to say, it seems like a long time ago now. We didn't really talk about it much, you know what Julie's like.'

'Well I'm glad things are alright with the pair of you, I wouldn't like anything unpleasant to happen.'

'I don't think so, not for the time being anyway.'

'It was all so different in my day. You were supposed to find the man of your dreams and marry him and stay with him forever. Women like you were called bad names and treated as being sick. I remember there were two or three like that who lived in our street. My mother used to tell me to stay from them, that they might want me to do things and play games, but she never told me what games. I was fascinated by them. They looked so different from the other women with all their funny clothes. But they seemed to have a good time and I always wanted to go and talk to them. It was just my mother, she would have thrashed me good and proper for that!' She chuckled and rearranged herself in the armchair and Cathy could see her eyes starting to close.

She slept a lot these days and the others were

beginning to get more and more worried about her health. Sue had spent days damp-proofing the house and putting up insulation and double-glazing in Elizabeth's room, but the winters were still very cold and they knew Elizabeth would not survive many more. They all found it hard to imagine what life would be like without her.

The children loved her, and many of the older women would spend hours listening to her stories and being surprised by the strength of her opinions. Sue, in particular, adored her. It was almost as though Elizabeth had taken the place of whatever family Sue had had and never spoken of. The two of them talked and laughed for hours, as though they shared the same world of dreams.

Cathy tiptoed softly back into the house so as not to disturb the old woman, and started chopping up some vegetables in the kitchen for the evening meal. Sue was off again, but had promised to be back as the following day was the evening of the meeting and she had finally begun to take more part in the community.

When Sue arrived she sat in silence for ages before they could get her to talk about what she had seen. Her green eyes were cold and she stared at the wall in front of her. Julie hadn't seen her in that state for months and felt a shiver of fear. Elizabeth, too, was shaken by Sue's behaviour. She tried to put her arm round her to comfort her, but Sue shrugged her off and stalked round the kitchen with a cigarette in her mouth.

When they finally got her to talk, they all sat feeling waves of shock and terror rise up. Men. Young healthy men. They were a reality again!

Bit by bit, they got the story out of her. She had been down in South London when she heard the news that had travelled north from Kent. A community there had been visited by a group of about fifteen young men. They had only stayed the night, camped a mile or so away from the women, and had not ventured near them, but the women were left in a state of panic and confusion. They had managed to find out only a little about them from a scout who had been trailing their progress since they were first sighted. They had come from a laboratory on the south coast, one in which the scientists had tried to produce enough test-tube boy babies to save the male race. But these projects always failed because over the years there were no healthy men left, men whose chromosomes were unaffected by The Death, to give sperm for the babies. However, some had been born and the last men that most of the women had seen were the results of these experiments.

This group spoke some English, but had clearly been left isolated for so long that they had no idea about the world they had been born into. They spoke of a man who was their 'father', someone they looked up to almost as a kind of god. The women reckoned he must have been the last of the scientists to be with them, to look after them sufficiently, so that they could survive after his death. These men were hunters, not farmers, and as they had hunted the area around the laboratory dry, they were forced to move on to new lands. And now they were heading north, straight for London.

Sue was flushed with anger by the time she had finished telling the others.

'Why now, just when things were coming together? Why did they have to come back!' She ground her cigarette end beneath her boot and rolled another, her eyes flashing round the room. Julie felt an enormous exhaustion settle on her shoulders. Sue was right, they had achieved so much, removed so much of the scars of the past, actually made a place where they could live and be happy and now to be faced with more men! She felt like crying.

'But how do we know they "will definitely come to London"?'

'Apparently their "father" left them some papers, which they carry round like a bible, even though they can hardly read, and the papers tell them about what has happened and talks about London like a kind of religious shrine, the heart of THEIR country. It sounds like they think they're coming to claim their inheritance!'

Julie looked round at the others. Cathy was white faced, clutching her mug in one hand and biting what was left of her nails on the other. Elizabeth looked grey, she seemed to have aged about ten years in five minutes. She reached her hand out and took Sue's. This time Sue did not reject her.

'Will they really come, Sue? All over again, it couldn't be. They wouldn't be interested in an old woman like me would they?'

'Don't worry Elizabeth, they won't hurt you, we'll make sure of that!'

Julie was surprised at the force of Sue's voice, this was a side of her that none of them had seen.

'Why don't you go to bed Elizabeth, Caroline will make you a hot water-bottle and we can sort all this out better in the morning.' Julie thought Caroline needed something to do, since she looked as though she might cry any minute.

'Yes, that would be nice, if you don't mind, my dear.'

'Of course not, I'm tired anyway, I'll come up with you.' Caroline took the old woman's arm and the two of them left, leaving Sue, Julie and Cathy facing each other round the table.

'I think we should leave talking about it till the morning, till we can tell the others what's going on.'

Cathy could see they were all too devastated to deal with anything that night. Tomorrow was soon enough to drop the bombshell on the others.

The news was met with horror, and panic spread throughout the community. They held meeting after meeting to discuss what should be. done. Scouts reported that the men were moving northwards again and were now camped at Blackheath. They seemed to be able to tell where the communities were, and always camped nearby, but as yet had made no approaches to the women. The Hackney women had to face the fact that there was a very good chance that they would come to them.

In the course of the meetings three main opinions developed. Firstly, that they should just ignore the men and hope they would go away and bother someone else. After all they had neither time nor energy to deal with them. The second was that they should try and make some contact, try to incorporate them into the world of which they were also a part. The third was that they should attack them at the first sign of trouble and wipe them out. The arguments went on far into the night. Julie felt helpless as she saw women being divided by men yet again, as they had been in the past. She felt unwilling to decide anything, too unsure of how much she was driven by her emotions. She was quiet in meetings, unusually so, letting the others go over the issues time and time again.

Sue was virulent in her attack on the men. Suddenly she had become outspoken and totally involved, her thick curls shaking as she thrashed out the arguments.

She had been down to Blackheath and watched the men, and had little hope that they could ever fit into society.

'They're like a pack of wild animals! They spend their time hunting and fighting each other. Once they've used up everything around them, they just move on to the next place and do the same there! You should see the mess they live in! You must be mad to think they could ever change!'

'But just to slaughter them! Isn't that just using their methods to deal with the problem!' argued Jenny. 'If we turn to killing now, won't that set a dangerous precedent for our community?'

'If we don't do something, I doubt we'll have much of a community to worry about!' retorted Sue. 'Do you really think these men are going to sit down and accept our way of doing things? It's all very well for you to go on, you never saw what they were like, the things they did! They're just not human!'

'That's not fair!' cried Jenny. 'Of course we know about it, just because we're young doesn't mean we don't understand what you're on about. It's just that that was before, when the world was run so differently, maybe now all that is gone, men will be able to live decently, maybe it was the old ways that sent them so crazy!'

Sue scoffed, 'I've heard that one before and never seen any truth in it!'

'We're never going to come to any agreement if we carry on like this,' said Julie. 'As far as we know, the men have not yet committed any acts of violence against the women, not so far anyway.'

'Do we have to wait till it happens before we act!' Sue turned on Julie. 'You, of all people, surely you must know what men are like, why should this lot be any different!'

'I know Sue, I know! But surely we must wait and see where they go, maybe they won't come to Hackney at all. They might go west from Blackheath, across the river further upstream and miss us. I just don't think we should prepare ourselves for the worst until we know it's going to happen.'

'Maybe we can make them different. They are still very young, hardly more than boys, and they've had so little contact with the old ways.' Allison was still doubtful but wanted to support Jenny.

'Well I don't think it makes any difference what they've learnt or not learnt! They're still men. Don't you remember what Barbara used to tell us about the real old days when women did rule and then men took over? Are we going to let it all happen again without putting up a fight!'

'Come on Sue!' interrupted Julie. 'All these women have been fighting in some way for years to free this world from all the harm that men have caused it. I don't really think you can say they'd give up without a struggle!'

Sue stopped short and looked at Julie. She knew Julie was right, but she just felt so angry all the time these days.

'I'm sorry, I didn't mean it to sound like that, maybe I should just be quiet for a bit.' She sat down abruptly and spent the rest of the meeting staring at her boots.

Finally Allison and Julie managed to sort out a compromise that everyone agreed would do for the time being. The guns would be got out and cleaned and anyone who wanted to learn to shoot would be taught, though the guns would be stored under lock and key in Julie's study. Meanwhile, another group, led by Jenny, would try to work out a way of communicating with the men if they did come, a reception party of a sort. Sue volunteered for nothing, she could already shoot and sneered at any idea of speaking to the men. Most of the time she prowled the streets between Hackney and the river, alone, watching out for any sign of them. The food stores were locked up and the animals penned, children no longer ventured further than their own street to play in, a sombre, waiting atmosphere filled the air.

A month passed, and then another. As New Year grew closer, many of the women had begun to think the men would never come. A slight relaxation of precautions had begun, especially as they had kept up the tradition of a festival in mid-winter, for the New Year, and the children were growing excited and impatient with the restraints put on them. The problems of the winter also took up much of their time. Elizabeth was bed-ridden and needed a lot of attention, the news of the men, on top of the worsening weather was a real blow to her health. Now her ramblings were more and more confused, she was losing contact with the present. Sue sat by her bed for hours, talking to her and nursing her. But as it grew colder, Julie knew the men would come, and that they would come north seeking the shelter of the buildings north of the river. For all she knew, they might have scouts out now, have already found their safe little haven from the winter weather. They had been at Blackheath for months, surely they must have exhausted the natural food supplies. Julie lay anxiously awake at night for hours, listening to Cathy's even breathing next to her.

In fact, it wasn't until the middle of January that Caroline pedalled furiously back to Hackney, after one of her routine checks, with the news that the men had crossed the river and were travelling north through Stepney, heading straight for Hackney. Within an hour the streets were empty, children were kept in and a system of lookouts on the roofs was arranged. The women grouped themselves together, locked in their houses, peering out behind drawn curtains, watching and waiting. This time the men did not camp outside their area. They wandered up and down the Hackney streets muttering to each other, pointing at the ploughed fields and gazing at the smoke curling up from all the chimneys. At the wide end of Broadway Market they built a huge bonfire and sat around it as night fell, singing their strange songs while they roasted some hapless calf. They looked sick and hungry and were obviously suffering from the winter cold.

The next day Sue and Caroline watched them from round the corner, each armed with one of the rifles Sue had found. A group of about six women, led by Jenny, approached the men nervously, carrying a box of bread and vegetables. They left the box twenty or so yards away and withdrew. The men watched them in silence. Slowly one of them approached the box, sniffing at it like a hunter, suspicious, but also desperate. When he realised it was food, he called to the others. Four more came forward to look at the box and then carry it back to where the rest of the tribe sat waiting. They talked rapidly amongst themselves until some agreement had been reached. The first man walked away again, toward the women, followed by a bodyguard of three others, armed with efficient looking spears.

Jenny gulped, feeling sick with fear and anticipation. She and the others stood their ground until the men were only a few feet away from them. For what seemed an eternity they just stood and stared at each other. Finally the man spoke, holding out his hand in greeting.

'I am called Fox. I am the master. We do not hurt you. We are hungry and sick and must find food. You will help us?'

Jenny stepped forward, her mouth dry, she stammered as she spoke.

146

'I am Jenny. We will not harm you.' Then she didn't know what to say. She had never seen a young man before and the sight of one so close blotted out all her carefully prepared speech. He was close to six feet tall and had blond hair and the beginnings of a beard and moustache. His clothes, like those of the rest of them, were an odd mixture of pre-Death clothes, boots and a pair of faded jeans, and then an assortment of skins made into a rough coat, finished off with a wide-brimmed hat, decorated with feathers.

'Where is your tribe? Are you master? We can meet and talk?' Fox moved a little closer and smiled.

Caroline and Sue came up the street, their guns raised. Jenny tried to concentrate, as the others in her group were clearly struck dumb by the proceedings.

'We do not have one master here, but we have come to talk with you on behalf of our people.'

'No master,' Fox frowned. They had read of women in the father's book, but it was hard to understand. They looked so different, so weak. He turned back and whispered a few words to his bodyguard, they nodded in agreement.

'You will come and eat with us and then we talk. We have good animal meat, my men are great hunters.' He grinned and nodded back to his companions, who bowed to the women.

'We do not eat meat, but we will come and sit with you,' replied Jenny. Fox frowned, suspecting an insult, but after another consultation, he beckoned to them to follow him to the camp.

Caroline and Sue sat in the street for three hours, watching, as Jenny and the others sat round the huge fire talking with the men. Finally they rose and, waving goodbye, made their way back down the market and round into Brougham Road. The other two waited another half hour to make sure they were not followed, then rejoined the others at No. 98.

They could hear the babble of voices from halfway down the street, and when they got in they found Jenny and her friends sitting in the middle of the floor with questions fired at her from all sides. Sue crouched on her haunches in the corner, while Caroline sat close to her mother, feeling horribly young and insecure. Julie managed to bring some order in the room so that they could hear what had happened.

'Well,' began Jenny, 'they certainly seem friendly enough, quite anxious to please, almost like children. Most of what we found out is the same as what we already knew. That they have come to London because of what this "father" told them to do. They don't seem to know much about what has happened and they wouldn't let us see his notes so we don't know what their attitude to us is.'

'I wouldn't have thought you'd need notes to guess that!' interrupted Sue.

'Oh stop it Sue! Let Jenny finish, you'll get your say!' Cathy snapped at Sue, amazed and impatient with the stream of bitterness that came from Sue since the men had arrived. She had never contributed so much to a meeting and, equally, been so negative and so unhelpful in finding a solution.

'Anyway,' continued Jenny, 'the scientist, or whoever, must have died when they were still very young. They can hardly read, and have turned the whole thing into a kind of religion. The papers gave them enough information to survive, to learn to hunt and fish, but what else it says is still a mystery. Since they left their home they've run into a lot of problems, already three have died because of rat bites, and their knowledge of medicine is non-existent. I think they had some drugs left for them, but once

148

those were gone they had nothing else to fall back on.'

'Why don't they go back to the countryside then?' asked Cathy.

'Because of this business with the papers. They keep talking about the Centre and Westminster, that's where they're headed, just because that's what they were told to do. Maybe their "father" was a bit mad by the time he wrote the papers, there hasn't been much left of Westminster for years. But they will go there, you can see they're determined. They just want to stay for a few weeks because of the cold and the sickness.'

'But what are they going to live on? Are we going to have to feed another fifteen out of our winter stocks? It isn't as though Hackney is bursting with wild animals for their wretched spears!' Cathy leant back against Julie's legs, remembering how proud they'd been of the harvest. It made her choke to think of just giving it all away to men.

'We don't have to give them much, and after this summer surely we can spare something for them without going short ourselves.'

'And you really think that after we've fed and nursed them, they will just go away and never bother us again! You must be joking!' Sue was red in the face with anger and frustration.

'Yes! Because the "father" says they must, don't you see!'

'But Jenny,' Julie tried to speak calmly. The thought of men hanging around for "a few weeks" filled her with an old dread. 'What happens even if they do move on? They will go to Westminster and find it's a ruin. No one can live there. Then what will they do? Surely, if we've fed them, they'll come back here and stay again, maybe try and move in for good!'

Jenny looked round to her group, waiting for support. Most of them sat silent, half doubtful, half intimidated by Sue and Julie. Finally, Vivian spoke up in Jenny's defence.

'I really feel that there is a chance these men could be different. They are so little touched by the past, so in awe of us and what we have achieved, that if they did come back, it would be worth trying to educate them more, teach them our ways.'

'Yes, teach them to read and then they'll understand their stupid papers and won't that be great! God knows what's in them about women if they were written by some half-crazed scientist!' Sue dragged hard on her cigarette and withdrew into the corner of the room.

Julie sighed, this discussion could go on all night, she had never seen such antagonism flying around, so little hope of agreement. The community had never had to face anything like this, even the hunger and the sickness, nothing had divided the women so much. She leaned forward, her hands on Cathy's shoulders, trying to listen, trying to work out her own tangled emotions. Only Caroline sat silent, her allegiance to Julie and Sue making her feel powerless to support the women who were her closest friends.

As night fell, the debate continued. More women came until the room was packed, full of smoke and words. They finally fell silent, restless, fidgeting.

'Tea?' suggested Cathy, wanting desperately to get out of the stuffy room and do something.

It was as she counted round to see how many cups she would need that she realised Sue had gone.

'That's odd, Sue's gone.'

Julie looked round. 'Are you sure she hasn't gone for a piss or something?'

'I thought she said something about going to get her jacket,' said Caroline

'But that was ages ago!' Julie got up. 'It's not like her to leave, not the way she's been behaving recently.' Something was wrong, Sue was such a strange one. Julie felt panicky. She suddenly looked round to the corner of the room. 'The gun's gone, she's taken the machine gun!'

Over the babble of voices that followed, they heard the first burst of machine gunfire. As they scrambled out of the house and ran down the street, they heard the second. When they turned into the market it was already all over.

Sue was crouched in the middle of the street with the gun cradled in her arms. At the top of the market the flames of the camp-fire crackled, illuminating the bodies that lay strewn around. As the women stood and stared in silence, the scene seemed a fantasy of the past. The flames danced and flickered, making wild silhouettes of the women as they tried to take in what had happened. The flames lit fuses for many of them, bringing back memories of fear and rage, their eyes narrowed as they watched rivulets of blood glistening, flowing down the cobbled street. The air smelt of gunpowder and death.

Julie and Cathy went over to Sue and gently took the gun out of her arms. She looked up at them with calm, open eyes and smiled. She was singing softly to herself, songs the others had never heard. Her old smile had come back and she let herself be carried back to the house without complaint. The rest of the women stood and sat and walked around the scene for hours, till the fire had died out and only the cold moonlight lit up the contours of the living and the dead. Before they departed, each one had approached the bodies and looked into the faces of the dead men. And each one accepted that, by whatever route, the final emotion that gave them a dreamless sleep that night, was relief.

EQUAL RIGHTS

She was late. Too late. The contract was lost. Her boss was not pleased.

'Why didn't you come in on time?'

'Module fault.'

'Why didn't you communicate?'

'Communication fault.'

He was not impressed.

'You know you could lose your job.'

She knew he would say this. She suspected he enjoyed saying it. They had not wanted her here. A woman in a man's job they would say. He was no different. She felt tired, the walkways had been crowded, too many people pushing and shoving their way to work. She did not want to lose this job. It had taken her years to make them give her a chance to do it. She had proved her worth. She looked at him across the desk. She knew she made him fell uncomfortable. Uneasy. The wrong role for her. The wrong role for him. She knew the law. The law said no discrimination. He knew the law too and knew it did not apply here. It did not apply much anywhere but certainly not here. She could see he was hiding a smile. Smiling at his own words. Smiling because he thought she could lose her job. He was new. He did not understand her yet. She would not lose this job.

'Perhaps I can still save the contract.'

'I doubt it. He's gone to Westmer's.'

'I'll catch him up. I'm better than Westmer, you know that.'

'You haven't got a module.'

'Lend me yours.'

He paused. She was better than Westmer. He wanted that contract. He didn't want her. He didn't like her but he could hardly say no.

'Take it.'

She caught him up outside Westmer's. He had just arrived. She talked to him, told him she was better. Insisted he listen. He listened. He thought she sounded better than Westmer but he didn't think he wanted a woman.

'I'm cheaper than Westmer. Cheaper as well as better. Did you know that?'

He gave her the contract. Promised her a bonus if it was completed immediately. Invited her to lunch and watched her over the table.

'Why do you come cheaper if you're better?'

'Because I'm a woman. It's harder to get the work.'

He nodded. He still felt uneasy himself. He thought she was pretty. Not beautiful. Pretty. Ordinary pretty. Short pretty. He wondered if he had done the right thing. She sighed. It was always the same. They never believed her. She was good, one of the best, even her boss had to admit it. But the image was bad for business, they couldn't do without her but they wanted her to go.

'Why do you do this work?'

'Because I like it. Because I'm good at it.'

'Will you take anyone?'

'No. I like to check the cases. It's easier if I agree. Westmer does anyone, that's his style, not mine.'

'Because you're a woman?'

'Maybe. Because that's the way I work.'

She left him and went back. She dropped the

module off at the office and took the walkway home. She took her time. She needed time to think. Time to iron out the last details. The walkway was not so crowded now, she could enjoy the trip. After all she had won the contract, she would not be losing her job, not yet. She smiled and settled down with a hot drink to watch the televiewer.

The contract was dead by tea-time the next day. Found dead in his module on its way through the streets. No one mourned, except Westmer, who had wanted the contract and had lost it to a woman.

NIGHT LIFE

1.1 Out there, beyond the stars, did they worry about what to wear on a Saturday night? Around her feet lay a mottled collection of last week's clothes, witness to her attempts to make herself halfway presentable for the club. She sat on the window ledge, staring blankly at the sky, twisting yesterday's dirty tee shirt round her wrists, pulling it so tight she could feel her pulse throbbing. She didn't really want to go, she never really wanted to go, but if she did not it would be noted, another mark against her name, another drop in the yearly rankings she could ill afford to lose. There had been a time, somewhere distant in her past, when she had swanned around her world, glided through the social whirl with ease and elegance, always ready for the night, always relaxed, always dressed for the part. Now, when it was so vital to hang on, when the alternatives were ever more bleak, she knew she was losing her grip.

2.1 The thin light from her window shone out through the dirty glass across the roofs of the city, fading as the tower blocks obscured the night sky. The light would never reach another window facing another way, where another woman sat alone waiting for a non-existent lover to come and hold her close in her tiny world. She did not look out of the window. She had given that up many years before. Instead she sat curled in an old armchair, her cheek squashed against the rough fabric of the covers, examining her own fingernails. She went out to her office job, spoke to no one except the computers and processors she serviced and then returned home each night to nothingness, to high-rise loneliness. The day would come, she knew, when her job would no longer be there, when age would stand against her and the world would give her a pot of gold, but no rainbow, and bid her farewell. Then she need never go out. She curled up deeper in the armchair.

3.1 Down, down, from the dizzy heights of depression into narrow streets where sounds of life are still audible, to the basement flat where two bright young things are getting ready for the night. Like Cinderellas with new ball gowns, their excitement fills the tiny flat. Washing, brushing, preening, fixing, forever changing their minds, forever checking with each other, swapping, gazing in mirrors, back, front, eyes, hair, hiding spots, hiding those pounds of flesh that keep them warm on winter nights. They practise walking up and down, talking, laughing, sitting down, standing up, and then collapse giggling into each other's arms. For them this ritual is a new one, their first season, first introduction into life. Ahead a glittering time of gaiety, dancing, and, they hope, romance. It stretches so far, so far they cannot see an end to it.

1..2 A cloud crossed the moon, blotting out some of the light that had briefly enveloped the city beneath her in mystery and allure. She turned away and reviewed the mess on the floor. Out of that pile of clothes she would manage something, she would not give up her thin hold on life, not yet be condemned to society's graveyard because her hair was beginning to lose its colour, because years of tedious underpaid work had left her with wrinkles of fatigue and frustration. With care she dressed herself, amending last month's clothes to suit this month's fashions, as near as she could. For half an hour she sat at the mirror with powders and creams brushing away the years, as best she could. She fixed her hair, still thick and strong. Unhurriedly, she plaited it tightly with the ribbons and silver thread that was so the rage that week. Her fingers skimmed in and out, weaving the hair with the deftness of years of experience. A last touch here and there, and, for better or worse, she was ready to go.

2..2 The squeal of the kettle woke her from her reverie. Unwillingly she pulled herself out of the armchair and shuffled into the kitchen to make herself a cup of tea. It was all such an effort. The kitchen was small but well-equipped, her salary was a good one, her allocation had been high, hence this comfortable three room flat. Every labour saving device had been installed. The home computer connection meant she could save herself the drudgery of shopping, everything ordered arrived, glowing with efficiency, to her hatch within minutes of her order. She did not know why she bothered to keep the old kettle when there was a gleaming tea-maker shining with disuse next to the microwave. It really was such an effort making tea the old way, but something from the past held her to it, some desire to remain a part of what was gone, maybe what had never been, at least for her, but she could pretend, she could believe, there was no one left to question her memories.

3.2 At last they are decided on their outfits, satisfied with their hair and faces, ready to go. Wrapping warm woollen cloaks round them, they hurry out into the yard and up the area steps. The winds whip round them, draughts coming down from the high blocks that surround their little estate of bopper dwellings. A scarf comes adrift and an icy blast chills through every layer, filling the young skin pores with a taste of the future. But they are oblivious to such things in their eagerness to be out, to enjoy their world. Their sharp heels clatter along the pavement and across the playground at the bottom of the street. In good weather they always stop to take a turn on the swings. Only then, flying backwards and upwards, do their eyes catch the tops of the high blocks, glimpse a pale face peering through net curtains. Tonight their heads are bent down against the wind as they make their way to the neon lights of the club.

1.3 She had to wait a good twenty minutes for the lift to make its creaking way up to her floor. She had complained many times about the service but little notice was taken by the authorities. After all, she had no clout in these matters. It was merely pointed out to her that she was fortunate to be in one of the blocks that still retained its lift, and if she complained further she could be transferred elsewhere. They knew, and she knew, the long term effects of being trapped so high up with only stairs, particularly as she got older. As she descended, she read the graffiti that never changed, that dated from a time when the blocks were used for families and young people. Once she had been tempted to add to them but knew she had already lost the will to protest; survival had become the only priority. Out on the streets she faced the long walk to the nearest club, trying to shield her face and hair against the weather so that the winds would not expose her age, and her fear.

2.3 The tea was strong and sweet and woke her up, allowing her a temporary burst of energy. She wasted it tidying the flat and changing the smooth silk sheets on her bed. She had been lucky to get such a flat. Of course it had nothing to do with luck and everything to do with her job and the status quota of her family. She knew she should be grateful for that, but at the end of the day she still had to pay the price for the failure of her youth. Drawing the thick, velvet curtains she allowed herself one brief glance out, far across the city to where, between the central blocks, she could see the sparkle of lights in the suburbs. She had always assumed she would be living out there.

3.3 This is the first time they have seen it at night, its lights sparkling round the entrance, reflecting on the shiny metal portico. Above, the neon letters blazed with electric glory, leaving the cold brick-work behind in dark shadow. Simma stops on the opposite corner to rearrange her cloak, feeling her blood pound through each artery. She grabs her friend's hand to hold her back, afraid to be left to go in alone. They laugh into each other's faces, taking courage from each other, giving love to each other. The wind whistles behind them, pushing them on across the road, driving them into the future. Not since their blood had come on the same day six months ago and they had been paired together had they felt such a thrill. So much preparation for this premiere occasion, and now it had arrived, and they need only cross the street and through the gleaming arc to reach their fantasies. Meril cannot wait any longer, she pulls the other with her and they are gone out of the wind.

1.4 It was a long walk from her block to the Razz through the empty, windswept streets of the city, deserted at the end of the working day. She did not qualify for a travel permit and so could not use the rumbling overhead trains that creaked their way between the blocks. She did not mind, preferring the relative security of the open spaces to the closed compartments with their late night occupants, oncer-city stragglers with despair and hatred in their eyes. Out of the deep shadows of the blocks, she entered the bopper estate, the estate where she had lived, a time that seemed so long ago now. Not just in years but in feelings and hopes. Then, her eyes only looked outwards to where success and security was built in neat rows of houses with grass around them, and shops where people never queued.

160

2.4 Back in her armchair she tried to shake such
thoughts out of her head. It did no good dwelling
on the past and she knew it. She flicked on the video,
spent the next hour watching the nightly series of
soap operas and quiz shows that were the staple diet
of every channel. But in the mood she was in, they
only served to reinforce her depression, each one a
statement of the order of things, each one a reminder
of how small a part she played. Families, children,
housewives and soldiers, vicars and tea ladies, all
enthusiasm and smiles in their efforts to pursue the
only goals in life worth achieving. Every night the
faces were different but it made no odds, they were
all out there, following paths that ended in social
acceptance and social rewards. The screen became a
blur, the sound of laughter and excitement a babble,
and she switched it off with a flash of rage. She had
not wanted what she had got. She had tried to play
that game and she had never worked out what had
gone wrong, or when. Distantly she could remember
her parents and the little white house she had spent
her first years in. Had she been happy there? Something seemed to have been wrong from the start.
She could remember her mother crying over her, she
could remember screaming the day she was first sent
to the girls' play centre and had to have her hair
curled up tight with ribbons. She had not understood.
They should have explained it to her better, they
should have told her what was to come if she did not
conform. She straightened herself in the chair, maybe
they did, she probably had not listened. And later,
well that had been another story.

3.4 Now they are inside and it's a time for final
checks and giggling in the cloakroom. In the reception
their identity cards are stamped for the first time

and slotted into two sparkling new folders; each with their name embossed on the outside. Already light-headed with excitement from their walk in the wind they find it hard to absorb everything. The lights in reception are bright, everyone seems busy, knowing where to go, while they stand, still hand in hand, wondering where to start, how to start. Meril is surer, whispering confidence, she leads the way through the heavy curtains and into the club. This is going to be the most important time for them, this is their chance to find their way into the adult life that the girls' centre had prepared them for. This is where they would meet, court and marry and so fulfil the dreams that had been planned out for them. It might not be tonight, although if they were lucky...

1.5 Finally she emerged from one of the small enclosures of the estate to be greeted by the fiery, yawning mouth of the club entrance. She stopped at the corner opposite the club, breathing deeply to compose herself, as she felt for a second the old buzz of excitement. This place was once all she had lived for, the one chance in the week to make the break. When she started going it hadn't occurred to her that fifteen years later she would still be there, know-ing that every week might be her last. Now she hated the performance of it but could not give it up until they made her. Maybe it was conditioning, she knew she had no chance of meeting anyone now, maybe it was just an old habit that was hard to change, that would mean accepting an unsavoury fact about herself: failure. She pulled her collar straight and headed across the road into the club. At reception her card was stamped and replaced in a battered old file, she could sense a few raised eyebrows in the cloakroom as she teased her hair back into place and covered the crinkles round her eyes with a little more cream. She stared icily back at one woman who was openly sneering and pushed out through the curtains. She needed a drink.

2.5 She had been asleep, dreaming odd dreams full of images of her girlhood, full of sharp words and tears that came with the fury of frustration. She wandered round the apartment, touching her possessions as though trying to get some warmth, some communication from those things that had followed her to this, her final home. Amy, that's what they had called her. Her parents had told her it meant love, friendship. Now it sounded hollow. No one had said that name to her for years. At work there was no need for names, no need for any speech beyond what was needed to keep the computers whirling, the lights on the console blinking in their correct order. She stopped to examine a small green mug that sat by her bed. Holding it in her thin hands she felt tears start to trickle down her face as the evening's depression overwhelmed her. She had had the mug at the girls' centre, it was a present from her blood pair, Jenny. Jenny who was gone after only a few weeks of the social, married to a smiling blond bore who had pursued her from the first night in the club and was probably pursuing her to this day. She couldn't bear to keep the mug, couldn't bear to lose it, it was her only link to a time when she truly cared about someone. She threw the mug at the wall, then, transfixed with horror, stared at the broken shards that littered the carpet. She did not know what was happening to her, she remembered others like her who had suddenly failed to turn up for work. Was this it? — the breakdown that would remove her from the population statistics? Another tiny battle won in the computer's war to even up the sexes. She forced herself out of the room and back into the armchair; rigid with fear, she kept her back to the window and the calling winds.

3.5 Meril and Simma are sitting on bar stools in the corner, sipping at their drinks through curling multi-coloured straws. So far, so good they think. The bar is not yet full, behind them the vast dance-floor stretches away empty and the computers are only playing quietly. Across the open floor half a dozen boys sit watching every new arrival. Meril is watching them too, amazed at how they have changed since the last time she saw them in the child centre. They are dressed brightly, like peacocks, strutting to and fro with an ease that astounds her. She does not realise yet how their status will affect her. She does not know the things they have been told, how easy things will be for them in the club. After all it is simple, they are the catch, the few for whom the girls must compete if life is to hold anything for them. She thinks one of them has picked her out and nudges Simma, whispering in her ear, feeling drops of sweat creeping out of her armpits as he makes his way across the floor and asks her to dance.

1.6 The barman smiled at her and presented her with a drink before she asked. She was grateful to him, a familiar face that had aged alongside hers. Once she even asked him his status but of course, he had long since taken his pick of the clientele. Still, he counted almost as a friend to her, although they both knew that it was a friendship soon ended. Every week it was a challenge for her to get in the door. She took her place on a bar stool at the end of the bar and gulped down the drink, feeling the alcohol burn her throat and fill her stomach with an artificial warmth that would help her through the evening. The barman poured her another. She watched two young girls sitting in the opposite corner, so young, so excited, this was clearly their first visit. One had already attracted the attention of a boy, whilst the other sat shy and nervous, waiting hopefully. She felt her heart tighten with envy for their youth and hope, and yet she could feel pity for them, for the lessons they would surely learn.

2.6 Amy, Amy, Amy, she spoke her name out loud to no one, trying to hang on. She would not give in, not yet. The television screen blinked back at her across the room. A family had just won a new washing machine and spin dryer and a woman was sobbing with gratitude. Her husband stood beside her, glowing with pride, the audience clapped and cheered and the noise filled her head, flowing through each vein, making them stand out beneath her thin skin, rivers of agitation beating against her skull. She forced herself out of the chair and crawled across to smash her fist against the control knob, silencing the babble. But then she was left with silence.

3.6 The boy holds Meril close as they dance, his arm tight behind her, his hand feeling up and down her back, his mouth closing in on her neck. He knows she is new and vulnerable. It is time he made his decision, and her warm body excites him. He could take her as his choice and start his journey to the top, to the power that would be his. She is suddenly frightened, disturbed by the sudden closeness, she pulls back to look into his face. She sees his flashing eyes that give off little warmth, smells his breath, heavy with alcohol and desire. His hands are too big, too strong, his touch too rough. The music goes on, one tune into the next allowing her no time to rest, no time to think things through. Everything is happening too fast. She wants to be back with Simma, her quiet, her shyness now seem so attractive, so peaceful. Simma is still alone. She is watching a woman who is also alone at the bar. A woman who is much older and who is smiling at her, raising her drink in toast as they sit at each end of the bar. Simma would like to go and sit with her, but dares not leave her place in case she loses sight of her friend. But it seems the woman knows that as she picks her drink up and comes over to join her. Sitting beside her without speaking, she gives Simma courage. After the next drink, the next record, then Simma will manage to speak to her. She peers through the crowd to find Meril and the boy, sees him pulling her towards the exit. Sees her try to turn away, sees her frightened face, hears her own name called as both figures are lost behind the curtains. She turns in anguish and confusion to the other woman who takes her hand and silently guides her out of the club following the fading echo.

1/2/3.7 And then all is, was, confusion and horror. They are running down black streets to find Meril who is sobbing, beating against the boy's back with helpless fists as she is pushed down on hard concrete, her skin crawling with pain and rage. And Amy has smashed her windows and screams out into the darkness, a great bellow of despair that is carried by the winds of the night down into the alley-way, making the boy stop for a moment, thwarting his violent triumph. And her bellow is answered by his yelp of surprise as the woman crashes into him and drags him off the girl and down the deserted alley steps, till his voice is silenced and the blood that oozes from his broken skull congeals with the rubbish in the gutter.

The morning that comes is calm and cold. The wind is content to sweep the rubbish into spirals below the tower blocks. They have found a safe place to hide, a deserted flat that is still habitable, only one of the windows is broken. Meril and Simma sit huddled together, while the other woman makes tea from an old kettle in the kitchen. Meril has bathed herself many times to wash away the memory of the boy, but she is safe. Simma holds her close, stroking her face, warming her heart. They are still young, still whole. The other woman returns and gives them tea and smiles at them. My name is Beatrice, she says, finding the sound of it novel in her ears.

Across the city there is an office where computers whirl and lights flash a thousand figures. Where tape strews out of machines, listing numbers and quotas and inputs and outputs. Where there is a tape that has recorded one less unwanted spinster but has failed to record the survival of three others.

167

THE COMET'S TAIL

PRELUDE

General Harding took the long quill pen and, still with some hidden doubts, added his name to the four others that were already signed to the heavy white paper. After years of planning it was done, decided, the fate of the project sealed after hours of financial wranglings as the members of the Eura Confederation fought over their different monetary investments. Operation EDEN could now proceed.

The boffins would be happy at least, he reflected. After ten years of technical trials and experiments, volumes of reports and evaluations, the Confederation had been finally convinced of the viability of the project. The politicians had always been enthusiastic. Space had presented the ideal fodder to take the minds of the people off their everyday fears and problems, and this one also held the carrot of a potential escape from the nuclear threat that lay at the back of everyone's mind. Maybe he was just too old to see the idealistic hopes they churned out in the daily presses from Lisbon to Siberia that had resulted in such popular support for the scheme.

Over the last fifty years he had watched the world try and wriggle out of its self-made suicide mission. He had seen the results of the nuclear disaster in Central America that had terrified the world blocs into the almighty shift that had created not peace, but a new drawing of lines. These now fell geographically, allowing the formation of Eura, the weight of the whole of northern Europe and Asia against the Americas tied together by the military power of the north. And, to counter-balance, the might of The Third that took in all of Africa, the Indian sub-continent, China and south-east Asia. Such an alignment had been the subject of speculation for a century, had been written of as a possible future that had now come to pass. It was still the same old mish-mash, as far as he was concerned, the same fighting over fields and oil-wells, the same prejudices against colour, class, religion, still filled people's minds. But he was an army man, not his place to dictate policies, just to put the politicians' plans into practice. So here he was, signing away the skills and time of his men to train two women to go on some expensive, pointless space trip to absolve his leaders' guilt that they were doing nothing to give the people any hope for eventual survival and expansion.

Outside the conference chamber he paused, beyond the glass doors he could see the hordes of pressmen clamouring for a story, a picture, and he needed time to collect his thoughts before their onslaught. Still, they would get the answer they wanted and then maybe they would leave him in peace for the time being. After all, they would have plenty to go on once the full training schedule really got underway. To make two women fit for such a trip, he shook his head, still amazed at their decision, this was certainly going to be a task.

Robert Hartman mixed himself a large gin and tonic and sank back into the dark green velvet sofa, letting the tension of the day drown in the alcohol, and the slow warmth of success fill his bones. He had won, after all those years of specualtions, meetings,

169

accountants and scientists rowing and complaining, he had won. As one of the early Eura astronauts, he was only sorry he was too old to go along. And of course, following on the reports of the psychs and the sociologists, he was also the wrong sex. It was still the one element he felt unhappy with, their insistence that if you put two men together for so long it would be a disaster, and that if you put a man and a woman together the combination could be fatal, so it would have to be two women. It seemed an unlikely choice, given the nature of the project, a kind of Noah's Arc try-out should surely represent both the sexes. But he had had to agree or the Confederation might not have been pushed into signing, and with the amount he had invested, he could no longer afford to let the project fail at this stage.

His intercom buzzed.

'General Harding to see you Mr Hartman.' Outside his secretary smiled blandly at the general, who was feeling hot and unenthusiastic about this necessary meeting with the project head.

'Send him in please, Sandra, and some coffee too.'

She inclined her head towards the office door and disappeared to make the coffee. The general entered Hartman's office and tried to make himself comfortable on one of the luxurious armchairs that always crumpled his uniform.

'Well, General, let me get you a drink to celebrate.'

'A whiskey, no water.' He didn't feel much like celebrating.

They sat silent for a few minutes, each examining his drink until Sandra had come in with the coffee, chewing her lip in irritation as she knew it would not be drunk, and was allowed to leave after the stock leery smile from her boss.

Then, for hours, they thrashed out the timetable

for the next six months, the selection procedure that must tighten the choice from the six standbys down to two, the preparations in Spain for the launch. The choice of sites had been made and the small island of Gran Canaria must be prepared for the invasion of scientists and engineers who would create a launch pad and monitoring station where the air was as clear as anywhere in Eura and where the weather was so good that cloud cover would rarely be a problem. Two divisions of General Harding's crack battalions would be used for the iron-clad security that would shroud most of the preparations from the public eye and make some attempt to keep out too many spies from America and The Third.

'I see no way of making this operation watertight, but we must do our best, eh.'

'Indeed.' The general knew what Hartman meant was that he must take responsibility, that any serious leak would be blamed on the army. He sighed, in his heart he wished he had been born in some earlier time when armies marched on their stomachs and wars were won or lost in an afternoon.

As that afternoon faded into evening, the two men shook hands and parted, each with their pink folder of plans and agreements, each with their private dislike of the other. Both were relieved that, barring disasters, they would not need to meet for several months.

LIFT OFF

Out on the track a sharp wind whistled across the grass. Caught in the great athletics bowl, it whirled round, swirling dust and crumpled programmes from the meeting at the weekend. Amongst the rows of

171

seats a few early cleaners competed against it with brooms and black plastic bags, each one enveloped in a cloud of dust that caught the early rays of the sun like a halo. Winter was beginning to bite home and soon the stadium would be closed over and iced, in preparation for the savage games of ice hockey and ice racing. Then it would be filled with the screams of the supporters and, frequently, the screams of the competitors as the games took on every personal, political and racial tension alive. But now, in the early morning, it still lay at peace, with only the minute scrapings of the cleaners' brooms to disturb the song of the wind.

Deep at the base of the stadium a door opened and three figures emerged, two tall, one slight. The slight figure began to jog out onto the track, running first with the wind, in the sun and then turning with the arc of the stadium to run round against the wind, resting her eyes from the glare of the beams that streamed so low in the sky. Of the two men, one was dressed like her: tracksuit, running shoes. He did not run, but stood beside the track, stopwatch in hand, his eyes following her progress closely. The other man was in uniform, weighed down by a machine gun that he shifted from shoulder to shoulder, as though worried about developing a permanent list. He wandered up and down between the rows of seats, stopping to stare at the cleaners, to drop his cigarette ends where they had just swept. They ignored him, although registering the gun and what that represented. As for the cigarette ends, the wind merely lifted them up and blew them back high in the stands where the afternoon shift would deal with them.

The soldier settled himself at the end of the fifth row, knowing he would be there for an hour at least. He had been coming out now every day for over a month, as part of his duties, watching this woman run round and round the track, stopping only to consult the man with the stopwatch. It was boring, but he was used to it.

Fletcher was the man on the track. He was chief coach to the South Eura athletic team and resented bitterly being dragged away from their winter training to spend his hours with this one woman. With the Olympic Games coming up next year, his last chance of training a winning team was at stake and now, because of some flap from the army, he had been sent out to this godforsaken spot to waste his time on a project that they wouldn't even tell him about. He had been training the woman for two months now, and he had to admit she was good, and getting better every day. Maybe with a bit more of a push, he could be back in Milan by the end of the month. He yelled at her to pick her feet up more, stop her shoulders from crashing up and down, elbows in, chin out. She had reached the times set down for her on the program, really all she needed was a maintenance trainer and hopefully they wouldn't make him stay just for that.

She could feel the beginning of pain in her muscles as she speeded up round the bottom bend. It would last until after the long straight, building up into an agonising burn through her chest, splintering her ribs, gripping her heart, until a new surge of adrenalin pumped through and carried her round the top bend and down the home straight. It was the worst, the part of the training that filled her with fear that one day she just would not make it, that her heart would give out and she would join the ranks of those who had already died in the pursuance of this mad project. She could hear Fletcher shouting at her and let her hatred of him distract her from the pain. His small mean ways had caught at her like rose thorns from the first day they met, and she was amazed at how he had risen so far in his profession, when his dislike of people was so obvious. After the first week of training she had felt like giving the whole thing up, as though that were even possible, just because of his constant remarks about her appearance, her dress, her everything. But today she could take it, today she knew something he did not. Hartman had contacted her last night, today would be her last at the stadium, tomorrow she would start the journey across Eura that would end up on the little island in the sun and her first meeting with her partner. She kicked on down the last circuit and finally came to a halt beside her trainer, smirking as she forced him to admit she had bettered the times set for her.

Vivienne Redna
Age: 26
D.o.B.: 5.8.13
Born: Moscow
Educated: University of Moscow, Paris Institute.
Major: Electro Engineering
      Biology
      Chemistry
Military Training: Hamburg Unit, specialising — small arms, unarmed combat Grade I
Personal: Parents both dead. Unmarried.
      No siblings. No children.
Political: No dissent record.
Clearance: Grade I.

The bare outline of the woman headed the fat orange file that lay on Hartman's desk in his new headquarters in what had been a tourist resort on Gran Canaria.

Inside lay a thick report on Redna which covered every detail of her life and training. Somewhere she was travelling the thousands of miles across Eura. Trains were often safer than planes in these unsettled times, and he had this time to acquaint himself with a woman who was deemed fit to carry out the project that was his life's dream. And with a voyeur's soul he enjoyed sifting through her childhood school reports, her early medical records, her sexual contacts, all listed, filed, checked, researched for the smallest sign that she was other than what she appeared, a brilliant student, a hardworking dedicated patriot who had fought to give most of her life to her country.

Outside another sunny day was happening, same as yesterday, same as tomorrow. The noise of tractors and demolition workers filled the air as a great tract of land was levelled and concreted, ready to take each new instalment as it was shipped in from the mainland of Spain. A fleet of submarines and destroyers cruised the sea passage between the island and the African mainland, helicopters turned and swept back and forwards across the island like buzzards, looking for their prey amongst the mountains, across the banana plantations, while the population grew accustomed to the continual need to produce documents at the checkposts that sprang up overnight like mushrooms.

Hartman's office was dark and cool. Air-conditioned and double glazed, it allowed him plenty of time to peruse the orange file at his leisure. So far, so good, this woman had fulfilled all their requirements. He was still waiting for the second file.

In a small bleak cubicle a woman sat naked, shivering, despite the central heating. Endless medical checks had left her tired and irritable, her arm sore from blood tests, her muscles exhausted by exercise, her head whirring with endless questions and checks and double checks. Now she waited for them to bring back her clothes and let her go home. Well, not exactly home, which seemed very far away now, but at least to somewhere she could close the door and be alone. They had done all these tests before, and she supposed they would do them all again on the island, and that was just the way of things, but in that cubicle she wondered for the first time what on earth she was doing. There had been so much competition that, since she was put forward, she had only thought of winning. That was her way, the desire to win, to compete. Now she had won, she was chosen, she was going, her heart was asking her whether she really wanted to go at all. Her life was little enough, but did she value it so low as to throw it away on some politician's pipe dream?

The door clanged open and a man handed her a crumpled pile of clothes. Uncaring as to her naked-ness, he stared at her like a zoo animal. She turned her back on him as she dressed. Something to tell his grandchildren, she supposed, if he lived to have any.

'Knock when you are ready.' The door banged shut behind him. She knocked when she was ready.

'Follow me.' She followed him.

Several corridors later she was escorted out into the driving rain where the awaiting jeep drove her back to the unit where she had been living for the last three months.

'The transport will call for you at 06.00. Make sure you are ready.'

She nodded and watched the driver depart, tempted to wave at him, at least he had been a familiar and not totally unattractive face since she had been there.

176

Inside she gathered up the small personal allowance of luggage ready for the morning. Well, now she was going, whatever her doubts there would be no turning back, she already knew far too much to be allowed that option.

In bed that night she dreamt of her home, of the wild wet hills where she had played as a child, stargazing with her grandfather, always wanting to be out there, beyond the confines of earth's gravity. It had felt like claustrophobia to have her feet rooted on the ground and only when she had taken to flying, in her teens, did she begin to feel the freedom that would let her breathe. But in her dreams, that black earth was warm and comforting, full of her mother's softness, her brother's laughter calling her back to play some more, and when she awoke her face was buried deep in the pillow and her fists caught tight in the sheets.

The transport came early and left her no time for reflection as she swept up her bags and papers and let herself be led out in the still dark morning into the armoured car. The driver was different, but the same. Dour, moustached, eyes glinting, he appraised her carefully, a phenomenon this woman. He did not know her function, but so much care over one woman, he shook his head, she looked just the same as they all did to him. The drive to the station was a short one and the transition to the train swift and silent. As it pulled out of the station, she left the last of her regrets on the seat of the armoured car.

Frances Duke
Age: 28 years
D.o.B.: 18.2.11
Born: Cornwall
Educated: Bonn University, Prague Centre of
    Astro-physics
Major: Computer Science
        Astro-physics
Military Training: Athens Unit, specialising —
    bomb disposal Grade I
Personal: Mother dead, father hospitalised (terminal),
    one married brother. Unmarried, no children.
Political: No dissent record.
Clearance: Grade I.

The second file slid across Hartman's desk to cover
the orange file. This one was green. The colours bore
no reference to anything other than the whim of
Sandra, and Hartman was used to it by now. He sat
back with a cup of coffee to reflect on this second
candidate to fulfil his dreams. Again the file was
impeccable regarding details of a young woman
whose life seemed to have been a monastic search for
knowledge that had taken her away from home
before she was ten years old. There seemed even less
of a person within those pages than with the other
and although all the information was duly registered
on the part of his brain that operated as a computer,
the other part that looked forward to asking Sandra
for yet another cup of coffee was uninspired. As far
as he was concerned, they would both be perfect for
the job and it seemed the world was scarcely going
to miss them.

He had not wanted to be part of the selection
procedure, just as he had not wanted the women to
meet until they arrived on the island. After all, the
three of them would be closely tied for the next

twenty years and he did not want to have to live with any mistakes for any longer. And they would just have to prove the sociologists right and get on with each other and the work in hand without all those feminine moods he could see daily in Sandra. He buzzed her needlessly to ask whether the women's quarters were ready, which they had been for days and to get another cup of coffee.

Travelling by train felt anachronistic to Vivienne after years of flying everywhere. She sat silently gazing out of the window as the hours rolled by on her journey across Eura. She had travelled backwards and forwards across the landmass all her life. She could barely remember her parents, or the tiny flat she was brought up in, somehow her childhood now reached her as a collection of schoolrooms with serious faces in front of her. She chewed her fingernails as the train burst through a tiny village and she caught a brief glance of a man and woman, sitting by the side of a field of something, eating their lunch. She turned her head to follow them as the train sped on and maybe for a moment she saw something that might have been, that was for people she had never known, would never know. But they would soon hear of her, even in these isolated villages they would hear of her. For better or for worse.

She felt isolation, fear, loneliness grip her, but shook them free with the anger that burned bright through her bones. She had had good times, all over Eura she had studied and learnt, not only of science, but of how to laugh, how to run and play and she would not forget those times now, when she needed them most.

A knock at the door of the compartment. The soldier brought his machine gun up to his shoulder while his companion opened the door a crack. The guard pulled back, then whispered gingerly through the crack.

'A call's come through, switch in and I can connect you.'

'We are not expecting any calls.' The soldier had his orders.

'He said to say it was Hartman.'

Vivienne looked up in surprise and reached for the phone switch. The soldier pushed her to one side and picked it up himself, after some mutterings he almost grudgingly handed it over to her. She had never actually spoken to Hartman, coded messages found their way to her, contacts that slipped commands and schedules into her life with his name stamped on the bottom. Somehow this seemed an odd time to make first contact. Maybe something had gone wrong, maybe her fellow guinea-pig had fallen through, maybe it was all off. She thought again of those people by the side of the fields and took the phone.

'This is Redna.'

'Ah, very good. I did so want to make sure the travelling arrangements were going according to the plan.'

'Everything seems fine.'

'Yes, so the officer assures me.'

If he was already assured, then why did he want to talk to her? She could almost feel the slick touch of his voice, a kind of curl in his speech that settled softly, chokingly round her neck. She did not think she was going to take to Mr Hartman.

'And how are you Miss Redna, ready for the trip?'

'I hope so Mr Hartman, I really hope so.' He missed the irony in her voice. She did not miss the inevitable leer in his.

When Hartman had rung off, the two soldiers unpacked one of the many meals and spread it out on the seat. They hadn't said much for the first five hours of the journey and, as the whole thing would take nearly three days, Vivienne decided to make some effort to be friendly. Out of her bag she pulled a pack of cards and they grinned. The three of them spent the next forty-eight hours alternately sleeping, eating, attempting to stay clean and winning and losing mythical fortunes at poker. Vivienne wished they had a fourth for bridge but the guard in the corridor only played snap.

Franni loved trains but only spent a few hours on that one till she was transferred to a ship for the main part of the journey. She thought she would enjoy it because of the sense of space, the distant empty horizon would give her, but what with the constant buzz of patrolling helicopters that kept interrupting her view, and the pitching and rolling of the keel, she spent most of the trip in her cabin, feeling green and pathetic. She thought little about the past and most about the state of her stomach and whether, if space sickness was like this, she would ever survive the trip. The crew were courteous but boring, offering her tea and sympathy but shrugging their shoulders when she demanded details of their progress. Later she learnt they had been instructed not to tell her in case she wanted to change her mind, even at this late stage. Ignorance breeds obedience, breeds acceptance. She was no exception.

Hartman also contacted the ship, but during one of her worst attacks so she did not speak to him. Again, it was merely a check by the master to see if his pawns were moving into place. They were. By the time land was beginning to appear on the horizon, and the rough weather had given way to brilliant sunshine, Franni Duke was feeling more like the woman who had fought her way past dozens of others to reach the last six in the selection. More like the woman who had thought nothing of the bitter disappointment her last rival had felt after months of trials and examinations, flushed with her own success. She lay on the deck, accustomed now to the helicopters, letting the sun soak into her body, even the consciousness of the men watching her body, noting the curving shadow she cast against the glaring metal, did not unsettle her resolve. This was going to be a moment of triumph for her, no one would spoil it and she would not spoil it for herself.

Still, when she climbed onto the helicopter for the final jump to the island, she knew that that was the nearest thing she was going to have to a holiday for the next twenty years, or the rest of her life, whichever came first.

And for both of these women there was another thing, another issue that dominated so much of their thinking that it had become a part of them. A speculation, a suspicion, an enthusiasm, a wariness, a grudging admiration that was tinged with mistrust and jealousy about the other woman. The only woman in Eura they had not triumphed over. At least not yet.

At different times they each stepped out of different helicopters and climbed into armoured cars that blasted them down the empty motorway to the space complex. Each felt the growing presence of the other as their meeting became imminent. Like a great computer dating agency they had been plucked out of so many others as the two women most likely to survive twenty years on a space ship. To themselves they seemed normal enough, but what must the other one be like. To themselves, this project was the capping of all their intellectual ambitions, for the other was it merely a chance for fame and fortune? Wrapped up with such speculations, neither woman noticed much about the journey. Franni caught a glimpse of the mountains to the west where a white flash in the sun signalled the great disc that would follow their progress. Vivienne watched two heads bobbing in the sea, two black dots unconnected to any visible bodies disturbing the sheen of the water. Neither woman would ever see the almond blossom that grew wild in the mountains next to groves of palm trees. They would not sit drinking wine outside bars that were decorated with geraniums and cactus, flashing with the flowers of the jacaranda. Tiny coves where boats rested on gleaming black sands away from the treacherous rocks that guarded the island from the west. All this would be lost for these two women who travelled blindly down a straight tarmac road built for tourists from the last century through a flat desolation of scrub and decaying buildings to the start of another journey.

Vivienne arrived first and was escorted from the armoured car into the foyer of the hotel Hartman had taken over as the centre of his operations. Inside it was dark and cool. Men and women hurried by her, ignoring her, brusque and efficient in dark blue uniforms that hid the sweat oozing through armpits and groins, tracing snail lines down backs that bent over consoles and digital feedbacks. Everyone had their place, knew their place, except this one strange woman who stood, vacantly looking round her while the guards who had brought her handed over their responsibility with much arm waving and bored exasperation to the hotel guards who nodded and looked blankly at her. Somehow she had expected something of a red carpet, but she was too tired to care, she sat down in the corner and waited until they had sorted out whose head would roll if anything happened to her.

Finally an officer approached her, bowing slightly, half-saluting, (he clearly didn't know how to treat her), and took on that responsibility.

'Welcome, Miss Redna, I'm sorry for this delay. I will show you to your room now, I am sure you will want to rest before you meet Mr Hartman.'

'Thank you.'

She rose and followed him out of the foyer and up to the first floor on a kind of rampway that went right to the top of the hotel and was festooned with hanging plants that had gone wild. Right at the top was a skylight that let filtered sunshine down the length of the building. It must have been a nice hotel for a holiday, she thought, imagining children running up and down the ramps. A flash, a past childhood, where a little girl ran up and down a steep staircase counting the shadows of the bannisters cast by thin sunlight through a frosted window, she paused, but only for a second.

The flat was serviceable, comfortable but as sterile as every other unit she had ever lived in. The balcony was a pleasant extra, though the view was nothing more than an empty swimming pool and a dying palm tree. She could see over the scrubland to the rest of the empty town and the sea. She leaned over and looked up, the sky was darkening and a few stars blinked through the evening haze. In the distance a helicopter made its round over the mountains, buzzing through the silent valleys like a mosquito looking for its prey.

She woke early, suddenly full of an exuberance that had seeped out of her during the journey. Standing in the shower, letting the warm water cascade over her, she felt revitalised. Now, finally, she would be a real part of it all, would belong in a way that the months of training had not given her. She examined her body, stroking the water down her arms and legs, watching the soap bubble up and drift down over the swell of her stomach, forming channels that ran into her groins. She felt in tune with every part of herself, every vein and artery, every muscle and bone responding to her will. She was ready to go.

The guard from the previous night brought her breakfast, a starched new blue uniform and a map of the hotel and told her to buzz when she was dressed. She wanted him to stay, she wanted to talk to someone, to pass on her good feelings, but he merely backed politely out of the room. It was as though she had already left, as far as everyone was concerned, after all, what was the point in getting friendly, when it would be twenty years before any conversation could be concluded. After she had eaten and dressed he returned at her call and led her down the inner balcony level, back to the central spiral and up to the next level. There he left her in a similar unit to her own with the news that Mr Hartman would be along to see her there, and that her fellow flyer would also be arriving later in the morning.

She fidgeted for over an hour, feeling an explosion of energy building up in her, until the door finally opened and a man and a woman came in to join her.

The bed had been too soft, she had not been able to make the shower water come hot enough and she felt as though another eight hours sleep would not have been too much. Frances Duke was not feeling like a flyer that morning. Her relief at being off the ship and onto land again had been only a temporary break from her mounting anxiety about what was to come. Lying in bed, watching her coffee go cold as the sun crept above the edge of her balcony, she wondered at their choice of her for this role. All her life she had done things on her own, only far off lurked memories of playing with her brother. Shadows of other children were meaningless reminders of friendships she had not enjoyed. She had learnt early, the benefits of being top, being first and had been prepared to accept the price. Loneliness had become a way of life to her, fitted her like a cool plastic skin that made outside contact acceptable but unimportant.

Now she was to be pushed into a close relationship with one other person, and for so long she did not know how she was going to manage it. As she dressed herself she realised she was trying to make something more of her appearance than usual. Did she want to impress both Hartman and the woman? It was almost as though she was going on a blind date for the rest of her life. She pressed the buzzer for the guard and, by the time he arrived to take her to Hartman, she was back in control.

The guard paused in the foyer, watching as a car drew up at the entrance and a man got out wearing the kind of dark glasses that give off a perfect reflection that Franni hated. He was calling something over his shoulder as he came in the door and then, as he turned, he saw Franni, stopped and examined her from a distance before he approached, dispatching the guard with a nod of head.

'Miss Duke, I presume.'

'Mr Hartman.' She took his proffered hand, dry, firm, powerful, in hers, small, cold, wary.

'I'm glad to see you. I hope you have been looked after satisfactorily.'

'Everything's been fine.' She couldn't be bothered to mention the shower, she would not be staying for long, after all.

'Well, in that case let us go up to my office, I think Miss Redna's already waiting for us and I'm sure you two ladies are looking forward to meeting each other.'

She half smiled and nodded in agreement, thinking how much he was enjoying this and wishing he need not be there for the first meeting. She walked up the ramp slightly behind him, watching him, trying to work him out. Forties, fit, an empire-builder, his clothes looked expensive, had almost too much taste, as though he were trying to disguise something. He still wore the sunglasses, so she could not tell what his eyes were like, the rest of his face was so like those of his type, lined but still conventionally good-looking. Two hundred years ago they might have called him dashing, now he was just another technician who'd got into politics and money and made good, his face might have been moulded out of polystyrene, it showed so little of a real human being.

Hartman turned to face her as he reached the door, pausing to relish the full theatre of the moment.

'And here we are at last, Miss Duke.' He opened the door with a flourish to reveal Vivienne standing, silhouetted against the light from the balcony. 'Allow me to introduce you.'

'I hardly think that will be necessary.' Vivienne came forward with her hand outstretched, 'I think we know who each other is.' She took the other woman's hand in hers, pressing it with an urgency that transmitted her desire to keep her embarrassment/nervousness/suspicion away from Hartman's sharp eyes.

Frances responded with a firm handshake, a quick

smile and a tacit agreement that any further conversation would be saved for later. The two women turned back to Hartman, who, disappointed at this meeting, was obliged to start dealing with the business of the day that would set the timing for the launch the following week.

Later they would look back on that first meeting, first sight, first impressions that lingered on. Vivienne always said that she was the first to offer the hand of friendship, Franni used to say that she hadn't been given a chance to do anything else. Mostly they just thought about it all to themselves, an unimportant moment really, just a marker where an image became flesh and blood. In a way, neither woman looked at the other very closely during that first meeting between the two of them and Hartman. For both of them it was their first proper meeting with him as well and his function now gave him centre stage as he expounded on the progress of the mission and his major hopes and fears.

'You must fully realise how important the communication between you and me is going to be once you are up there. You will represent the hopes of Eura, maybe even the world, what you learn will ensure the survival of our people, should we ever need to evacuate. You must never forget that.'

Vivienne couldn't stop watching Hartman's reflection moving about in his sunglasses that lay on the desk. It was like a figure in a crazy mirror place in the fun fair and she wanted to giggle, especially as his speeches went on and on. Both women had had similar stuff drummed into them for months and to be still listening to it now was becoming tedious.

'But what I want to know, Mr Hartman, is what plans have you for the extension of the greenhouse block which is essential, if we are not to die from lack of oxygen? I telexed from Prague to say that what had been planned was not sufficient.'

In fact Franni already knew the answer to this question but it brought Hartman's spiel to an abrupt end and allowed all three to get back to the business of the meeting.

Everything was going to plan, the launch site was ready, the monitoring station was tuned in and set to go. Everything had been checked and re-checked, the tv cameras were set up, the advertising moguls had finished fighting over slots and sponsoring. Hartman looked at the two women. He led them over to the window that overlooked the launch site, where the rocket stood waiting. He arranged it so that he stood between them, allowing himself a feeling of triumph that the whole thing was coming to fruition.

'There you are, ladies, your transportation, your chance to do great things for mankind.' He allowed himself to slip an arm round each waist.

Both women stiffened, then, well, it was an amazing sight and as, after the next forty eight hours, they would only have each other to talk to, neither could see the point of rowing with Hartman now.

There would be no time wasted. All the preparations had been done, with the weather perfect and the accountants eager to get this expensive project going, so they could cut down on the massive costs already incurred, there would be no delay. The women had passed through the medicals with no problem, the final countdown checks were fine. Procedures were familiar, practised, second nature to all those blue uniforms. The Launch would be the following morning.

Back in their units, now united by a connecting door that stood ajar, both women sat attempting to make the final personal preparations for the trip. Vivienne ran through everything that had made her want to go so much in order to block out the voice that sang a love of mother earth through her bones. The experiments, the animals, so much to learn, so much time to do research in peace without the distractions that normally dogged her progress. It was all very well to get romantic now about the wide rolling lands she had journeyed through on the train, but she had never wanted to go there when she had had the chance, just because now she could not go, might never go at all, she had no right to demand that of her life. She clenched her fists, she had demanded things all her life or she would not be here now. This was the ultimate achievement, as Hartman had said, her work over the years to come could help save mankind in many different ways, she would be a heroine. She laughed out loud at her ridiculous thoughts and went over to stand in front of the entrance to the next unit, watching the smaller woman who was bent over the table writing something.

'So, we're going tomorrow.' Stating the obvious was the only way she could think of to break the silence.

The other woman twisted round, smiled.

'Yes, seems a bit strange doesn't it. I mean, well, you'd have thought they might have given us a little longer to get acquainted.'

Vivienne took this as an invitation and wandered through Franni's unit to stand on the balcony, gazing out over the swimming pools to the faded tourist centre. In the distance she could see a small fishing boat on it way back to the harbour after a morning's fishing. She turned back.

'Are you sorry to be leaving?'

'Sorry? No, no I don't think so. It's what I wanted to do after all. And you?'

'Me, no, it's been my dream ever since I heard of the mission.' Her voice sounded full of enthusiasm and confidence, she wondered why.

Conversation fizzled out, neither knew what to say to a person they were to spend virtually the rest of their lives with. Franni went back to fiddling with her papers on the desk, Vivienne to staring out to the sea. When the intercom buzzed, announcing lunch, it surprised both of them. Somehow eating together made a connection again, a topic, reflections on the diet awaiting them in space, a beginning of relaxation.

After the meal lay an afternoon of checking and practise runs down on the launch pad, but all went without hitch and by nightfall there was nothing left to do except watch the glittering lights of the launch pad out-dazzle the stars. An early meal and an early night had been prescribed for both of them, so there was little time left for more talking. Soon each one was lying alone in her own single bed in her own unit. The last night on earth.

Franni lay curled on her side, wondering about the future, trying out the other woman in her mind. She seemed okay, certainly very competent, but twenty years? Her brow wrinkled. She pushed back her doubts and regrets, she had wasted enough time on them already, it was much too late. Her last night, she pulled the blankets closer under her chin. Well, no one would miss her, her family were little more than a shadow, that would not quite leave her. There had never been any time to fall in love, no time for all that passion and romance churned out in the media. She had not minded, did not mind. It just seemed odd that there would be no one to wave her goodbye. When sleep came it was empty of dreams, a heavy sleep that blanketed out the soft slap of the waves on the beach, leaving her with the solitude of space.

In the other unit Vivienne was lying on her back, filling in a final areotext to the one person she wanted to write to, her old tutor at the Paris Institute. He had told her she would go far, she laughed to herself, even he had not known how far. Of course he would know soon what was happening, but she wanted him to hear it from her own hand. Marcus had been more than a tutor, he had been a friend, sometimes a lover, he had wanted to help her and when she left, he had cried. She had not cried. She had not loved him as he loved her, could not give him what he wanted, but still she was fond of him and so she wrote, allowing her flippant style to carry her through till her eyes were aching with tiredness and she could sleep without feeling the earth pull at her bones to hold her to the ground.

The next day was as bright and beautiful as the day before and in a blaze of sunshine both women were driven to the launch pad and boarded the great white metal bird that perched on the runway, wings swept back ready for the swoop up into the stars. Hartman met them on the runway with final instructions to a couple of changes made in the layout that differed from the mock versions they'd trained on. He shook hands with them, gave each a special squeeze to give them confidence in his control of the mission and gestured to the steps that led up to the pre-board room and then into the ship.

Inside the pre-board room a few technicians stood around watching dials, the countdown had been going since before dawn and everything was under control. There was no press, no crowds, no excitement. They might just as well have been getting the shuttle back to the Spanish mainland. They both felt a sense of anti-climax, sitting on a bench in their ship suits as though they had made the top team but no one had come to watch the game. The interview screen flicked on and Hartman's face appeared in startling magnification.

'Ladies, I'm proud to pass on a message of hope and thanks to you both from no less than the President of Eura himself.'

He went on to read out an obviously prepared speech that sounded like one of Sandra's best efforts, and then the formalities were at an end. The two women boarded the spaceship, allowing themselves one last gasp of the polluted, dust-laden, hot air of that sunny little island, before the door slid shut and there was no time to do anything except prepare for take-off.

When it came, Franni felt grief and self-pity and fear meet and flow in her blood till, as the huge machine ground upwards beyond the clouds, an overwhelming relief filled her and let her relax into her body as the automatic pilot shot them forward. Vivienne had forgotten there would be no chance to bid earth goodbye, until they were out of its grasp and felt tears pricking at her eyes. No, she did not want the open fields of Eura, the life of an ordinary woman, but they should have let her say goodbye, somehow. There had been no time for goodbyes. On the ground Hartman rubbed his hands and turned his back on the launch pad to return to headquarters where the progress of the flight could be monitored. Like a proud father who had just wedded off his two last and ugliest daughters, he felt suitably pleased with himself. Operation EDEN was finally off the ground.

FLIGHT

Diary Extract V.R.

I've been keeping this diary for so many months and suddenly I don't know what to put down. Just the normal report of experiments, figures, drawings and reports will not sum up what is happening up in this flying goldfish bowl. We've been up now for a year and, as far as the mission goes, Hartman is well pleased. Apparently people are still interested in our progress, so we continue to furnish him with mundane reports of our day-to-day lives for telecast. And mundane it is on the whole. It took months for the animals to settle down and start breeding, so our diet has been limited to dried food brought from earth that can never be anything but tasteless whatever we try to do with it. F.D. does most of the food preparation and, now her greenhouse is improving, we can look forward to a more interesting menu. So much time is spent talking to machines and computers that now it's hard to write as to another human being, if anyone will ever read this, which sometimes I doubt. Space is so vast, so empty, I can feel it sucking us into some void that will tear us away from any hope of a return to earth.

Daily routine keeps us from going crazy with it all. Daily routine will surely start driving us insane. Perhaps it already has. I lie for hours on my bunk wondering what is happening down there. Each day we pull further away from home, time twists reality further from my mind. Like a smooth pebble, I have been thrown out from the safety of the beach into the deep ocean, and I am sinking fast. Hartman is our only link, and his contacts are ever more infrequent, more crackled and faint. His face looks grotesque on the screen, his voice a parody of the smoothness that lifted my hackles on earth. I cannot believe he is still down there, on that tiny island, sitting in his office, drinking Sandra's coffee.

Maybe Sandra has gone, finally made the break and set up home up in the mountains. Maybe she runs a bar where locals sit for hours over tiny glasses of alcohol and the smoke of cheap cigarettes fills the air. Maybe in nineteen years I will be able to go and sit next to her on a high bar stool where the sky stays above your head like a safe canopy and the stars keep the places they held when I was still a child.

Up here I spin round in this fairground toy. The observation panels are smooth and curved and give a never-ending vista of blackness pricked with light. There are no clouds, no rain, no blue skies to rejoice over, only the sharp lights move around, giving new insights into the same web of eternity. Sometimes I think I will die out here, sometimes I think I already have.

I should say something about my work, about my workmate. My work is all that keeps me sane. Bent over the microscope, I can be anywhere I like. The animals are doing well, no one ever told them they would be stuck up her for ever. Their eyes are warm, their needs are real and beyond what a computer can give them. Sometimes it is an effort to leave them for other tasks, or for my quarters. So far there has been no disease and now they are breeding, we can start using them for food. I cannot kill the old ones, those that came with us will not be used. I feel like a murderer to take any and curse any flight that cannot survive on vegetables but Hartman was unyielding and, for what it's worth, Hartman is God.

As for her, well, I have given up on anything more than the contact I have with the computer. She hardly ever speaks to me, unless it is about work, and then she is brisk and direct allowing no room for expansion. She spends hours at the viewing panels, playing with spatials and drawing graphs that tell me nothing. We have compulsory sessions set up by Hartman where we are supposed to 'relate', give each other companionship, hobbies, entertainment. She will only play chess or scrabble with the seriousness of a grand master. Mostly, she makes an excuse and stays in her quarters. Sometimes we talk, laugh, I feel communication has started, but then it is switched off. It is as though she can see exactly how much I need before I crack up and gives me that, no more, no less. We have been here for a year and I know no more about her than I did on the island. What have they done to us!

Diary Extract F.D.

My god, they really didn't know what it was going to be like when they planned this trip. Twenty years, virtually to the day, and we've only done one. Let me describe this floating coffin to you. A huge round disc really, just like the flying saucers people used to imagine a hundred years ago. Round the edge are the viewing panels that close and open as we want and as the computer decides. In front of each panel a bank of electronics, wires, lights, buttons, inputs and outputs. A thousand miles of wire runs under the steel floor to the central computer that stands in the middle, the axis of our world. With weighted boots it takes me exactly fifty four minutes and eight seconds to walk round touching each panel as I pass. Six months ago it took me sixty three minutes and twenty five seconds, in another few years I might be able to do it in half an hour. Beneath the operations room lies the domain of Vivienne's animal kingdom, where the cages are just a bit smaller but their occupants seem happier. Above my head is the greenhouse level, where a thousand light tubes shine to keep my plants alive and maintain the oxygen flow.

And if you are wondering where we sleep, eat, shit, squeeze that last smear of toothpaste out of the tube, smell the stale smell of period blood on an old tampon, wash dirty knickers and try and remember who we are, then follow me up to what I laughingly call home. I sleep in my bubbly above the computer tower in what are described as private quarters. Two rooms little 'bigger than cupboards, equipped with bed, chair, drawers, table, all bolted to the ground in case of gravity lurches. There is a disposal unit that takes care of anything you want to dispose of, but is fortunately too small for any contemplations of suicide. Even if we do not return, I like to think some floating remains of two human lives are now scattered along the track of our orbit and may one day be sighted by some future, more intrepid, explorer. There is no place to stamp any identity in those rooms. I tried putting photos up on the wall, but they just sneer at me with their images of an earth I believe I will never see again. If she has done better with her rooms, I do not know. I have never seen them. We eat in the operations room, sometimes together but mostly apart. I cook and she sits and watches me, trying to make conversation with eyes like a starving puppy. I think she is cracking up, but what the hell can I do about it. We are here for a long time, we have to be able to look after ourselves. I have done it all my life, I cannot change now. I feel outraged with Hartman and his gang, how they could have thought it would work with two such different individuals. Six months ago I told him it was a disaster, they should bring us back, but he just smiled. I am beginning to wonder what this project was really meant to prove.

Report to Eura Council. Operation EDEN.
R. Hartman

Timedate
Mission now at launch + 3yrs.

Technical Progress
Oxygen feedback experiments proving very successful. Work developing on species development, use of infra-red and ultra-violet to promote leaf expansion in progress. For further data re figures for future planning see sub report No 87.

Animal breeding now established: work to start on genetic reconstructions to enable evolution of rodents suitable for computer controlled production.

Astral sciences already expanding, giving vast new areas of knowledge to units on earth. Studies of behaviour of matter in meteor belts of particular interest.

Communications
Still very good, though now becoming affected by astral storms and imperfect conditions on earth. Tracking via Observatory in order.

Personnel
One reported breakdown at launch + 2yrs. No follow-up. Work rotas still following as planned. No psychiatric disturbances apparent as yet.

Hartman flicked the switch of his dictaphone off and sat back, easing himself in the deep armchair at his desk. No psychiatric disturbances, but he knew that was not true. Something was going on up there that he could not work out. Both women reported in as regular as clockwork, both went through every medical check-up without a sign of trouble. It all seemed too smooth to be real. He went back through the tapes and replayed the one where Duke had complained so bitterly about their choice. For a few minutes he listened to her sharp accusing voice calling out to him from space to make an end of it, to bring them back before she went crazy. When that tape had come in he had considered complying for a minute, knowing he had been proved right. Two women, it would never have worked. But he knew that there would never be an EDEN Mark 2, at least not under his control, and so he had ignored the tape, omitted to send it in to Eura Council. And since then there had been nothing to glean from the tapes except business.

With the six-monthly report to prepare for Eura Council he was tied to that desk, surrounded by all the reports sent in from the different sections. Technically the mission was a triumph, already fortunes had been made based on research results sent down from EDEN. His own status had been vindicated, and he loved sitting at Council like a magician who always has a new trick to amaze his audience. World-wide, the mission had already shifted the balance in power towards Eura even though EDEN was bound by international agreement not to work on military projects. Already it had assumed mythical proportions for a desperate population, on what they saw as a dying planet. And he was enjoying playing God.

He pressed the intercom button.

'Lisa, more coffee please.'

For once Vivienne had slept well, no edgy dreams or earthbound nightmares that so often woke her sweating, beating the walls with her fists. For a few minutes she couldn't work out what had woken her, until her conscious ears heard the whine of the alarm above her head. In panic she shot out of bed and pulled her overalls on over her naked body, swearing as the zip got stuck, staggering from side to side as a series of gravity lurches hit the ship, lifting her off the ground as she struggled with boots and belt. Finally, she got out of the cubicle and clambered up the steel rungs of the ladder to the operations room.

'My God! What's happened?' She still felt half asleep, in shock, as she saw Franni running around the perimeter, flicking switches and dials in an effort to stabilise the ship.

'Just get the damn equi-drum back on sync before we start turning somersaults. Hurry woman, I can't keep the control for much longer!'

Vivienne made a dash for the bank of dials that held the gyroscope that monitored ship movements. The needles were haywire, spinning round through the danger zones. Mechanical madness reigned as the two women attempted to quieten their unwieldy monster before it succeeded in committing silent suicide. Sweat ran down Vivienne's back, a mixture of fear and effort, until finally, the gravity lurch subsided and the drum began to respond to her command. The console lights changed from red to orange and then to green, till the two could collapse in their seats, feeling the ship once more resume her contemplative course as though nothing had happened.

'It's the worst one we've had, doesn't augur well for the future.' Franni broke the exhausted silence.

'Unless we find out what causes it, or a way to

program the comp to deal with it, we could be in for quite a few sleepless nights.'

'Do you think it could throw us off course?'

'Well, this one hasn't, but who knows, they seem to be getting more violent the further out we get.'

That proposition was one neither wanted to think about. Yes, they had rocket fuel in reserve, they could use some of it, but for how long? What was it that made the ship suddenly plummet through nothingness and then get shot back like a yo-yo? What would happen if they did not come out of it?

Vivienne poured out two cups of de-caff, giving one to Franni and holding the other in both hands, trying to let the warmth soak through to melt her fear away.

'You'd better check the animals, I don't suppose they took too kindly to such a rude awakening. I'll start drawing up a data run on it to send to Hartman, maybe he and his goons can make some sense out of it all.'

Franni was brusque, seeing the other woman's fear so visibly, knowing that her own lay only a hair's breadth below the surface. She needed to be doing something, not sitting around considering a lingering death in some starless void. Vivienne flinched at the order, at the apparent lack of concern for herself and left the room in silence.

An hour later she was back. All the small mammals were safe, although by experience she knew their breeding patterns would be disturbed for a few weeks. But two of the chickens were dead, one had been with them since the start and she had allowed herself to cry as she sent its body out into the icy cold of space. She reflected grimly on the morality of using these animals for such experiments. Taking them away from their natural habitat, and sentencing them to a lifetime of cages and artificial light. She had told herself she would treat them better than on some factory farm on earth, but somehow that seemed little justification. After all, for whatever reasons, she had made the choice to come on this mission, they had not.

She started feeding the information into the computer, and the familiar buzzes and clicks as the reels spun round, settled her nerves and got her back on course. Dumb creatures after all, what would they know of choices, how would they tell if life would have been sweeter in a chicken run back down there?

'Hey, Vivienne, I think we've got another problem. I can't tune in to Hartman, something's wrong with the beamer.'

Franni was truly worried this time. Without that link with earth, to continue the flight would be a nightmare. Vivienne joined her at the main console and listened for the familiar crackle that announced their connection with the observatory on Gran Canaria. There was nothing, not so much as a flicker.

'Look, Franni, it's the beamer, it's not turning with the dial, that gravity lurch must have shook it free from its main socket.' Vivienne felt her stomach sink, a hole replaced by a new dread.

'Shit! Three years up here without so much as a murmur, and now all this! It means one of us will have to go out there and fix it up, it's too fiddly for the robotool.' Franni was shouting, frustration bursting out of her like darts. 'And it's no good you sitting there with those great cow eyes of yours, that's not going to help anything! God! I'd better get out there and do it myself, you can go and feed the chickens or something!'

She stormed out of the room, wishing the doors were manual so she could slam one. Three years, two months and four days she had spent with this woman, and she had still not learnt to be able to tolerate her for more than an hour or so at a time. In fact she was finding it more and more difficult as time went by. She stomped down the tube to the pressure chamber, letting her masochistic self dwell on the thought of another sixteen years, nine months and twenty eight days until their orbit would bring her back, release her from this captivity. The trouble was, she reflected as she pulled on her space boots and started checking the safety equipment, she could not simply murder Vivienne and send her body out in bits to join the rest of the flotsam and jetsam they had littered space with, she could not actually run this ship on her own. The thought might be pleasant sometimes, but it only made her feel more frustrated because it was out of reach. A year ago she would have given in, gone home, even started looking towards death as a release, but recently she'd determined to survive, and to survive mentally as well as physically, and for that she needed Vivienne.

Sometimes she wished Vivienne would shout back at her, relieve her guilt at what she was doing, but she never did. Maybe that was her defence. Franni shrugged, couldn't really be bothered to think about the ins and outs of it. The woman was simply not up to it, not tough enough, a wimp through and through. She pulled the oxygen tube down over her shoulder and clipped it into the filter system, before pulling the space helmet over her head and switching on her radio contact before de-pressurising. Now she would have to work, switch into contact.

'Vivienne, can you hear me? I'm ready to de-pressurise.'

'Just as well I'm not feeding the chickens. Yes, I can hear you.'

Franni could not see that Vivienne had been crying, she could afford to make a more snappy answer, sound more convincing.

'Okay, okay, I snapped your head off, I'm sorry. Now let's get on before this aerial starts heading off for Mars!'

How was it that whatever she said, Franni always managed to get the advantage?

Vivienne started turning the dials that operated the vacuum chamber, storing the valuable air in pressurised cylinders ready for re-pressurisation, and then switched the radio viewscreen round to watch for Franni to emerge.

Outside the blackness was as deep as ever. There were points of light, clusters and speckles like the outside of a blackbird's egg but somehow that light was no light, just icy chips in the darkness. Vivienne watched Franni jet out of the vacuum tube and start making her way round to the aerial bearing. She waved a greeting to Vivienne, just a check that everything was okay. Vivienne flashed the radio beam and sat back to wait for her to finish. Idly, she watched the red spacesuit floating awkwardly above the silver rim of their craft. She wondered for the thousandth time about the woman inside it. So sharp, so unfeeling, and yet Vivienne had heard her up in the greenhouse almost crooning over those plants, and she was not the only one to have nightmares. She knew Franni thought she was too weak, potentially dangerous, potentially mad, and she knew herself, knew she could be too soft, too trusting, unable to withstand such solitude. But Franni was so stiff, still so unyielding after all this time. What on earth would happen if she started coming apart at the seams? Vivienne pushed her hands through her thinning hair and shook her head, returning her eyes to the screen. To her amazement she could no longer see any sign of Franni.

She whirled the tuner round in an effort to trace the red flash to its source. She yelled into the communicator only to find it was dead. There was no link, no answer, no person anywhere in the universe she could communicate with. For a moment she was paralysed with shock, fear, the desolation of her nightmares swept over her as she envisaged the tiny red spacesuit rolling and turning away from her through space, leaving her so utterly and completely alone.

No, it could not happen. She ran round the operations room, switching up every panel till all the screens were down and the panorama of space encompassed her. And far off, at the opposite edge from the aerial position, she caught sight of a red fleck, drifting out beyond the flaps, seemingly out of control. She screamed out through the plastic, beat her fists against it in a meaningless effort to discover if Franni was still alive, then, pulling herself back inside her head, she bolted down to the pressure chamber and started to pull on her own spacesuit, hurrying through all the safety routines with fumbling fingers so she could get out. It seemed to take hours to get the programmes through that would allow her to leave the ship unattended and finally press the buttons that would jettison her into the void she so hated.

Once outside, her heart rate began to slow back to normal as the mechanics of controlling the back jet took over and she made steady progress round the rim of the ship to where she had sighted Franni. There was no sign of her and as Vivienne started a search of every area round the ship, she began to accept the horror of the truth; Franni had gone, maybe sucked down by a minor gravity lurch, maybe had her suit punctured by a meteor fragment and sent off like a burst balloon to whirr through space to her death. By the time Vivienne had made a complete circuit of the ship her brain, trained so well to be logical, had already started planning how she could manage the ship on her own, reverse the orbit and return to earth. So it was almost a shock, a disappointment, to see Franni's face grinning out at her from her helmet as she hung waiting outside the pressure door.

'So you decided to come out as well, it's amazing out here isn't it. I just couldn't believe how beautiful it was.' Franni's voice was just a crackle to Vivienne's fractured nerves.

She made no reply and both women remained silent until they were back in the operations room, sitting opposite each other, surrounded by the blind eyes of space.

Franni was bubbling with an openness that Vivienne had never heard before and she was struck dumb beside the woman's constant stream of feeling about the outside. In her heart she felt a storm brewing, dark clouds gathering over restless waves, winds that began to howl spitting drops of water against the clouds. Her eyes began to cloud over and fill with a passion of rage against the arrogance and selfishness that faced her.

'Oh, shit, it was so extraordinary out there. Like being born again, I know that sounds mad, but do you know what I mean? Just all the endless space full of stars and suns and planets. It was like when my grandfather took me out so many years ago, God I'd forgotten everything he told me, and then out there it was like he was beside me, pointing out everything. I had to be there, stay there, and then, after I'd switched the radio off, well it didn't matter, I'd fixed the aerial, well then it was all so silent I could hear his voice again, telling me all the names, reminding me of all those gods and heroes and whatever, and then, all those other stars. God, if he could have only been able to see them as well, to feel that space, shit, they should bring everyone up here, just to get out there and see it all for themselves. Hartman was right, it *is* worth it, every minute of it, to have had that chance.'

Slowly, Franni dried up as she realised the other woman was barely listening to what she was saying. She looked at her quizzically, was this going to be another pathetic reproach? Was she also in a state about being out there? She opened her mouth to punch out some smart remark and then just left it out and waited while the silence fell back in the room.

'Well, I'm glad someone managed to have a psychic experience in this floating tin can.' Vivienne enjoyed the slight flinch she produced in Franni and carried on. 'You realise, of course, that you didn't bother to tell me you were off communicating with the stars before you switched the radio off, leaving me to think some fate worse than death, but that would end up in death, had got you and left me to drive this crate back to earth with only that damn computer, which can't even cope with the odd gravity lurch, and a few white mice to help me. You realise of course that for the last three and a half years or whatever it is, you have never bothered to tell me a single thing of any value except which knobs you might want me to twist and when, that as far as I'm concerned you are about as much support, company and help as the dead chickens I had to jettison this morning when you were so busy with your dataruns!'

'Oh, come on, Vivienne, for God's sake don't let's start all this again. You know what I think, twenty years is a long time, we've got to be careful about how we handle getting any closer, we could drive each other mad.' Franni's reply was nervous. Somehow Vivienne wasn't reacting in form this time.

'And you think you're not driving me mad now. I've tried everything I can think of and you only push any contact away. I'm not saying we have to be lovers or anything,' her voice died away, 'just some room to talk, to share something.' She wished she hadn't shouted, but it was out and it created a silence that burned round the room.

Franni lay back on her bunk and examined the skin on the back of her hands, watching for age spots. She wondered when getting older would become notice-able, given there were no younger women to make comparisons with. She was still trying not to think about Vivienne and the incident of the spacewalk three days ago. After the row things had just gone back to normal, except that it wasn't normal, both of them knew it, but this time Vivienne wasn't trying to push anything either, so it was just a matter of routine work, a couple of new experiments, reports back to Hartman on the gravity lurches and that was all. The lurches were getting more frequent, although a little less severe, and that was plenty to worry about.

And so time passed. There was always something to be done, new programmes sent up by Hartman, new tests to aid his research on earth. They dissected the space around them, counting atoms, measuring neutrons, establishing fresh data on the origins of the universe, naming stars that no other eyes had ever seen before, breeding plants and animals that proved the mechanics of genetic engineering beyond the wildest dreams of every earth-bound scientist. They learnt to deal with the gravity lurches, adapted to a certain kind of gait that left them prepared for the sudden drop as the ship fell into an empty lift shaft, only to pull up just before it got to the ground floor, and return to its unconcerned course.

Neither made any allusion to what had happened, both moved about the ship clothed in a plastic bubble that protected them from the other. Vivienne's eyes had lost the softness that searched for companionship now. They carried a diamond brilliance that flashed for her creatures and remained ice-cold for anything else. Franni's tongue was quieted, muttering figures and equations into the computer, her head bowed over print-outs and calculators. She no longer crooned to her plants, though they seemed not to mind. And the ship flew ever outwards along its pre-ordained track through an endless night.

ORBIT

Diary Extract V.R.

So this is what it's like to be mad. I know I am now, and it's better than before when I just worried I might be becoming so. It makes life so much easier just to float within this ship, roll as it rolls, spin as it spins with that certain knowledge that there is no return to a state of mind and order that was lost somewhere in my past life. I should say that I count my life only from the time this flight started, a single orbit of this one tiny galaxy, just a stone's throw in space from a lump of rock where another woman with my name once lived, perhaps happily, perhaps not, I do not remember now. Even my dreams are space-bound, full of star bursts and brilliant eclipses that fill my head with shadows, taking over the softness inside my skull till space exists only inside me, a figment of my imagination. And then when I wake and go up to the chamber and see it all around me, I know I am just a thin membrane between the meeting of the two, and already I can feel the skin pulling ever tighter, till one day it will slowly rip, letting the stars within my head go out to join their sisters.

I could recount so many interesting discoveries, brilliant research that must be making advances for those that I travel for. Hartman, Hartman, Hartman. He still calls out with promises and gifts, like a genie in a bottle he comes when I choose to pull the stopper out and must return to his lair on my command. I watch him closely, seeing how age is creeping up on him, deepening the wrinkles on his face, and yet he seems to have grown no wiser, cannot answer the questions I ask him as a genie should, but only pulls on a ridiculous beard and begs to be excused for other business. What other business is there I wonder, what else exists but him and us, what else matters except our tiny spinning world? But I humour him, feed him what he needs or he will learn to escape my bottle and haunt my every waking moment, so I give him facts like sweeties, just one or two each time, otherwise he will get spoilt and greedy.

And her, I have to watch her like I watch my rats and mice for she is mad too and I must be sure she does not get too near me and disturb my spirit. I know they sent her with me as a trial for my strength. They knew I would find her too hard to deal with, but I have proved them wrong. I have learnt how to protect myself from her power and now I can just watch how she is, a crazy, who does not roll as I do but just sits and stares at the stars as though they will listen to her now that I don't. Sometimes she spies on me, comes into my room when I am sleeping and touches all my things. But it does no harm because I know she is there and can guard against her with the power that comes with the sunbursts, rises with the moons of Jupiter, flashes with the force of the comet that streams somewhere ahead of us.

Now, for the first time, I feel happy to be here, happy that others may follow in my footsteps, it's just a matter of tuning in.

Diary Extract F.D.

All I can do is keep churning out the data-runs. All I can do is keep watching the plants, cooking the food, counting the seconds it takes to get from A to B, to get one task done, then how long till I can find another. The mission is a disaster, but we've gone beyond any hope of turning back, of escaping whatever fate awaits us. I long to go back outside, to feel again that divine touch, a floating freedom, a blaze of the universe that carried me into a different world. But I cannot, for fear that I will let myself go, or that she will close the door behind me and I will die a suffocating death, cut off from my last link with reality, humanity, solid ground. Every day gravity lurches shake me, my nerves are torn apart. One day we will not come out, surely surely, we will slip away off the dials, off the scopes back on earth and they will just make an empty tomb for us down there while Hartman looks for another job. He pushes, probes, always wants more information, more material, but for what? What uses is he putting our souls to, in this struggle to survive? He never answers my questions about what is happening down there. He gives us no solutions, no explanations for the lurches, no guidance. He is a leech and yet I cannot live without his contact.

Vivienne has gone somewhere else, into a world I cannot reach. Maybe it was my fault, shit, they never told us how to do this. I know I should have tried harder at the start, but the thought of it, twenty years, I couldn't help her then and now it seems like it's too late. Sometimes she scares me, at night she has terrible screaming nightmares and I go to her cubicle, but as soon as I go in she is quiet, just lying frozen still as though she knows I am there. I have fixed a bolt on my door, she watched me do it with those huge eyes but made no contact. God! I wish this was over. Only my plants keep me sane, now I listen to them, feeling their natural growth, getting some comfort from the bright green leaves that unfold and reach up towards life, they have not given up hope, and I can only feel it would be a human arrogance to give up now.

Report to Eura Council
R. Hartman

Timedate
Mission now at launch + 5yrs

Technical Progress
Experimentation still producing useful data on both animal and plant species development. For application in increased food production in East Eura see attached report.

Work on matter control and rearrangement in seed production has proved crucial in development of Mutant Ray that allowed Eura to force through agreement on forestry control in the Third. Both crew members recognised for this work with honour of the Order of the Eura Cross.

Communications
Data-runs received without problem although direct links are more erratic. Importance of base on G.C.

is still vital to sustain mission.

Personnel
Physical health reports are still good. No disease, no physical injuries either reported or monitored.

Signs of mental stress are evident though no clear picture has emerged. Psychiatric reports are enclosed though main pattern seem to be withdrawal from personal involvement resulting in first signs of psychosis. Erratic personal contact makes close judgement impossible. We must be able to maintain our connection with the ship or future research may be lost.

Hartman was worried. With the increasing possibility of major conflict between Eura and the Third, there was pressure to cut the program down to just a computer intake bank to receive data from EDEN. To have to leave now would be the end of his career, his hopes, his whole personal ambition which had become tied up with the fate of the ship. As long as he could use the information he received to offer new war technology, he could justify his existence, but recently the data-runs had become more bitty and stilted, repetitions of old experiments, lists and lists of facts and figures with no theory or research to fit them.

He could not bear the possibility of failure, he would not let it happen and so he spent hour upon hour writing his reports, trying to fix up the banks of information into enthusiastic new projects. They had sent the two best scientists in the field, the two fittest, most appropriate candidates to take the strain, and they were turning out material a college kid would be ashamed of. He wanted to shout out at them, show them what they were doing to him, his head was on the block for them and they didn't even seem to understand what he was saying any more.

Leaning back in his armchair, he let his gaze take in the brilliant sunshine outside, his ears heard the bustle of the office, the click of typewriters and computers. Sometimes he even envied the lot of those ants that worked for him, without responsibility, without culpability. All day they filed and processed and served him and the project, but if he could not produce the goods, then there would be no future for any of them, but they would not have to face Eura with that failure on their plate.

He would just have to keep on pushing, keep hoping that another phase of activity would start and the data-runs would start flowing again. And as for the dream, the dream of EDEN that had fired the imagination of the world, he turned from the window and buried himself back in his work.

'It's communal time, Vivienne, do you want to play scrabble?'

'Okay.'

'I've made us some tea for a change, would you like some?'

'Yes, such a long time since we had tea. I think I'll sit here, is that alright?'

'Yes, of course, here, take the cup, careful it's a bit hot.'

A new phase. Politeness, careful, false, exhausting politeness. The two women sat opposite each other, avoiding eyes, the clean polished surface of the table between them bearing the square scrabble board. Vivienne dipped her fingers into the bag of letters, letting them slide into her hand, taking them out, one by one and arranging them on the stand in front of her. Once she didn't like playing scrabble, but now she loved the feel of the plastic squares on her fingers, felt a thrill when she pulled out a blank. She had favourite letters, an S made her feel warm, a P gave her hope, Es were useful but a little humdrum. A, ahh, that was her best letter. This time she had none, but had picked out a T and a W which always made her feel more determined to do well.

Franni chose hers quickly, almost uncaringly in her effort to get the game started so that there was something to do, something to think about. They had played so many times, it was hard to make it anything more than a routine. She drew a good selection that included a blank and managed to draw out a spark of enthusiasm. She watched as Vivienne sipped her tea and studied her letters, waiting for the first word to hit the board.

'Here's a word, look,' Vivienne put the word out letter by letter. TWINE. She laughed and clapped her hands, 'That's a good start. Shall I score?'

'Yes, of course, if you like. Here's mine. EDGE.'
DARE
RAT
TRANCE
BRANCH
FOREST
FISH
HARTMAN

'You can't have that, you can't have proper names.'

'Why not?'

'You just can't, it's the rules. You know that, we've always played that way.'

Vivienne sat back and looked at the other woman suspiciously. She didn't like it.

'Why can't we change the rules? Anyway, I don't think Hartman counts. He's more like a thing than a proper name anyway.'

Franni laughed. Vivienne laughed. Franni said okay, that Hartman didn't really count and she would let it go this time. They carried on playing.

MIME

END

ICE

TIME

EMPTY

'Shall, I make some more tea?' Franni was beginning to need another task, another distraction.

'No, let's go on a bit more, I've got a good word, then we can have tea.' Vivienne put her word down.

YEARN

Franni got up to make the tea, thinking that suddenly she hated scrabble, all those words that just mocked them, meaningless up here, where words were so useless, so incapable of summing up what was happening.

'Don't you want to play any more?' Vivienne was disappointed. 'I think I was going to win this time.'

'I'm sorry, I just don't feel like it. Here, have some tea.'

They sat on, the board staring up, the stars staring in, silent. Communal time.

The communication panel flashed, announcing a tape from Hartman. They sat and listened without comment as he railed at them from the screen for their lack of commitment, lack of work, pleaded with them for the project, for the hopes of the free people of the world, for children and old people, cajoled them with promises of rewards and medals, fame and fortune.

Without a word Vivienne got up and took the letters from the board that spelt his name and arranged them on the screen.

'You see,' she announced triumphantly, 'he is just a thing. He can't see us or hear us, we don't even know if he's really there. All he does is give us more words to play scrabble with!' She started grabbing all the letters, making the words as Hartman crackled them out across the void.

EFFORT
DEDICATION
WORK
GOALS
SUCCESS
MONEY

Franni sat in her chair, feeling a huge desire to giggle as Hartman's face slowly disappeared under the letters. Then she could resist no longer and reached for the rest of the letters to completely cover the screen with any nonsense words she could think of. Then they turned the sound off, so that the only thing left of him was the dull glow of light that seeped out from between the square letters. At the back of her mind Franni told herself she would replay the tape later, just to make sure he hadn't said anything important, in the meantime she could not help but be sucked into Vivienne's mood, an exuberance neither woman had felt for a long time and that neither really knew how to handle any more.

Vivienne's eyes were bright, 'Let's play something else now!'

'What about cards, racing demon?'

'Yes, okay, I'll get them, and why don't we have some of the wine.'

Vivienne flew round the room pulling a double pack of cards out of the communal time locker, a flagon of wine from the store and two glasses. She did not know why she was feeling so good, feeling the roll of the ship go with her, feeling the other woman respond to the mood. Suddenly it was all so important to hold on to, she would do anything to sustain this moment.

She looked across to where Franni was sitting, waiting for her, a smile still on her face that made her seem like a stranger, as though this was their first meeting instead of that one so long ago on the island. She realised she had never really looked at her, absorbed those sharp features and small, wiry build, appreciated her tenacity and perverseness. Maybe now they were both crazy, it would be easier to find some common ground.

They played the first hand in silence. Both pairs of eyes fixed on the table, as they flashed the cards out as fast as they could. Vivienne drew her breath in sharply each time Franni beat her to a card. The piles mounted on the table as, with one frenetic flourish, she managed to get rid of the last of her cards.

'I'm out, I win the first round!' She felt triumphant, sitting back sipping the wine, while Franni collected the cards and sorted them back into their packs for a second hand. Franni smiled, equally determined, she dealt out her pile of thirteen with a concentration she normally reserved for her beloved spatials. The second hand was noisier, as the temperature of excitement rose. Both women could not restrain themselves from calling out as they made their plays. That time Franni won, and won again before Vivienne could recover her attention and beat her in the fourth hand.

And so they went on playing and drinking, laughing and shouting, while outside the solitude of space gave them little attention, two noisy specks in an ocean of space. The ship drifted on its course, pulling them further and further away from a world that was too busy creating its own destruction to bother about two souls it had thrown away so many years ago. The computer lights flashed as it carried them along, drawing its power from the eternal energy of the forces that surrounded it like a careful mother with two children to look after who have just discovered how to play.

Finally, Vivienne could not go on any longer. The wine was beginning to affect her and the cards slipped between her fingers. She giggled and stood up, slightly weaving her way, she wandered round the room, pressing all the shutters so that all the viewing screens were down and the cabin was flooded with stars. Again she felt the stars inside her reach out to touch their fellows beyond the perspex wall, only this time it didn't frighten her. She stood in front of one with both her hands pressed against the cool plastic, her eyes hazy with wine, flicking from star to star, blackness to blackness. Franni went over to join her at the screen, wondering at this woman who seemed so lost and crazy and yet carried a strength in her body that she herself could never have. As they stood there together, the space between them seemed a little less than the space that surrounded their tiny craft. And then a gravity lurch hit them with unexpected force that sent them spinning across the floor, ending up in a pile under the table that had spilled playing cards all over them. As the equi-drum managed to get a hold of the ship, and the computer buzzed and flashed re-establishing the course, Vivienne managed to struggle into a sitting position and started picking the cards off her. Franni was sprawled across the floor conscious, but infinitely drowsy with the effects of the alcohol that had rushed through her system as the shock of the lurch had hit her. She let her head lie back on the floor, looking up to where Vivienne was sitting.

'Well, that was well timed wasn't it. Are you alright?'

'Yes, I'm fine, just a bit bruised I think.'

'Here, let me see, I'll get some spray for you.'

She managed to crawl over to Vivienne and tried to focus her eyes better to look at the damage.

'No, it's okay, it's nothing much.' Vivienne felt self-conscious as the other woman reached out to touch her. And then Franni knew that she wanted to touch her anyway, that she wasn't really bothered about the bruises. She let her small hand go out across the void between them and rest on the other woman's shoulder, let it slide across onto her collar bone that lay bare where her tunic had ripped during the lurch, let it feel the sharp rise of breath as it passed over a redness that would soon result in the deep purple of internal bleeding, let her fingertips trace the contour line that led it to the deep pit at the base of Vivienne's throat.

Vivienne sat rigid, each bone, each blood vessel paralysed, her eyes empty, her stomach a drain where all the collected fears churned and clotted till it became a cauldron of heat. In her head the madness roared and the membrane that had grown so thin began to tear from top to bottom, burning out in a rage of energy that could only be cooled by this alien touch. She turned her face to meet Franni, her eyes now starful of brilliance as she forced one arm up to close it round the other woman and pull her into her body.

For an eternity they just lay in each other's arms without speaking, letting their fingers play, ranging over skin and bone, hair, muscles, the tension building, the rough nylon of their overalls sliding and sparking with the static they created. Each felt alone in her head as the contact allowed a flood of personal emotion to run free. Franni heard again the thunderstorms of her childhood, the great waves breaking on the seashores that had been the centre of her existence so long ago. Vivienne retraced her steps through the open plains that surrounded the city of her youth, smelt the red poppies that grew wild along the railway embankment as she buried her face in the soft curls of the woman who flicked a thousand memories with every touch she made. She felt tears begin to slide down her cheeks as the knowledge of crashing, overpowering homesickness hit her and made her hold on to Franni with the strength of years of loneliness.

Franni let her tongue taste the salty tears and lifted her face to see her.

'Hey, don't cry, it's okay, I'll stop if you want me to.'

Vivienne simply shook her head, letting her long hair create a soft screen between them and pulled her closer. Franni knew she was finally losing control, finally being absorbed into the insanity that she had reserved for Vivienne alone. But it didn't seem to matter much anymore. As she gently started undoing the zips and poppers that would release them both from their overalls, she vaguely remembered a training session where this possibility had been explored. At the time she had found it ridiculous, a complication that would defeat the purpose of choosing two women for the trip. Of course she had known about such women, though few still existed since the social controls after the alignment, but they were just sick, suffering from some physio-social disease that was now readily and compulsorily treated with the new genetodrugs. They were not like her and so she should not be behaving like them, even though she felt overcome with desire to let her hands run over this woman's breasts, a desire that gave no comparison with the sexual fumblings of the male students she had slept with back on earth. They had told her that even if she did feel some sexual urgings, a simple dose of Genna 1 would solve the problem, and she knew they had several sealed packets of the drug, but now it was all so different, they would just have to realise that up here the same rules could not apply.

Finally they both lay naked and silent, stilled by the enormity of what they were doing. Around them the smooth circular walls of the ship gave shelter, a familiar comfort where soft lights flashed on the computer banks and the vastness of the space beyond the screens hid them from prying eyes. Vivienne rolled onto her side, her head raised on one hand, the other tracing a path across Franni's smooth stomach, wondering at the softness, the gentle curve of her hip down onto the taut muscles of thigh and leg. As each minute passed new discoveries were made. Vivienne cried out to the stars as Franni buried herself deeper against her breasts and let her fingers explore the curling hairs that gave protection for the softness that lay beneath. And as the ship turned and rolled, basking in the ocean of space, they let their limbs strain and relax as their mutual desire drew them up, until they fell into a gravity lurch of their own making and finally surfaced to the sound of their own breathing and the feel of each other's sweat drying on their skin.

Franni was the first to speak, needing to hear the sound of her own voice to make sure she still existed.

'Well,' she rolled onto her back, letting her hands feel her ribs rise and fall, 'I don't think I'll be putting this onto the next data-run to Hartman.'

Vivienne got up and weaved her way to the console to get some water to kill the thirst and unlock her tongue. She leaned back against the unit and looked down at her exhausted companion.

'I think you might be right, for once!' She giggled and returned to sit beside her, enjoying the soft contact of thigh against thigh, shoulder against shoulder. She waved her arm expansively. 'But this is our place, no one knows what we do here, no one can watch us, we have only ourselves and the animals, and after all they've been doing it for years!'

And so another phase, another warp, where they found a new way of surviving, of holding back the nightmare of loneliness, the madness of isolation. Like adolescents, they spent days and nights with their eyes turned away from the screen into each other, delving into every corner, learning new tricks, new games to play. Daily routines were started and then dropped at the touch of a hand. Franni forgot all the myriad of little tasks that had sustained her for so long, Vivienne stopped screaming her fears out in the night when she slept curled close against such warmth.

The new energy their passion gave them also unleashed an old desire to work, and for the first time for years, both women worked long hours on projects dropped in a haze of disillusionment after the first years. Both strove to show off to the other with fresh discoveries and experiments. The ship was alive, the computers overworked with untried spatials covering star patterns traced across heavens they had never even dreamed of. Franni would drag Vivienne up to the greenhouse where they could sit in the branches of trees planted when the ship was still on earth that now curled their way around the starlit chamber, making her admire the skill of her green fingers that created new and radiant plants that held the valuable genetic keys to problems long thought insoluble.

Both of them treasured this new contact like a rare stone discovered beneath layers of earth and mud, dazzled by its brilliance, shocked by its strength and yet aware of its fragility in a universe of rock. They examined every facet of it, each effect on pulse rate, blood pressure, skin texture as though it were a new science, compiling a data store inside themselves that produced ever more questions to be answered by curling fingers that darted and probed, lips that sought out every crevice formed by the rolling, sweeping, curving flow of two bodies.

DATA RUN

Diary Extract V.R.

I can't believe we've been up here so long, ten years, nearly half the life I lived down there and yet that life is forgotten, so far off it's hard to imagine ever going back. So much has happened, so much has changed, and yet we are still those same women who met on a sunny little island and barely spoke to each other for years, dominated by the task we had set ourselves, overshadowed by the weight of the project, by Hartman, by the everlasting space that drifts by us. I thought we were lost, going down some great empty hole and now I don't know if that is what has happened and this is the result, or that we have pulled out of a nose dive into an equilibrium that can give us hope for the future. I thought I was mad and now I don't know. I thought she was a threat, a danger to my madness and now I don't know if she is a saviour or a witch who has cast her spatials over me, and to be honest I no longer care. We treat each other with a familiarity that is so strange, I am shocked at how easily I have adapted to it. I always wanted the contact, was always hurt and afraid of her sharp tongue, always conscious of her feeling of superiority over me, and now I have that contact and can feel how much she needs it too, I am afraid again.

We have kept to our own quarters, sharing only the narrow bunk space when work allows us both to sleep at the same time. She has not taken off the bolt she put on her door, I have not ceased to feel a smear of fear when I sleep alone, knowing she is working above me. The space outside is so endless but the space inside is infinitely precious and we must follow careful, unspoken rules in case the claustrophobia of our world drives us apart and out.

With my work I can find a release, a new expression of unleashed potential that has resulted in the flourishing of my animals. We no longer use them for food, as though the human bond we have made has given us more respect for their tiny lives so, although I must control them, prevent their eagerness to breed from outstripping our limited resources, I need no longer gag on the products of my own inventiveness.

And we have fun, simple fun of a kind I have never experienced. Away from any constraints of social pressures we are released, free from the time barriers of days and nights, work and holidays. There are no appointments to be kept, no account of time spent needs to be made, no one to answer to except each other. Hartman is just a name, a flicker on the screen. Now he is the puppet and we are the puppeteers, he must dance to our tune, listen when we speak. We have told him nothing of what has happened up here and that gives me a childlike thrill. He has become like the old man who lived in the flat below me who I tormented as a child, a representation of unwanted authority, a spook who has lost his power to frighten me as I grow older and more confident in the power that runs in my blood.

Sometimes we turn the telescopes back towards

earth, seeing it as a tiny orb, dim and unimportant against the vista of the great planets that now dominate our screens, wondering that he is still down there, tracking our path with his leering eyes, knowing they are blind to our reality. And she, she has become a compilation of all I never had and all I miss from that half-forgotten world. She has taken the place of the wide fields and sunlit streets, the evening shadows that crossed the square and made magical patterns against the apartment blocks. She is one of the stray cats that made their home in the acres of garbage dumps beyond the grey estates and forayed far into town, slipping in and out of dirty alleyways and crumbling buildings that failed to diminish their glowing coats.

I do not know how long this magic will last but it is of our own making, our own experiment to extend the quality of our survival. We still stand or fall on our own ability to roll with the changes, to create new realities that can sustain us.

Diary Extract F.D.

Well, it's been a crazy couple of years, it hardly feels like the same trip, the same women as before. I still can't work out what it's all about. We don't talk about it too much, I think I'm afraid if I do it might all evaporate and we could be back to the horror of before. It wook me much longer than her to stop worrying about the morality of what we were doing, even though, as she always points out, I was the one to start the whole thing off in the first place. I even tried taking some of the Genna 1, though I never told her. It didn't seem to make any difference, I just felt a bit dozy. I looked up her reports on it in her trials on the hamsters and it seemed it didn't affect them much either, which doesn't say a lot for the drug. It also made me wonder about how they have used such drugs down there, how I saw all those people then, queueing up in experimental labs to be tested on because they would not fit into the 'normal' way of things. They always said it worked, but now I think it must have just been a way of escaping from the white coats and the hospitals and camps where they sent the so-called failures. And what would I do? How would I feel if we were back there? I know I just escape from those questions because we are here, because it is still so long to our return that it seems irrelevant to worry about such things. And she never talks of that reality, we are so locked into this spaceship, no other life exists. I can forget my nagging earth-bound logic in hers that carries her so smoothly through our world.

I know that things will change, that we can't keep up this burst of energy for ever. What will happen then, God knows, I can only cope with it from one day to the next, amazed I wake every shift and want to feel her body rise against mine, amazed she still seeks me out with her wet tongue and unleashes a power I never thought I was capable of.

And of course, now I can go out again and float free with the stars, watching the sun rise on Jupiter, its rings glowing with such a primordial force. I'm no longer afraid she will shut the door on me, leave me to such a lonely death.

As for the project, I suppose all this make me feel more optimistic on one level. If we can survive, just the two of us, then maybe there is hope for a larger, more stable community to make it if they had to. Although with no solutions yet for the problem of distances, I wonder where they envisage going to, after ten years we are still within spitting distance of earth, given the mammoth dimensions of space. Hartman has spoken of trips that could take generations, children who would be born and die before a trip was completed, I am only glad that I would not be a member of the crew for that mission. The thought that we will and can return home is still one that saves me from total lunacy. Maybe Vivienne doesn't feel so much that way, she seems so much more able than I to cope with this life on a day-to-day basis, so much less concerned about earth, about the connection with Hartman that still feels like a lifeline to me.

Report to Eura Council
R. Hartman

He couldn't even bear to start reading off the preliminary sections of this, his final report to the Council. He could not believe what they had done. Lying at the side of his desk was the fat report from the financial bureau with its accompanying letter from the president outlining his death, the end of his career, his removal from Operation EDEN.

He had spent months, years, begging and pleading for the extension of this, his life's dream and was not prepared to accept that finally they had not listened to him, had allowed the pressures of the accountants and bureaucrats to stifle him, suffocating all the new work in a blanket of figures and debts and political expedients. He knew they had had a phase of the doldrums, when the data-runs from the ship had been empty of promise, but over the last couple of years all that had changed and some of the research coming through had amazed even him. How could they be so stupid as to allow this opportunity to pass them by. Oh, they had taken great pains to assure him that all would not be lost, the computer terminals would be maintained, a basic crew kept on to service the data-run input, the operation would not just be abandoned, but from now on those runs would be sent out across Eura to be developed by unknown scientific establishments already in existence, his own highly trained staff, his own research and work would all be disbanded. And he would not be needed any more.

He poured himself another glass of the sticky banana liqueur which he had become rather too fond of during the years he had spent on the island. Looking round the office he would shortly be vacating he tried to think about the future in a world that seemed to have little use for him, now it was set into a militaristic course of self-destruction. They had offered him various different posts that would allow him to work until his pension became due, but he would be head of none of them and had refused the lot. They could not expect him to become sub-servient again after all these years. His mind turned to thoughts of the two women up in space and he felt anger and resentment pound through his system. How dare they treat him like this, it was all their fault, their lack of concern for his welfare, their lack of dedication to the work he had set them. After all, if it wasn't for him they would never have had this chance. Men would have understood, would have responded to his need. He had sent them so many ideas they could have given the answers to, and all they sent was new types of vegetation, new star patterns that meant little to a world intent on creating ever more productive methods of death. Men would not have done such a thing, would not have become so removed. It was as though they thought themselves somehow superior to him just because they were up there.

He paced the floor, his heart rate building up as waves of self-pity and rage took him through the rest of the bottle.

Franni's red spacesuit bobbed up and down against the pull of her anchor bond as she tried to direct her hand-held camera to catch both the curve of the ship and the distant glow of the sun. They had automatic cameras, but she loved to do them herself, like taking holiday snaps rather than buying ready-made postcards. It had been a good shift and she had felt an urge to go outside that had been lost for a few months. Inside the bubble of her helmet she could hear her own breathing, the air escaping from her mouth, hitting the perspex screen and then sucked back into the oxygenator on her back. Away from the ship, from Vivienne, she concentrated on pulling herself back into an equivalent, tight, close circuit formation, weaving her frayed tiredness so that the worn holes closed up under steel strong mesh. The next shift they would work together would mark a day she had never thought they would reach, she wanted to feel good for it, wanted to be able to control her frustrations, her growing insecurities that were probably worse because of this particular day.

Far ahead the comet drew them along in its trail, like a mother duck who has unknowingly adopted one more duckling that has tagged along after the others for want of another direction. The comet was now headed back towards the great star that held it in thrall. And so they too would turn away from the further reaches of space and begin the long path back to where they could unhitch themselves from the free ride and return to their own mother planet. This was a day they had planned as a celebration of

230

their survival, of the love that had grown between them, a statement to each other and themselves, that they were going to make it home. And now that time had come Franni felt more unsure than she had for months, more unable to deal with the relationship that had created so many possibilities for survival. She tried not to think about it as she drifted above the monitor panels, avoiding looking into the viewers in case Vivienne was already up and about, maybe looking out for her. She took a last photo and made her way back into the air-lock, carefully checking her suit as she relinquished its protection for the thin cotton suit that allowed every contour of her body to show through and waited a few extra moments before re-entering the operations room.

Vivienne was already there, rubbing sleep out of her eyes, sitting at the food, hunched over a cup of tea before starting her program of work for the shift. She had slept heavily, dream-free, but had woken with a stomach full of anxieties and a leadeness in her legs that was making it hard to get into motion. She looked up as Franni came in and stretched out a tired arm towards her. Franni let herself be encircled, wanting the reassurance, even though part of her mind pulled away from the contact.

'Anything to report?'

'Nothing much, a couple of small lurches, nothing the drum couldn't handle.'

'I see you've been out taking snaps, more for the family album!'

'Yes!' Franni laughed, feeling embarrassed, like being caught out, a grown-up playing children's games. She turned out of Vivienne's embrace and replaced the camera in the store above their heads. Vivienne's eyes followed her, taking in the signs of unease, wondering at the sudden flush of shyness that had prickled across the woman's face.

'Would you like a cup before you go off?'

'No, it's okay, I'm pretty tired.'

That wasn't true really and Franni stayed, lingering on the other side of the counter. She wanted to stay and talk, aware that despite herself she had become dependent on this contact, but frightened of where the conversation might lead to.

'I wonder what's going on down there, what's happened to Hartman?'

Vivienne shrugged, since the news of Hartman's removal from the project, his last hysterical tape, she had become aware of how little she had ever valued his presence. As long as they were not completely forgotten, as long as someone was aware of them, even if it was only a computer bank, she didn't really care. It astonished her sometimes that Franni was still going on about it. After all, they had hardly known him before the mission started, and over the last five years his contacts had been more and more infrequent.

'Does it really bother you that much that we don't hear from him anymore?'

Franni sat down awkwardly on the stool opposite her.

'I suppose it does. I don't know why, just the human contact, just someone who's bothered about what happens up here.'

'Isn't it enough that we bother?' There was a thread of acid in Vivienne's response.

'Perhaps for you, you handle things so much better, it's just that I feel like we've been deserted or something.'

'By him! You know what he thought of us, how he treated us! God, we've been through this so many times. As far as he was concerned we were just an experiment, a way to make himself important, a success. He didn't give a damn about how we were, as long as he got his precious data-runs! At least knowing there's only a computer to listen to us, it's clear that's all that is expected, there's no pretence of anything more!'

Franni sat with her head turned away from Vivienne's accusing stare. She didn't want to continue with this, afraid that unspoken feelings might seep out into words, into statements that would lay bare the gripping in her heart that stopped her from letting go of Hartman and what he stood for. Finally, she galvanised herself into escape.

'I know, you're right, I'm just tired, it'll be alright, I must go and get some sleep.' By the time she had finished she was already across the cabin with just a wave of her hand to bid the other woman goodnight.

And Vivienne was left, wondering how you could lose someone so easily even up here, even locked up together for a lifetime. Dreading a return to the madness she had found in isolation, she worked furiously all shift and disappeared to her cubicle before Franni emerged, unwilling to see the face that held such a key into her own time-locked soul.

They met again for their sad celebration of the turning of the orbit. Both worked overtime to keep everything light, to laugh at each other's jokes, be interested by each other's stories, trying to ferret out any last piece of themselves that would appear new and fresh. They let their bodies touch each other with a contrived casualness that could give an illusion of harmony. Franni had cooked a dinner of fresh vegetables with rich sauces and dressings that filled the room with smells of home. Vivienne fetched bottles of wine that served to remind them of another time, another life, when they had got drunk together. And with such effort they managed to find a level between them, a space where they could feel some of the strength of the past. Inevitably, they talked of going home, playing familiar games, about what they would do first of all, what they would eat, where they would like to live. Vivienne recounted her dreams of the open fields, of crops growing where the land was so flat and the sky so big. Of how she would take Franni there and show her the wild flowers that grew on the railway embankments as they streamed out of the city of her youth. And Franni talked about the rocky coastline that had edged her childhood with its beauty and its danger, of watching sea birds screaming in the dark skies, and of her grandfather and his tales of the fishing boats before they had all gone. Each women spun her own story, half remembered experiences laced with imagination and an unspoken homesickness. They never talked much of their later life, of the course that had led them to this point. That was an understanding, a tacit agreement to forget a block of their lives in case, by remembering, they felt a responsibility for where they had got to. To each it was as though a wave had swept them up from the arms of a forgotten mother and out into space, and now that same wave was pulling them back on an ebb tide to be left like foundlings on the beach.

They stayed together for endless time, eating, drinking, sleeping stretched out on the foam loungers in the operations room, unwilling to give up on this game where they dealt carefully with each other, avoiding areas that might cause pain, allowing the effects of the alcohol to dull their consciousness that something had changed, while the slow effect of the turn of the orbit took its course and the ship began to move back into the heart of the solar system.

Finally and slowly they surfaced to take stock of

234

themselves, a little more ready to deal with the shifting of their world. Vivienne was the first to feel the need to move back into a present reality, taking herself off for a shower so she could let the water wash away accumulated sweat and grime and allow her skin to breathe clean again. She sat in the chamber wrapped in a towel, letting the water drip off her hair onto her bare shoulders as she held Franni secure between her thighs still half asleep in a world of nostalgia. She ran her hands down over the woman's face and onto her shoulders, giving her a gentle shake.

'Come on, Franni, we've got to do some work.'

'Why?' answered Franni sleepily. 'What's the point?'

'Because, because the animals must be attended to, and the plants, and all your precious spatials. You know that, we've still got a long way to go.'

Franni pulled herself up and turned round to face her.

'Do you still think we're going to make it back to earth?'

Vivienne laughed and reached forward to kiss her lightly.

'Of course! What else is there that I can think. I thought we'd never make it this far without either me going completely crazy or you taking an axe to me, so it seems we can if we want to.'

Franni blushed with the memory of how she used to feel about Vivienne and clambered to her feet.

'You know, I still feel funny about Hartman and all that.'

'Yes, I know. There doesn't seem much I can do about it, does there?' she replied, with a mixture of resignation and fondness. 'I don't understand it, I don't think I ever will, but as long as it doesn't make us row or whatever, I'll just have to put up with it, after all it's your problem.'

'But I want you to understand, maybe it's because you don't that, well, that things have changed between us.'

Franni could have kicked herself, she had fallen into the fatal trap of allowing the words to come out, to admit something she didn't want to deal with, and after they had spent such a good time together. As she waited for Vivienne's response the logic of her old position, that communication was dangerous, that emotional space must be guarded day and night came flooding back to her. She turned her back on the other woman and stood in front of the viewer panel, her knuckles white as she gripped the steel edge of the console. Why couldn't she have just kept it in, maybe things would have come right in their own time. The silence between them hung heavy, loaded, like a thunderstorm that is unwilling to break.

'Maybe, maybe you're right. But things have always changed, will always change, we can only go with the roll of it.' Vivienne pushed her drying hair out of her eyes, trying to find her balance before some unknown vortex sucked her in. She could hardly see Franni, she seemed so far away, a speck in space.

'My God! Are we so helpless! Do we have to live our lives at the whim of this fucking spaceship, spinning through every different variation on one insane theme until it decides we will be released? Can't we decide what we want and then just do it!'

'It seems like the problem is we don't know what we want. For a while we wanted each other and that was enough, but maybe it just blocked out everything else, now it's not enough anymore, but we can't go back to how things were and I don't know where to go from here.'

Franni stared out into space, straining her eyes

to pick up any sign of the planet they had come from. Dreaming in her head of a little sunny island where at least one human being had sat and waited for them, listened to them with whatever hatred in his heart. Now he was gone and she was still here, locked up for another ten years with a woman who had become everything to her and all she wanted to do was get away from her and her madness.

'I just want to go home.'

Vivienne let her head drop back, feeling the skin on her neck stretch out the wrinkles that had crept in over the years. She could not help Franni, could not comfort her, could only sit and watch her shoulders shake with stifled crying until Franni tore herself away from the panel and disappeared into her cubicle. She stayed sitting on the floor after Franni had gone, idly running the towel over her hair, letting her eyes take in all the familiar details of her surroundings, running her fingers across the floor. Examining the minute layer of dust that clung to her skin, clogging the tiny pores as it mixed with the last lingering drops of water from her shower. She did not know what was expected of her except to survive. She did not know anymore whether the love she felt for Franni was just a means of survival or something more. And if it was just survival what then? Should she go to her, try and comfort her, let her own irritation with this drama about Hartman stay within her skin, do anything to reassure the other woman so that she could reassure herself and stay alive? And if it was more than just about survival what did that mean, about herself, about the life she had led up until the mission? If they did get back to earth what would happen then? Would they just go their separate ways, rolling with the change of things down there or could they make it different. Was Franni right after all, was rolling just surviving?

The next few months passed by with no further reference either to their relationship or the possibilities of going home. They had both learned to use their work as a way round confrontation or communication and so their work went well. Vivienne spent most of her shifts either down with the animals or bent over her microscope in front of a table covered with boxes of test tubes and slides. She was working on a series of new vaccines and had little time to observe what Franni was doing, although she registered the growing pile of computer printout that was building up on her desk beside the spatial controls. Sometimes she felt the urge to ask her about it, wished Franni would volunteer the information, but she was too afraid of unsettling this precarious equilibrium.

For her part, Franni had become totally locked into her research and had rediscovered her ability to shut out any interference, either from Vivienne, or from herself. She knew she was on the verge of some kind of discovery, an explanation for something that had plagued their trip and, like a child that will not show her mother the home-made toy she has made until it is finished and can be presented with triumph, she kept herself secret from her companion. And when it was done she felt only fear for the reality.

She looked up from the fat wodge of printout on her desk to where Vivienne was just emerging from the shaft having given the animals their feed before going off duty.

'Vivienne, can you wait a minute, I think I've got something here we both need to take a look at.'

She beckoned Vivienne to join her at the main console and started unravelling the streams of paper.

'What is it, Franni? I'm really tired. Can't it wait until next changeover?'

238

'No it can't. I think I've worked it out but I need to explain it through just to confirm things in my own head.'

She started pushing different discs into the computer input slot and waited while the different programs she had set up were digested by the memory and flashed up on the screen.

Vivienne was not as familiar as Franni with the finer points of space computer science, the construction of spatials had become a speciality for the other woman, but she knew enough to begin to follow what these different tests and calculations were leading to.

'You're talking about the lurches aren't you, this is an explanation of what is causing them!'

'Yes, exactly. I've been thinking along these lines for years, but there was no proof and I could never get Hartman to take it on seriously and do the research down there that would have speeded the whole process up.'

She looked up at Vivienne and grinned suddenly, 'I know, don't say it, I didn't really need him in the first place! But listen Vivienne, if this is true, if this really is the cause of gravity lurches well, then it must mean that there's a chance everything just goes through!'

Vivienne sat back, trying to sort out all the data in her own mind, listening while Franni went through it again and again, thrusting different papers at her that backed up different features of her observations and experiments. She had to get it clear before she could start thinking about the consequences. The gravity lurches had dogged their footsteps ever since the mission began. For years they had done tests on the ship, questioning the workings of the equi-drum and the gyros that held the ship in balance as it swung round on its own axis. Hartman had followed up their tests on the island, building identical models to try and create the same situation, they had got nowhere. Then had come the doldrums when they had done little work and simply refined their equipment to deal with the lurches so that as little disturbance as necessary was caused. Part of her had got so used to them she hardly cared any more what caused them. And now it seemed that Franni had found the answer. And that answer was in itself so simple it almost seemed amazing they had not hit on it before.

'You do see, Vivienne, don't you. It's just like we're on the end of a firework, that's why it keeps happening. We just keep travelling along behind a comet that is spewing out x amount of matter and gases that are burning out and at the point that they do they just explode and then implode, pushing a hole in space, a pinprick, that just for those few minutes can pull in whatever happens to be passing at the time, like us for example. We don't go through because the hole isn't big enough, the pull isn't strong enough. It's like driving over a pothole, you don't disappear but you feel the dip that rocks the suspension.'

'But surely that phenomenon only happens with stars, the creation of black holes.'

'Yes, of course it does. But with such an implosion the hole is going to be huge and the pull that much stronger, lasting that much longer, so we can pick them up on our equipment down on earth. And comets are still such an unknown quantity, we couldn't do such detailed research on them without being up here and part of one. These miniscule holes wouldn't even register back on earth.'

'Are you saying, then, that any matter that explodes in space will reverse its pull and create a hole?'

'I don't know, I'm not sure at this stage, maybe

it's peculiar to comet trails. But I don't see why not, the actual mechanics should apply to anything.'

'So, if we blew up, for example, would that create a lurch for any debris behind us?'

'I think so, we'd create enough of a pull to take not only the ship through but maybe,' Franni feverishly pressed the computer keyboard, 'maybe seven or eight minutes of anything that was that close behind us.'

'And if anything ahead of us blew, that was sufficiently larger in mass than us, then we'd be pulled through instead of just having a bumpy ride.'

'Exactly!'

The two women looked at each other. Franni switched off the program and went to make them both a cup of tea. They were both unsure how to handle this new information, how to get to grips with the possible futures it held out to them. By common consent they both sat at the viewing panel that faced the way ahead, where on the far edge of the screen they could see the glow of the comet's head burning through space, as though at any minute they would be sucked away almost as a punishment for finding out that it was possible.

'And what would happen if we were sucked through?' Vivienne reached out for Franni's hand as though, if it were going to happen, she wanted no chance of facing it alone.

'I don't know, I don't think anybody does. Almost certainly you'd just be crushed out of existence, maybe you come out on the other side of the universe and start again, maybe you come out in a different universe altogether. God, Vivienne, how can we know that!'

'I suppose we should send the data-runs back to earth, even a computer would be interested in this, perhaps they could extend the research on earth and give us more information on the possibilities!'

Vivienne nodded but gave no response. She felt a chill in her bones that had not hit her since she had thought Franni was lost out in space. All these years she had worried about the lurches, dreamt they would suck her down to her death, but in her heart she had always hoped it had been a gyro fault, and one they had seemed to have conquered. Now she had to re-think, to accept that the course they were heading on took them on an endless chase, dodging whirlpools, always on the verge of suicide. Now every time a lurch occurred she would have to stop herself from waving her life goodbye.

Franni was held enthralled by her own discovery, it was the best piece of scientific research she had ever done. When they got home she would be famous, her mind raced on, all those scientists who had scoffed at the work that could be done by two women on this mission, now they would have to eat their words, if they were still alive of course by the time the women returned. The thought of being caught by such a trap didn't register with her except as a scientific possibility, and on that level there was even a part of her that longed for such a thing to happen, a child who wants to die to see if it's all true, but reserves the right to come back to life afterwards. She felt awed by the enormity of it but her eyes were wide open with the wonder of all the new questions that were spewing out of space as every minute passed.

During the weeks that followed Franni ironed out all the technical flaws in her report and prepared the data-run for earth. Vivienne helped her with the back-up she could provide even if it were only an ear which questioned different propositions. They worked together well, personal problems were dwarfed by this new enormity and the old familiarity seeped back into their blood almost without their noticing. Franni had so warmed to the work, she had the energy again to comfort Vivienne through the nightmares that had returned to haunt her sleep. They no longer talked of going home and the spectre of Hartman faded into the background as Franni's confidence surged, as she saw herself as the centre of this research. And although Vivienne found it hard to quell the panic in her stomach every time the ship slipped into the familiar pit, she could not help but be caught by Franni's perpetual enthusiasm and so be lifted back into the safety of her arms.

'I think I'll start calling them Franni lurches,' she giggled one night as they lay, bodies wrapped round each other on the narrow lounger.

'Oh, shit, no, sounds like some kind of chocolate bar! Or a new make of sanitary towel!'

'Or maybe a particular kind of sexual deviation found only among women astronauts!' Vivienne laughed and bent her head down to kiss one of the two soft nipples that were rising to meet her.

In due course they sent the data-run back to earth and waited with growing excitement for the response. As weeks went by and there was nothing except the normal message that the run had been received and was being examined, they fell back to playing scrabble and cards while outside space drifted past the viewing panels, endlessly uncaring.

RE-ENTRY

Diary Extract V.R.

It seems like Franni was right after all. Without Hartman no one on earth seems to care about what is happening up here. We haven't had any proper reports for months and months and it seems to have killed off once and for all any desire to do useful work. I thought I could just do it for my own pleasure but the kinds of things I have been trained to do need someone else's approval to give me any value. Franni tries to be interested, but I know she feels the same, so it's just like a short circuit, if we can't value our own work, how can we value each other's. The strange thing is, I don't feel like I have to go back to the stagnation I went through five years ago, I seem to be able to do other things that do feel good to me. I've started painting and drawing, something I haven't done since I was at primary school, before they realised I had a 'talent' for sciences and it's amazing how many things I can think of to paint, both from within the ship and out of my own imagination. Also I've been trying to get this diary into some more useful form, leafing through the bits I've written makes me wonder what anyone else would make of it, such an assortment of ramblings.

I feel a sense of calm at the moment though I know too well now how quickly that can all change. I've got used to the knowledge about the gravity lurches and although they still frighten me much more than Franni I don't feel such an urgency to escape from that possibility anymore. She spent hours and hours showing me how unlikely it was we would hit a big one, given where we are in the comet's tail, and without any panic messages from earth I can only assume that it's not that much to worry about. She spends all her time reading up literature on black holes, delving back into early theories that such black holes could exist, despite the problems of low mass and gravity strength. As far as I can understand the finer details, we just have to trust that the gravity pull of our ship and of the orbit we are in, outweighs the strength of the pull into these minute fractures in space. In my sleep I dream dreams of going through endless black man-holes but always wake before I know what lies on the other side, or even if another side exists. But they are not nightmares, it seems just an extension of rolling through this time, this life, of creating another theory that will allow me to survive. And Franni and I seem to have rolled through into another phase of existence that feels possible and pleasurable. Maybe we're just getting older, more willing to accept each other while more confident of ourselves. Fifteen years is an eternity to spend with one other person and we have had to learn the hard way that despite our necessary dependence, we must at least try and allow ourselves to be free, separate, to create gaps where personal idiosyncrasies can develop, unfettered by self-made bonds.

When we're back on earth I don't know what will happen. I wonder if we will just appear like crazies to them, a lot of things can happen in twenty years and we have been kept so ignorant of the world as it is now. I doubt we could survive long without each other, although sometimes I think maybe after all this we will be better equipped to go on to something else alone than ever before.

When I think about how I was at the outset, all that dedication and ambition linked to such insecurity and fear, I can no longer picture how I am now, but I can see that there have been so many changes that it is inevitable more will follow.

Diary Extract F.D.

The more I go into this new discovery about the lurches the more there seems to be to astound me. I find it hard to think about anything else and even though earth seems amazingly disinterested I can't stop sending off data-runs and requests for information in the hope that one day they will answer our call. The silence from earth frightens me, we've never gone so long without some form of contact and it makes me wonder what is going on down there that such revolutionary research can be ignored so easily.

As far as I can see, each time we hit a lurch we are reaching the horizon of a tiny hole but we are able to skate past it, using the strength of the ship's own pull and that of our orbit, so we do not get sucked right in. I have tried to compute what effect that might be having on our time dimension. Are these continual brushes with the limits of physical time going to create a relative lengthening of our lives in comparison with the continuum down on earth? But without relative data from earth, and the limits of the technology up here, I can't get very far with this.

As far as our life up here is concerned, we seem to be able to avoid most of our personally inspired black holes at the present. I thought I was going to withdraw back into myself because of the pressure of Vivienne's fears following the discovery of what was causing the lurches. For a while I found those huge eyes following me round the ship, asking for some kind of reassurance, intensely irritating, but instead of cutting off I just laugh at her and make her laugh at herself which seems to relieve both of us sufficiently to carry on. We still sleep together sometimes, allowing a spasm of energy to carry us along into a state where we can forget everything except the touch and feel of our bodies. But it seems like this part of our lives has become an orbiting moon rather than the central sun of our existence. When the tide pulls we go with it, but it no longer gives

246

off the brilliance it once did, it is instead illuminated by the light of fifteen years of familiarity and companionship.

As earth grows imperceptibly larger on our screens I cannot help but think more realistically about our return, as though some emotional gravitational force is already reaching out its fingers towards me. I daydream about every different kind of return, jubilant, desperate, unwanted, we are heroines one day, outcasts the next. I cannot think about a separation between us and wonder what that will mean, given social goals at home. But then twenty years is a long time and maybe things will have changed for the better. Maybe we will be allowed to retire to some seaside retreat where I can teach her to fish and she can keep rabbits in the garden. A sweet thought, but I am only too aware of my ability to romanticise, and up here twenty years is just spit against a tidal wave of time.

Hotel El Pacifico
Gran Canaria

Dear Sandra,

I can't believe that things would have come to this. That you would threaten to throw me out just because of some paltry bill that according to your, dare I say, questionable accounting, I have run up over the last few months. I have surely explained quite clearly that I have resources, that the council promised to pay me the miserable pension they offered which would more than meet this amount. After all the years we have known each other I find it hard that you could have become so calculating and unfeeling to someone who has always given you so much appreciation in the past. Surely you make enough profit out of the stream of locals that frequent this place to allow one old colleague to stay in this apology for a hotel and consume the odd glass of liqueur and bowl of salad and bread.

I would be the first to admit that times are hard, that there is no value in credit any more, but surely you must appreciate my position. I cannot leave this godforsaken island because I believe any day now they may need me back on the mountain to run the mission again and I must be ready. As a person who was once so important to the smooth running of the mission I am confident that once reminded of these particular circumstances you will withdraw my notice to quit forthwith.

I look forward to hearing from you at your earliest convenience.

Yours sincerely,

Robert Hartman

Hartman held the crumpled remains of his letter in his hands, seeing only the scrawled letters across the neat typing, 'forget it'. That was all she had written, and then had got the odious Pablo to bring it back along with a battered old suitcase for his few possessions and a look that told him only too clearly that his room would have to be vacated tonight.

Pablo stood in the room waiting for an answer, enjoying every minute of this triumph over a man he had despised ever since he had first come to the island. He knew, Sandra knew, even Hartman knew, that it was all over now and yet it seemed all the more reason to achieve those little victories over any representation of that race of men who had brought such destruction.

'Can I help you pack, Senor?' he asked, enjoying the play-acting that he was still subservient to this drunken fool. Hartman simply turned his back and sat down heavily on the creaking springs of the iron-frame bed.

I'll come back later to carry your things down-stairs, Senor.'

Hartman could hear his heavy laughter as he went out banging the door and clumping down the stairs to the bar. She would be down there, he thought, sitting behind the bar like some lady of the manor, issuing her directives to ruin the lives of men like him. To have let himself get into the clutches of such a woman, that had been his great mistake. It was all her fault, she had left him for no reason and was now wreaking some illogical feminine revenge on him. Well, he would go, she would not see him defeated. He would go back to the mountain, to the observatory where he would control his mission, his project that was now reaching its ultimate success as the re-entry year grew nearer. And then they would all see what he had achieved in spite of them.

First of all, he drank the remains of the bottle of brandy he had 'borrowed' from the bar. He needed the strength, a man in his position deserved it, but even though the brandy was rich and fiery, it did not stop his hands shaking as he packed the few clothes he had not sold and the dog-eared files they had let him take from the mountain. He made his way down the stairs and through the bar, ignoring the sniggers and prying looks of the locals and the steely glare of the harridan sitting on her stool. Then he was out in the dark safety of the alleyway. He turned his back on the village and began walking unsteadily upwards to where the alley became a narrow dirt road that would take him to the mountains.

He had only gone a couple of miles when the support of the alcohol failed him and he collapsed under a fading palm tree, gazing up at the stars with unfocused eyes. Without any further supplies he could not stem off the advent of soberness, could not control the shaking of his limbs or the nightmares that his brain concocted for him, and finally could not shake off facing the unbearable reality. It was all over, not just for him but for everyone on this nightmare island, everyone everywhere. Eura council had not met for months, the military had taken over and even as he sat there listening to the hot summer winds blowing through the palm above his head he knew there were matter reactors exploding elsewhere. M/Rs that would carry darkness and poison across the globe with a speed that would leave every soul gasping its life out in shock. Across the sky he could trace the flashing light of a probe till it disappeared over the horizon. He wanted to laugh, thinking it might be one of the escape ships that he should have been on, they should have taken him with them, he could not believe their foolishness in leaving him behind.

And further out, beyond where his bloodshot eyes could reach, he knew they were there. He wanted to reach out and shake them, make them see him, acknowledge him and what he had done for them. He hated them, those women that were surviving without him, uncaring, heartless. Tears of rage flowed down his alcohol-worn face and mixed with the radiated dust that was already settling on the island of his death. Exhausted, he curled up in the ditch by the road and closed his eyes.

'Jesus! Franni, wake up, you've got to wake up!' Vivienne had to shake the other woman to pull her out of sleep. She dragged her out of the bunk and pulled her, ignoring her sleepy protestations, up the ladder and into the operations room. Franni's eyes squashed up as she was met with a brilliance that seemed to blind her and she staggered away from

Vivienne in an effort to find her balance and grow accustomed to the unexpected light. All the viewing screens were down and it appeared on one of them that they had discovered a new star, a yellow/red disc that filled one of the screens and outshone any other body in space.

'What the fuck's going on? What's that?' She stared at the screen, then away as she felt the light burn into her eyes.

'It's earth, it's gone, blown, destroyed, finished!' Vivienne was nearly hysterical, running round the room playing with every panel she could lay her hands on in an attempt to make the computer change what they were seeing, make it into a nightmare that they could wake up from.

'What do you mean, it's earth? It can't be earth, it can't just blow up! My God it's a planet, planets don't just blow up! There must be something wrong with the viewer, the magnification must be wrong, it's probably just some little meteor fizzling out somewhere!' Franni was rooted to the spot, her mind whirring with alternative explanations.

'Vivienne, don't you understand, it just can't be earth, it just can't be!'

'But it is. They must have done something down there, triggered off a gravitational collapse in a nuclear holocaust or something. We're already picking up a huge wave of blast reaction and I don't know if the blocks will take the strain. I've plotted it out and it's the only possibility, you've got to help me fix up the final blocks before anymore hits us!'

As she spoke, she grabbed Franni's elbow and pulled her, yanking her out of paralysis and shoving her in the direction of the rear block controls.

'You finish getting those into position while I check on the forward ones. Hurry, we don't have much time!'

Franni uncoiled like a spring and shot into action, suspending her incredulity until the lead shields were in place and the ship a fortress against the invisible onslaught. For the following days they did little more than monitor the radiation, check on blocks that seemed to be holding and grab something to eat only when real hunger overcame their concentration. They left the screens down so they could watch this sudden new star burn so brightly and then, almost imperceptibly, begin to fade. The waves of the blast swept past them, moving out into deep space, till their dying ripples were absorbed into the huge ocean of background radiation. And then they did nothing, could do nothing, moved like zombies around the ship keeping the bare essentials going, saying nothing, thinking nothing, like robots with blind eyes unable to absorb the new program. When they were tired, they simply sat in front of the screens staring out at the fire that was eating up their world. When they slept it was brief, empty, unfulfilling, leaving them even more removed, vacant.

As time passed without record, clouds of dust drifted over them obscuring the screen. In the specks they saw leaves and trees, earth, buildings, flowers, cars, bricks, mountains. Each saw her own future, her own past blow past on space winds and evaporate.

Few words were exchanged, only that which had to be said in order to keep the ship fixed on its course, still turned back into the orbit that would take them back to nothing. They returned to sleeping in their cubicles, but alone, always alone as if any human contact would only cause a further fatal explosion. And outside the flame that had flared so proudly, burnt so brilliantly, was now fading into a dull glow, an ember in space that would soon be forgotten, that would have hardly registered on the master plan that ruled the destinies of every star and planet across the universe. Just one small globe that had upset the routine, disturbed the natural order for a moment, before time and space pulled it back into rhythm. And they, who had begun to feel themselves a part of that rhythm, they simply took on the mentality of space and worked on without any conscious choice, carrying out tasks set, filling forms, building data-runs, feeding animals and plants, plotting their course and counting the years till they would be home. There was a sense drifting through the ship that this routine was now set for eternity, that time had held still and they would simply move on without making any further mark on it. A sense that might have held them in thrall for a lifetime, had the unexpected and urgent buzzing of the computer receiver control not created a shift that pulled first Vivienne and then Franni out of their slow-motion existence and back into the world of sound, reaction, action, where time passed and all things changed.

The alarm had been built into the computer to alert the astronauts if they had not properly received a message from base. Hartman had joked that they might be asleep and miss his birthday, they had laughed. It had never been used, in the past they knew when the transmissions were due and over the last years there had been none. Now that it was whining out, its pitch rising until the noise filled the ship, it took them a few minutes to respond.

'Franni, do you realise what that is?'

Vivienne stood in front of the computer, studying the dials as though she had never seen them before. Franni nodded and blocked her ears to try and drown out the sound. The computer maintained its deafening attempt to get the women to pay it some attention, like a child in the night whose inarticulate crying slowly rises into screams before its parents are forced to answer the call.

'Christ! Can you do something about the noise? I can't stand it.' Franni crouched down below the level of the controls, burying her head in her hands.

'If I do, that means I'll have to switch it on. We'll have to listen to what it says.'

'Just stop that noise, do anything you like!' Franni was screaming to make herself heard.

Vivienne let her fingers rest on the income switch, feeling her skin vibrate against the metal as the whine flooded through her system. At the other end of that switch was a message from the dead, a connection to hell, a tape from a planet that no longer existed. She felt the tiny muscle in her hand flex as her pressure built up on the shiny rounded tip of the switch.

'Vivienne! Do it! Just do it!'

Franni's face was covered with sweat, her head exploding as the tone of the alarm met the tone of her own madness and swept her into a pit of pain and rage. She swung an arm out at Vivienne, triggering her into action, letting her finger flick the switch with a sudden surety that dissolved into silent panic as the noise stopped dead and was replaced by the preliminary buzz and click as the tape moved into position and prepared itself to play.

They sat on the floor, cross-legged, like schoolchildren, mouths open, eyes fixed on the receiver control, picking up the tiny movement of the tape as it started to reel off.

Report to Operation Eden

Launch + 15yrs

Final Transmission   Comet 1 Feeding In

Confirmation of data-runs received.
Data absorbed and computed.
Results support Eden conclusion. Inform-

ation fed to appropriate data banks on
mainline Eura connection.
Recommend highest scientific award to F.D.
Recommend highest scientific award to V.R.

****

**TRANSMIT DATA FROM EURA COUNCIL.
SWITCH ON INPUT THREE.**

Vivienne leaned forward and pressed the panel that
would record the rest straight into the computer
process disc. They turned their empty faces to
the screen.

EURA COUNCIL REPORT TO
OPERATION EDEN

Following the scientific reports contained in
data-runs 8/5289 and 8/5290, the results
of which have been thoroughly examined
and counter-researched by the top astro-
physics laboratories in Eura who have
confirmed the results and accepted the
challenge involved for known astro-
physics, Eura Council has great pleasure
in conferring the Order of the Golden
Star Cluster to Dr Vivienne Redna and
Dr Frances Duke.

The Council unites in sending its applause
to both astronauts and looks forward to
their return so that they may extend their
gratitude personally.

However, in the meantime, Eura Council
greatly regrets that due to more pressing
problems the main computer banks on
Gran Canaria must be harnessed to another
cause. The main observatory will stay on
tracking beam until such time as computer
contact can be resumed.

Eura Council trusts that the achievements started by this major discovery will be further developed on earth and that the two astronauts will be reassured by the confidence this Council places in them.

****

INPUT 3 CLOSED
GO TO END PROGRAM

The computer flicked them neatly into 'F'.

END PROGRAM

CLOSE-DOWN INPUTS 1/2/3
CLOSE-DOWN OUTPUT 5
TRANSFER TRACKING TO MAIN BEAM ONLY
SWITCH BACK TO MAIN PROGRAM
DISCONNECT

****

The computer buzzed and whirred, as though in its own brain it wondered at this severance, unknowing that its connection to its master computer had already been ripped away with a savagery that held none of the subtleties of its own language. Quietly, efficiently it shut down on all its links with earth until a complete panel of familiar lights faded out and the unwanted discs were refiled. Then the reels stopped and it sat back to continue with more familiar tasks.

Franni was the first to break the silence, overcome by a sudden fit of laughter that echoed round the room.

'Oh shit! the Golden Star Cluster! My God, Vivienne, I used to dream that one day I might do something good enough to get that! It was a dream, a dream! And now I could award it to myself anyway, make it out of silver paper and glue!' She marched up and down the room, mocking out an award, bowing to her reflection in the mirror, chanting the award speech so fast it became a gibberish, and collapsed hysterical beside Vivienne. 'And you too, my love, they gave you one too! Think of that, you can go and show it to the guinea pigs, I'm sure they'd be impressed. Now you're Dr Vivienne Redna G.S.C., they'll have to take more notice of you, jump to attention in their little cages whenever you go and clean out their shit!'

'But how did this tape get here? After so long?' Vivienne had not listened to a word of Franni's ramblings, still lost in the screen as though it was not really over, as though the contact would suddenly be resumed. She turned to the viewing screens, peering out into the blackness, as though between the pinpricks of stars she would find the blue-green planet still following its tiny orbit round the sun, still waiting for their triumphant return. Franni followed her and held onto her arms from behind, holding her close with the strength of urgency, fear and a love that was all that was left, feeling Vivienne pulling away, out into the madness that had always haunted her as two different realities collided, creating supanovas in her brain.

'Listen to me Vivienne, I don't know why it was so long. Maybe there was a delay in the transmission, God knows what's been going on down there over the last few years. Maybe the computer here had it for ages but just had more important stuff to deal with. After all, it's only been the last few days that we could actually stop and rest without worrying about the blast effects.'

'But Hartman would have told us. I know he would, he would have made them listen. They couldn't have done this, couldn't have let it happen, not while we were up here.' Vivienne's voice was

cracking, near to tears, near to screams as all the
nightmares came back and she struggled to free herself from Franni's grip. She pushed her elbow back
violently into the other woman's stomach and
wrenched herself away, leaving Franni doubled up
coughing, and made a dash to the exit chamber,
dragging her spacesuit down off the rack and forcing
her body into it. Franni pulled herself painfully
upright and then threw herself across the room to
try and stop her, hearing only the hiss of the vacuum
motor starting as Vivienne sealed the door against her.

Franni wasted valuable minutes fumbling to re-
program the lock controls to reverse the system so
that by the time she was in her own suit, Vivienne
was gone.

Outside she forced herself to check the levels
before starting the search. The ship was well protected
against excess radiation, their suits were not. The dial
was well up, nudging against the red band. They had
a few minutes before the creeping legacy of earth
would penetrate, but only a few. She started jetting
around the ship sweeping round to pick up the
familiar yellow flash of Vivienne's suit. She didn't
dare think about failure, about being truly the only
one left. And yet she knew that Vivienne was crazy
enough to do anything, to simply jet out until there
was no power left, to die in that space she had so
loved and hated. She counted the minutes left before
she too would be committing suicide by continuing.
Five minutes left. They had been up there for years
on end and now there was only five minutes to make
thing alright. Five minutes to think and say all the
things she had left in her head. It was just not enough
time. She tried to think where Vivienne might have
gone. If she had just drifted away it was too late to
do anything about it, she must work logically, as
she had always done. Hartman, she had talked of

Hartman, maybe she was trying to reach him? She suddenly changed direction and shot up above the main rim to where the high dome of the ship turned gently on its axis. And she found Vivienne huddled round the aerial, her hands in a vice-like grip on its main extensor, her visor misted with tears as her voice mouthed soundless messages into the metal.

It took her all her strength to get Vivienne back into the ship and out of the suit. Vivienne was babbling continuously, hitting out at her until Franni managed to get her to swallow a mouthful of sleepers before she took some herself and let drugged exhaustion overcome everything.

When she woke it was with that heaviness that sleepers left behind. She wasn't sure what had happened, what was happening. Everything seemed normal, Vivienne was making breakfast at the counter. Franni watched her cautiously as she poured out the hot tea with a seemingly steady hand. Feigning sleep she allowed Vivienne's call to her to go unanswered so that the other woman had to come over to her and shake her gently, calling her name. Only then did she let her eyes open properly to meet the gaze of those large brown eyes.

'I've made some tea, do you want some?' Vivienne's voice sounded normal, Franni sat up, pulling the blanket round her shoulders.

'Yes, thanks.'

Franni took the cup and cradled it in her hands, letting the steam warm her face. Vivienne returned to the counter and sat drinking her own tea, her head bent over some papers she was reading. Everything seemed so ordinary. Franni shook her head trying to get the lingering effects of the sleepers out of her brain. Draping the blanket round her body, she went over to sit in her usual place across the counter.

'Are you okay Vivienne?'

'Yes, of course, why shouldn't I be?'

'Well, after, after what happened before we slept.' Franni felt as though she was walking gingerly through a minefield.

'After what happened?'

Vivienne's eyes examined her quizzically, wondering at this woman. So much had happened, maybe Franni had begun to imagine things. She was always so logical, so practical, in the face of all this, maybe something had snapped.

'Vivienne! You must remember. You went outside, you tried to reach Hartman! I had to get you back in, I thought you'd gone for good!'

Vivienne put down the papers and rested her smooth forearms on the counter. She laughed and stretched a hand out to stroke the curve of Franni's face, fascinated again by the turn of the woman's jaw, the tiny lines that radiated out from the corners of her eyes and melted into her hair.

'Oh no my dear! That was a trick you played on me a long time ago, don't you remember. I spent ages looking for you and thinking you had disappeared off on your own trip, until I found you just stargazing. I wouldn't do such a thing to you, I know what it feels like. You must have just dreamt it after taking all those sleepers, I wondered why you'd taken so many, though I suppose it's understandable in this crazy situation.'

Franni felt lost, frightened of this woman like she had been in the old days. She jumped up from her seat and went into the exit chamber to find both their spacesuits hung neatly on their hooks showing no sign of having been used. She took her helmet down off the shelf and sat on the floor, hugging it in her lap. Had Vivienne gone to the trouble of covering the whole thing up, tidying up any sign of the struggle she remembered so clearly. Or had she

260

dreamt the whole thing, was she crazy as well?

Vivienne stayed in her place at the counter, worrying about what to do next. She never knew quite how to handle Franni when she was like this, so different from the down-to-earth cynical foil to her own dreaminess she had grown to love. Perhaps that was it. There was no earth anymore, nothing for Franni to root in, so now she was just drifting. She went over to try and comfort her, but Franni evaded her arm and disappeared into her cubicle. Vivienne heard the rasp as the bolt went home.

And out beyond their spinning insanity the infinitely vaster forces of space began to reassert themselves against one unimportant upset in a lesser part of one small galaxy. And in that corner of the galaxy a few easily forgotten planets continued their unhurried progress around the star that was their life-giver, turning in orbit with no memory of a flash in time that no longer existed. The dust of rock, the energy of matter, drifted out to be swept up into other, greater orbits, into storm winds that would carry it far out till it was swamped by time and space.

Slowly the fractures healed and a new reality existed outside and with a seeping power flowed in through the ship to the souls of the two who were left. They drifted carelessly round each other, waiting until their own orbits had settled down again, before they could look beyond to what was their future in this new time. They grew used to madness, to the mixture of dream and reality where they might one day discover a new earth on the screen, hear the sound of Hartman's voice on the tape, and another where all was silent and they could do no more than listen to the tapping of their own heartbeats. They learnt not to question the other's reality, knowing it would change from time to time. Bending in and out of each other's dreams and nightmares they could only give solace, give the physical touch that proved only their existence, their survival. And slowly, like snowflakes settling in a glass ornament, a new picture came clear that they could both stand and watch together, seeing the same thing. And the picture was death.

They found it together, cautiously starting to work again to give some substance to their lives, some shape to their world, they began the routine of scientific study of the new phenomena. Measuring the amount of matter that had been blown apart, the strength of the radiation that had bathed the ship, a spark of understanding of what the mission had discovered, flickered and burnt bright in both their minds until their eyes could meet in recognition. Franni could not speak the words she knew Vivienne was thinking, but the routine took over, and she typed them gently onto a new data-run.

PROBABLE RESULT OF EARTH EXPLOSION

Immediate wave of radiation — Ship's defences OK

Following wave of dust / small meteors — Ship's defences OK

Gravitational backpull leading to creation of small black hole — Mass 4.9352

Strength of pull creating event horizon at distance 98867.

Position of ship's orbit path — 47629

Time until arrival at event horizon — 725 hours.

She pushed the keyboard over to Vivienne who read what was written and deleted one word. The word was probable. Franni fed the run into the computer and asked only one question: evasion possibilities. The computer flicked its inner switches up and down as it digested the data and looked at the question. Weighing up the forces of a dying planet, intent on its own digestion against the tiny amount of fuel that could be used to attempt an evasion, the computer seemed scornful in its reply.

EVASION POSSIBILITIES – NIL

It asked for any further questions, any further information, but as there were none it clicked back into the monitor program and fed the disc neatly back out into Franni's hand.

She handled the disc carefully, as though within its smooth plastic shell it contained the thin grasp they held on life.

'That means we've had it doesn't it?'

Vivienne nodded mutely, feeling the blast of Franni's breath hit her face like a hurricane as she spoke, making her turn away to shelter from so crude an assessment. In a sudden rage, Franni hurled the disc at the computer, irritation overcoming her, as it failed to do more than give a hollow rattle as it bounced off the board and clattered across the floor.

'I don't believe it! How could they have been so stupid! They always knew what the risks were, just like children left to play with fireworks!'

She was hammering the viewing screens with her fists, railing out her fury to the dead perpetrators of the murder of her world, her eyes wild with hatred, red for revenge, hollow with despair.

'I thought they had learnt! I thought that was why they sent us out here; so the world could expand!' Franni grabbed hold of Vivienne's collar and was shouting in her face.

'He told us didn't he! Hartman told us years

ago. They got rid of nuclear weapons, they listened to the people, saw the sense of it. He told us, I remember. He couldn't have been lying! Not to us!'

Vivienne tried to untangle Franni's fingers.

'Yes, Franni, he did. And it was probably true.' She turned back to the screen. 'But you know what they're like. They would always have just invented something better. In fact I doubt they did disarm from nuclear weapons till they had something else. It was always so sick, we just didn't realise down there.'

'But they shouldn't have! They shouldn't have! I wanted to go home! I wanted to be with them!'

'And they left us behind.' Vivienne's voice was quiet, lost. A child who has missed out on something, however awful, because she had been forgotten. She remembered a time long ago when she had been a student on placement in a station far away from her home. There had been one of those war scares and she had rushed to pack her bags to get home, even though she knew her city would be one of the first to go. But she needed to be there, to be a part of what was happening, not left behind to survive in an empty wasteland. And now it had happened and they had had no warning, no time to make any decisions, no time to say any goodbyes. All that she had known, loved, hated, was gone except this floating tin ship and one woman who was still a mystery to her. She watched Franni in silence, watched her beat her fists till they bled, run crazy through the ship pulling out files and tapes till the floor was awash with the collected research of over fifteen years. She couldn't help her, could find no words that would make it all right for either of them. It occurred to her, as she slipped onto the floor to join the curling tapes that lay scattered there that only now, now that they knew their own deaths were imminent, could they begin to accept the death of a whole globe of humanity. The thought made her want to laugh, to share the joke with Franni, but she could only let the tapes flow through her fingers and spiral downwards into silent tangles on the floor.

After the despair came the anger, after the anger came the grief, after the grief came an almost hysterical desire to think and say and feel and hold on to anything and everything that confirmed their tiny existence. They slept for only a few hours at a time, begrudging their bodies' need to rest when there was so much to do. Vivienne opened up all the cages and let the animals run loose through the ship. She watched them for hours as they delighted in their new found freedom, climbing all over the machines, raiding the food store when Franni left the shutter open, chewing at the plants in the greenhouse. And yet, she noted wryly, they always went back to their bleak little wire cages when it was time to sleep. Home is home to a rat or a hamster or a woman.

Franni spent her time preparing a capsule that they planned to launch out with the last of their fuel in the hope that such a small craft could use the power to escape the fatal pull and survive to tell their tale to some other species that might have more sense than to blow themselves up. She had repaired the damage she had done to the files and was endlessly flicking through them, always looking for some clue, some sign, an answer to where their world had gone wrong. Vivienne frowned, unsure as to what Franni was doing, what she was looking for, mostly uncaring as she grew more wrapped into the feel of her own death.

They met, as usual, for communal time, playing

scrabble, cards, watching the stars, though always careful to avert their eyes from the sector that was drawing them home. They tried to love each other, hold each other's body safe, but their only connection was an electric fear and all their passion together only served to remind them that death was something that could not be shared.

With four days to go, Franni had finished the preparations for their capsule, had stocked it with all their reports and data runs. The last items to go in were their diaries, each with its final entry.

Final Diary Extract V.R.

And I thought that all you had to do was spin and turn with the flow of life, that all you had to do was listen to the rhythm in your body and you would find the answer you needed. But now I listen and there is only a chaotic crackle, there is no music, no pattern to follow. I feel like I am already dead although I know that to feel anything is a sign of life. I feel so alive, so healthy, that the prospect of death seems ridiculous. I wonder if we could have done anything, twisted strands of time and destiny to make a new ending, if we had been down there. But the machine was too big, the weapons were only one small part of it, we were another. Like some mythological monster, if only one head was cut off then ten grew in its place. I watch Franni, trying to remember every detail about her, as though she was the only one dying and I will be left with her shadow following my footsteps. There is no final message because this is not yet the end, and when the end comes there will be no time for words.

Final Diary Extract F.D.

So this time next week I'll be dead. Not even just dead but gone, finished, nothing left but an infinitesimal spark of matter in a furnace. Sometimes it terrifies me, sometimes it's just like that feeling at the end of the holidays when you know you'll be back in school and there's nothing you can do to stop it so you just have to accept it. Shit, I wish it wasn't happening, suddenly a lifetime in this tin tube with crazy Vivienne seems like a glorious option. We talked about religion once, seems like eons ago, wondered if when death creeps round the corner so does God, but to be honest if he/she is out there I just wish he/she would flash up on the computer or something because I haven't really noticed anything different going on. I think I'll just believe in the capsule, maybe it'll make it somewhere and give someone else a laugh at the farce we managed to make of everything. And, in a way, I'm glad we can't go back to earth, they wouldn't have let us be together to do anything down there, not even die.

The capsule spun away from the spaceship, its flaming jet forcing it out towards the edges of the system. It escaped by a whisker and started a vacant wandering through the stars until another force would hold it in a gravitational thrall. And as the computer ticked out the last seconds, two astronauts went home.

RELATIVELY NORMA
by Anna Livia   £2.95

Minnie flies to Australia to tell her mother she's a lesbian, and discovers, to her astonishment, that all the women in her family have their own lives to live, their own revelations to make.

"... fast, furious and teeters agilely on the knife-edge of feminist farce."

British Book News

"I was touched to the bone by the book's portrayal of the gropings for independence of both mothers and children."

Spare Rib

THE OPEN ROAD
by Jennifer Gubb   £1.99

A collection of feminist tales rooted in a far from bucolic rural Devon. Stories about growing up, growing old and being a woman in the country.

"... raw knuckled, unsentimental sensuality that the country has for those who live not only in, but off it. Along with the constant struggle against poverty and land, there is a war of the sexes being waged — brutal in its directness ... Gubb's writing, neither bitter nor romantic, conveying the rich-rough texture of a life without recourse to 'set piece' descriptions, has those same kind of qualities."

The New Statesman

CACTUS
by Anna Wilson   £2.95

A lesbian classic.
The story of Bea and Eleanor whose relationship broke up 20
years ago due to social pressure; of Ann and Dee who leave the
city to concentrate on theirs.

"I'm tired of always having to use cactus skills; as if that's all
there ever was for lesbians in the world — drink in the fleeting
support of the ghetto, grow a thick skin to withstand the
heat of a hostile environment, go sit in the desert for a year
drinking your juices meanly."

For a complete booklist including lesbian feminist poetry and
radical feminist theory, please write to:
Onlywomen Press Ltd.,
38 Mount Pleasant, London WC1X 0AP, U.K.